BASTARDS AND SCAPEGOATS

TWISTED LEGACY DUET

CORALEE JUNE

Cover by: HarleyQuinn Zaler

Editor: Helayna Trask with Polished Perfection

Cover Photographer: Marx Chavez

Cover Model: Roque Arrais

✿ Created with Vellum

For Christine Estevez. I am so thankful for your friendship and support. I couldn't do this gig without you.

*M*y mother used to tell me that death was just a monster she couldn't figure out how to conquer. At eight years old, I didn't understand what she meant. I just thought monsters were the creatures that hid under my bed and in my big brother's clenched fist. The day she died, Mom learned how to best the beast. I found her writhing on the floor with armor made of fentanyl while clutching a needle-like sword in her palm.

I remember how I pleaded. "You can't die." I clutched her hand while sobbing over her soft skin. Her hair was soaked with salty sweat and clung to her forehead. "You can't."

I refused to believe that she'd done *it* at her happy place. This was supposed to be the one place where the monster couldn't catch her. The place where she used to put Band-Aids on my scraped knees and bake my favorite pies. Not where we used to build her pillow forts in the living room and eat chocolate as she cried. Even though her moments of motherly affection were few and far between, they were special to me. This place was special to me.

I'd sometimes catch her sliding down the wall while biting her fist. She used to find the darkest corner of our house and settle there for a week or a month or my entire childhood. Dad said she liked to play hide-and-seek. We made a game out of her depression.

"Mom!"

She didn't answer me. She was too damn high— too lost—to make her mouth work. When I found her passed out on the ground and foaming at the mouth, I called an ambulance. It wasn't the first time I'd had to do this. Young boys shouldn't have to know the right things to say to a 911 operator. Young boys shouldn't have to know words like *overdose*. She loved things that damaged her. She loved to kiss death on the cheek.

She loved to make me feel terrible for existing.

Oh, she loved me, too. In her own special way. I was one of those damaging addictions she forced herself to love. It was the worst kind of love. Love wasn't meant to be forced.

"Mom?" She started seizing. "No!"

I did this crazy thing where I almost laughed. Because I was so fucking scared—so terrified of losing her that the adrenaline cracked my mouth into a manic, terrible, nervous smile. I wouldn't know until much later that the weakness in my expression would seal my fate.

I clutched her to my chest. "Don't do this," I pleaded as I shook her frail body.

She died in the arms of the bastard son she never wanted.

1

VERA

"I love you," Mom whispered in a voice that lacked conviction. Although her new husband ate those words up like apple pie, I wasn't sure if it was her affection that made him smile, or the idea of owning someone.

"Love you, too," he whispered back with equal

yet still impossibly lackluster enthusiasm. He leaned over and grazed her lips with his mouth. It was a satisfying sort of sadness, watching my mother kiss the *love of her life* on her wedding day. Her smile caused a pang of remorse to creep up my throat and settle on my tongue. I swallowed away emotions like I was drinking bitter, unsweet iced tea, and cheered at all the appropriate times. It was the right thing to do. I *always* did the right thing.

Lilah Garner—sorry, *Beauregard*—looked stunning. She was beautifully aware of her appearance and wielded it like a weapon. She poised herself like a goddess in the middle of the room, daring you to look at her until your eyes bled. Mom was rough around the edges. Her makeup was a bit too thick for her conservative husband, her dress a bit too revealing on her thin frame. This wedding was her grand performance. Romantic love was nothing but theatrics for the woman who birthed me. I'm sure in her own special way, she cared for Joseph. But it wasn't the sort of love you read about in books. It was a love born out of opportunity, and everyone knew it.

"Introducing, Mr. and Mrs. Beauregard!" the announcer said as the happy couple walked onto the dance floor. I politely clapped along with everyone else watching.

My mother and I were close. Only fifteen short years separated our ages, and we fought for our place in this world. She always wanted a comfortable life. I suppose spending all your existence clawing your way through bullshit made you wish that you didn't have to try so damn hard. Her new husband offered comforts neither of us had dared to even dream of, but the privilege of peace came at a price.

The smile stretched along my face felt sore and forced. I'd been wearing it all day, and the happy mask was just as foreign to me as the three-thousand-dollar designer lace dress clinging to my thin body, and the heels strapped to my throbbing feet. My light brown hair was swept into an elegant updo, my full lips lined with mauve liner and matte lipstick. I had red paint on my nails. My tan skin was buffed and shined to perfection. My brown eyes lined with smoky makeup.

I didn't want to be here. Not really. The makeup caked onto my skin had all but sweat off in the September humidity, and the lashes expertly glued to my eyelids earlier this afternoon by Connecticut's finest makeup artist, were now hanging by a thread.

But my mother wanted an outdoor wedding.

She wanted the fairy tale.

She wanted everything her unplanned teen pregnancy had been denying her all these years.

The only thing that could make her special day more perfect was if I weren't here.

No. That was an intrusive thought orchestrated by my deep-rooted insecurities. My mom loved me. She wouldn't have worked so hard to give us a good life otherwise.

The happy couple walked around the room, shaking hands with their guests and greeting attendees with wide, practiced smiles. When they got to me, Joseph awkwardly patted me on the shoulder, his lips pressed into a thin line as he stared at me.

"I love you," Mom whispered before kissing me on the cheek. Her glossy lips left a sticky residue on my skin.

"Love you too, Mom. Congrats, Joseph."

Ignoring me, my new stepfather cleared his throat, pressed his hand to the small of Mom's back, and whispered, "There are more people to see. The Vice President is here."

With a gracious nod and a pleased grin, Mom

squeezed my hand and followed her husband off to a group of guests to my right.

She looked happy, with her vintage dress and petite body gliding across the ground. The setting looked straight out of a fairy tale. Twinkle lights woven like thread and strung from poles towered above us and made the sweat on her face glow. Her breasts were spilling from her dress, giving onlookers a tease of what was underneath the sixteen-thousand-dollar gown she wore.

She wanted to feel like a princess today.

Don't get me wrong, Lilah Beauregard *deserved* to feel like a princess. We hadn't had an easy life. The day she realized she was pregnant with me, was the start of her misery, and she had earned the right to a happily ever after. The tenacious woman paid in blood, sweat, and tears. Lilah worked three grueling jobs while getting her GED. She also made sure I had food on the table, and I never really felt unsafe. Her creepy boyfriends never slept over. There were times we feared not making rent, but she didn't purposefully go out of her way to make me feel like a burden. My mother loved me. She wasn't abusive or cruel. She was just human, a fact that I had slowly realized over time.

Growing up meant accepting the vulnerabilities

of your parents. I learned to normalize their flaws because expecting more from her led to disappointment. I couldn't put my finger on the exact moment I realized that she silently resented me. Perhaps it was two years ago, on my sixteenth birthday. She got me a purse I'd been eyeing at the local thrift store and a prescription for birth control. She made me swear not to ruin my life like she did.

Or maybe it was the night of homecoming when she uncharacteristically sobbed at the sight of me in a dress. It hadn't occurred to me until later that she missed her own homecoming because of me.

Or maybe it was tonight, as I watched her clink her glass of champagne for a toast. The words *fresh start* escaped her lips.

She loved me. Hell, she devoted her young life to raising me. But everything was about to change. I could feel it in my bones. Up until now, life was nothing more than a long, slow dance with survival.

"You don't have to smile the entire time, Vera," my new grandfather said while settling at my side. I wasn't expecting him to chat with me. There were much more important people here than I. And didn't he know? I *had* to smile. The alternative was crying. There was no in-between. I let out a light chuckle while continuing to watch my mother. She was grinning broadly at something Joseph had whispered in her ear.

"I'm afraid if I stop, someone will take a photo and I'll end up in tomorrow's headlines," I murmured with a slight wince. I was forced to swiftly get used to the publicity of our new family. My new grandfather, Governor Jack Beauregard, looked around the room, frowning slightly at the various clicking cameras zoomed in on the happily married couple, pausing when he noticed a few of them trained on us. Like the skilled politician he was, Jack wrapped his arm around me for a comforting side hug.

"I know it's a lot to learn. There is a spotlight on my family not many can handle. You've adapted well." I resisted the urge to snort. If adapting well meant crying into my pillow every night, then yes, I was adjusting accordingly.

The Beauregards weren't just politically inclined. They shoved their hands into every money-making industry until they were up to their elbows in privilege and wealth. My mother would never admit it in polite company, but she chiseled at her rocky foundation with nothing more than a pin needle and somehow managed to strike gold. "Your love and support for your mother has been commendable. You moved across the state. Helped plan this monster of a wedding and are wearing a dress that looks tremendously uncomfortable. Honestly, you should look for a job in politics, because you haven't cracked once."

"At least not publicly," I whispered, making him chuckle. Jack liked to point out how mature I was for my age. I didn't have the heart to tell him that I was forced to grow up the day I was born. I was eighteen going on seventy. Smiling, I twisted to face him. Jack had salt-and-pepper hair and deep wrinkles carved into his pale skin. The tux he wore was polished and dignified. I noticed a nick on his chin, probably from shaving. He had genuine laugh lines painted around his mouth, like he spent his entire life finding everything amusing.

I had yet to meet someone who didn't like my new grandfather—including me. Though he seemed to know that the public always had their eyes on him, he still maintained a joyful disposition. Jack took the time to get to know me. He hosted barbeques and asked me about what books I was reading. He also got me into one of the best local universities so I could still be close to my mother during this strange transition.

"You're doing great, kid. I just wish my wife could

have lived long enough to see Joseph married. She would have loved you."

I inhaled slow and steady, trying to come up with a response. I never knew what to say when Jack's wife was brought up. "I'm sure she was lovely. She's here in spirit," I replied before reaching out to gently squeeze my new grandfather's arm reassuringly.

He patted me on the shoulder before looking back at my mother and new stepfather. "And you look beautiful tonight." The compliment made me dip my head. I never did well with compliments. I didn't really know the right way to accept them. That was my mother's expertise. "You're so supportive. I'm proud to have you join the family."

"I just want her to be happy," I admitted. It was a phrase I'd learned to use repeatedly when reporters asked how I felt about the shotgun wedding and her rumored pregnancy. Four months ago, they were just dating. Two months ago, they were engaged. Now? Mom had a rock the size of California on her hand. And as far as the pregnancy rumors? I'd found a positive test in the trash, but she hadn't told me yet.

"It's okay to want to be happy, too," Jack said while leaning over and tapping me on the nose. "I'm going to talk to my buddy over there. See you later, Vera." I inhaled his whiskey scent and nodded, like it was the appropriate thing to do, before turning my attention back to my mother.

The bride and groom's grand exit wasn't for another hour, according to the itinerary, and I needed to cool off in the main house for a bit before posing for the camera again. I also needed to find some lipstick.

I smiled while walking by senators, governors, diplomats, CEOs and other important people I knew nothing about. I wasn't raised in this life. I didn't know the first thing about what my mother was marrying into, but I was quickly learning.

Politicians lived their life on stage. They couldn't so much as take a shit without everyone knowing. Joseph was following in his father's footsteps, and Mom looked forward to posing at his side. It seemed appropriate. She was a modern-day Cinderella now standing at the side of a prince. But I didn't trust in their happily ever after.

After grabbing a glass of water and heading up the trail toward the large house, I guzzled down the chilled drink and took in our surroundings. Jack owned the estate where my mother and Joseph got married. Surrounded by sprawling lawns that were beautiful, the large home was surprisingly modern despite the overgrown vines and traditional landscaping. The blocky house with tall rectangular windows almost felt out of place. Jack had it built as a gift for his late wife and spent some of his summers here. He called it his second retirement home. It was crazy what money could do.

I passed the security guard, who gave me a subtle nod of acknowledgement, before making my way inside and upstairs to the bedroom I was staying in for the next two weeks while my mother and Joseph were honeymooning in Paris. Fucking Paris. Apparently, the Beauregards had a flat in the city, with an incredible view. The only time I'd ever been on vacation was when we went camping at the local state park.

My wobbling ankles ached as I ascended the stairs. Reaching behind my back, I slowly unzipped my dress for a bit of temporary breathing room before letting out a sigh of relief and loosening the smile cemented on my face. "Fucking finally," I said while walking up the stairs leading to my suite. It wasn't until I heard a distinct whimper that I stopped on the top step.

"Hello?" I asked. This place was supposed to be off-limits for anyone but the bridal party and families—not that Mom and I had anyone.

"Harder baby," a high-pitched woman demanded. "Fuck that pussy."

My eyes widened as a slapping sound filled my ears. Oh, shit. The sound was coming from my room. If someone was bumping uglies in my bed, I was going to lose it.

I instinctively knew I should have walked away. A wiser woman would have fled. But I was drawn to the loud moans. My hand went to the doorknob, and my heart twisted in my chest. I turned the handle slowly, slowly, slowly.

I expected a dark room. My fumbling experiences with sex involved a high school ex-boyfriend who wasn't worth mentioning. Our twisted experiments were always in the dark. Always while Mom was working a double shift at the restaurant. Always with the pillow clenched between my teeth to stop my moans from shattering the paper-thin walls of my bedroom.

But this wasn't two bodies seeking pleasure in the silent shroud of darkness. The entire space was drenched in light. It was like they didn't care if they were seen or heard. They were too lost in the power of pleasure. It was loud and chaotic. Intoxicating.

Directly across from where I was standing at the door, was an old vanity with a large, lit up mirror.

Two bodies moving on and against it. I immediately recognized the girl, the hard lines of her face a picture of pleasure in the mirror's reflection. She was a younger waitress who worked with my mom. They were acquaintances at best, just someone Mom liked to gossip with during her lunch break, but Mom needed people to stand beside her at the altar, and Colleen looked amazing in a dress.

Her partner pressed her cheek into the tabletop, and her exposed ass was angled toward him. Her moans were loud and harsh, cutting at my eardrums with splitting cries.

But my eyes were locked on the muscular backside flexing and poised at her back. He was thrusting into her from behind. Tan, broad, strong. He had dark hair and a tattoo of a detailed, shaded skull staring menacingly at me. With every thrust, his ass cheeks clenched, and the vanity slammed against the wall. "Yes, darlin' keep going," he groaned before pushing into her once more.

"Harder," she demanded back. I nearly snorted. Any harder and he would be sending her straight through the drywall.

I watched with an open mouth. The room smelled like sex, and clothes were strewn across the floor in a shocking display of passion. I looked up at the vanity mirror and gasped when I saw a pair of charcoal eyes staring right back at me.

His mouth was plump and framed by a light dusting of dark facial hair. His jawline was razor-sharp. The brown hair on his head looked like someone had been running their hands through it, my guess Colleen.

We were locked in an intense stare down. "You like that?" he asked, but I wasn't sure if he was speaking to me or Colleen.

"Yes," she moaned.

The man smirked while tipping his head back in bliss. It was a sight I'd always remember. His mouth parted. His eyes squeezed shut. Every muscle in his body was flexed. I could feel my heated pulse thudding at the sight of him. My legs shook. I gnawed on my lip.

"Get out," the man demanded before looking over his shoulder at me. All snarky playfulness had disappeared. Now he challenged me with his stare. My cheeks flushed in embarrassment. What the fuck was I doing?

I should have argued that this was *my* room. I should have screamed for the security team stationed at the front door. I should have done a lot of things, but instead, I ran out of the guest room and shot down the stairs like a bullet from a smoking gun. I heard them cry out in tandem as the pleasure of their mutual orgasms tore through them. I went outside as their screams seemed to echo around me.

The wooden boards creaked under my feet as I walked along the back porch of the Beauregard home. Some of the wedding decorations from the night before were still perched in the yard. The cleanup crew wasn't scheduled to arrive for another hour, so I felt comfortable sitting in my flimsy silk pajamas on a lawn chair.

The yard smelled like fresh flowers and insect repellant. I clutched my coffee in my palm, willing my body to wake up as I stared out at the yard. My heavy eyes itched from exhaustion and allergies. I didn't sleep last night, and though I wanted to enjoy the comfort of my bed, I also wanted to see my mother off for her early morning flight. We'd agreed to have coffee together before she left, and I was looking forward to some alone time with her. The last couple of months had been such a rush that I couldn't remember the last time we'd been together with just the two of us.

The back door sliding open caught my attention, and I turned to greet her, pausing when I realized it wasn't my mother coming outside but, instead, the man from last night. After the wedding was over, I had gone back to my bedroom with a sense of trepidation. Luckily, the couple had vacated my room, but I still asked the housekeeper for new bedding in case they took their wild night from the vanity to my king-sized bed. I spent most of last night thinking about our strange encounter and picturing his flexed body moving in and out of her.

I quickly smoothed out my petal-colored silk pajamas and sat up straighter, realizing my nipples were probably poking through the thin material of my shirt. Fuck.

The strange man looked handsome but

hungover. He looked like the kind of man to make cherry stems out of women and tangle them up with his talented, twisted tongue. His olive skin had a sheen of sweat on it, and his black eyes scanned the deck before landing on me.

"Well, if it isn't my little voyeur," he said with a grin before smoothing his shirt and licking his lips. "Did you enjoy the show last night? Come back for an encore?"

He bit his lip while sweeping his charcoal eyes over my exposed skin. I flushed at his words. "I didn't mean to watch," I stammered. Then, I remembered that I wasn't the sort of woman to be flustered fuckless by a pretty man. "You were in *my* bedroom, you know."

He sauntered over to me. "*Your* bedroom, huh?" he asked while scratching the back of his neck. The movement showed off the curve of his muscles. I exhaled. "Last I checked, that was *my* bedroom." He clutched his shoes in his other hand, eyeing the empty chair beside me. "May I?"

I wiggled anxiously in my seat, a fresh but foreign desperation dictating my movements, and he didn't bother to wait for an answer. The strange man plopped down in the chair beside me and started putting his shoes on. What did he mean, *his bedroom*? Did he live here, too? I spent three breaths watching the careless way he moved, like he was fully comfortable in his skin. Shockingly, he wasn't embarrassed about what happened last night. He effortlessly met the awkwardness like his life depended on it. While I blushed from my toes all the way up to the tops of my ears, he just shrugged the entire experience off, as if fucking for show was something that happened regularly for him—maybe it was.

I picked up my coffee cup and took a sip, mostly because I wanted something to do with my hands. He smiled as I did. "Is this going to be awkward between us now? I'm technically your uncle, but—"

My eyes widened, and I choked on the coffee I was drinking. Sputtering. Coughing. Choking on the truth. It was a long moment before I could respond. "U-uncle?"

He chuckled and pulled the cup from my hands, so I didn't spill on myself. Our fingers brushed, and a tingle of awareness shot up my arm. "I'm Joseph's younger brother. I'm sure they've told you all about me, right?" His tone had a sarcastic quality to it that I quickly processed. I had no idea that Joseph had a brother. The only family I'd met was Jack. And even so, there was no mention of anyone else. He must have seen the confused look on my face, because he forced a smile. "The name is Hamilton."

"Like the play?" I asked, brow quirked.

"My parents were fond of pretentious sounding names. They thought class was predestined and a healthy handful of syllables could determine the status of a man."

Hamilton Beauregard felt like a mouthful and completely contradicted his easygoing demeanor. "I'm Vera. It's nice to meet you," I choked out.

I had so many questions. Why didn't I know about him? The wedding was rushed but not *that* rushed. There was plenty of time for Joseph to tell me about his younger brother.

"I'm a bit of an outcast around here. You won't have to worry about seeing me at awkward Thanksgiving dinners or imagining me fucking some girl on Christmas morning. Most of the time, I'm working offshore on the rig. You know, there's no money in politics. Dad has to hide his fortune *and* his youngest child in old oil money." Hamilton laughed at his joke, but it didn't feel funny. "I have twenty-one days off. Figured I'd see my big brother get married, though unsurprisingly, the invitation got lost in the mail."

He lifted my cup of coffee to his lips and took a

sip while staring out over the yard. I didn't comment on the fact that he was drinking *my* coffee. "Offshore?" I asked.

"I'm a tool pusher on an oil rig," he replied.

That explained why I'd never met him. He was constantly gone. "Cool," I replied, not really knowing what to say. I knew as much about his career as I knew about him—nothing.

"It pays the bills," he said with a grin before handing me back my cup of coffee. "Plus, it keeps me out of the public eye." He winked, like I was somehow a part of some secret I actually knew nothing about.

"I-is that a good thing?" I asked.

Hamilton leaned a little closer. The morning light made it look like he had flecks of gold in his dark brown eyes. "I have a habit of fucking things up."

"How so?" I asked.

"Last night, I plowed a woman whose name I can't remember while staring at my new niece," he whispered with a secret smile I felt in my gut. Yep. I supposed that was fucked up.

I cleared my throat. "Let's agree to never bring that back up."

"Fair enough," he replied before licking his lips.

Despite barely knowing him, I surmised that Hamilton was inherently sexual. More time passed, and hot tension built between us. My skin pebbled as we stared at one another. "I should get going," he finally said. "Things usually go to shit when my brother and I spend too much time together."

"And whose fault is that?" I asked, my question surprisingly bold. I wasn't sure why I said it. Maybe I was looking for validation that my mother's new groom wasn't a good person.

"Usually mine," Hamilton answered before standing up and smoothing his shirt. "See you around, Vera."

He winked at me, then walked down the deck's steps and headed toward a parked motorcycle in the distance.

The sound of the back door opening drew my attention away from Hamilton, and I turned to greet my mother, pleased that I no longer had to navigate this awkward conversation with my *u-uncle* and that she had remembered our breakfast date this morning. Thank fuck Hamilton left before she woke up. I didn't want to explain how we'd met the night before. "Hey, baby," she greeted while adjusting her lavender robe and settling in the cushioned chair beside me.

My mother looked tired. Her brown hair was still curled from her updo the night before, and her smeared lipstick had stained the skin at the corner of her mouth. She slowly sipped her drink, and my eyes zeroed in on the glimmering rock on her left hand.

"I was worried you'd forget," I admitted.

"I could never forget you," she replied with a sigh. "Though I was moving very slow this morning. Perhaps an open bar was a bad idea, hmm?" she teased, her voice like a pack of cigarettes and church bells. I laughed. I hadn't seen her touch a drop of alcohol in a while. I eyed her stomach, trying to see the evidence of a pregnancy, but saw nothing.

Every Sunday, for as long as I could remember, my mother and I did this. We sat outside on our patio and drank coffee. Sometimes we chatted about life. Sometimes we sat in silence.

"I saw the pregnancy test, Mom," I admitted. "I'm happy for you. You don't have to keep it from me."

"You know?" she asked, shocked. Mom turned to face me with a grin. "I'm sorry I haven't told you yet. It's been a lot of change for you, baby. It's been killing me, not telling you."

I set my cup down and reached out to grab her

hand. "I'm happy for you. But we never have secrets."

Mom sighed. "You've always been more of a friend than a daughter. Hell, I don't even have any friends. I had to ask Colleen to be a bridesmaid, and I don't even like the bitch. She's too nosy." I cleared my throat. Colleen certainly didn't mind being a bridesmaid when Hamilton was balls deep inside of her. "It's always been you and me against the world, baby. I just feel guilty. This child is going to have all the things I couldn't give you. A father. A consistent home. It won't need toys from the bargain bin or goodwill clothes. I'm not going to have to work three jobs or worry where rent is coming from. I can't help but feel sad that this baby is going to get a completely different version of me than you did." She held her stomach and looked off at the tree line in the distance for a moment. "Heck, I'm about to have a honeymoon in Paris. You've never even been on an airplane."

My heart panged. The different upbringing this child would have was something I'd thought about ever since I saw the test. "I like *my* version of you," I lied. "And I want you to be happy. You deserve this, Mom." This baby might not have the same upbringing as I did, but Mom had earned the right to have a happy little family. This was just another pitstop on the road to accepting our new normal.

"You're too good to me," she whispered, her green eyes sparkling with emotion. "It's still us. You and me. We just have a little more help. I l-love Joseph. I really, really do. Promise. He's a good man. I adore him. He's going to pay for your college. He wants me to see the world. He buys me anything I want. I know the two of you haven't really had a chance to get to know one another, but he cares about you. He's really excited for you to attend his alma mater. Jack attended there too, you know. It's somewhat of a family tradition."

Had Hamilton attended there?

I forced a smile. I didn't want to attend the pretentious Greenwich University. Up until Mom and Joseph started dating, I had dreams of attending Brooklyn College for Social Work. My entire high school class catalogue was cultivated with the hope of getting a scholarship so I could attend. I knew that Greenwich University was a greater opportunity than I could have ever hoped to achieve. The tuition cost more than most people's homes, and only the most elite students attended. It was intimidating to think about, but once the engagement was announced, Joseph informed my mother and me that it would be better for everyone if I attended Greenwich, as it was close to home and more respectable for our family legacy. I didn't even know what that meant, considering I didn't feel part of the family.

I didn't know Joseph. Not really. He wasn't worried about getting to know me either. At least not more than what was politely required of him. I just had hope that tolerance for one another would at the very least grow over time.

I was determined to accept all the change thrown at me. I understood that the ability to adapt wasn't a gift most people had—hell, some people weren't even given the opportunity. There were entire populations that lived, breathed, and died in accordance to a routine given to them by society. Joseph might be an unexpected variable, but he was like every challenge I faced:

Conquerable.

As if summoned by my uneasy thoughts, Joseph came marching out of the house through the sliding back door with a scowl on his face. He looked like he wanted to punch someone. "My brother is such an asshole. Hamilton can't show up for the ceremony, but he can make it for the free booze at our reception? Dick. I mean seriously, to have a threesome in the dining room is just ridiculous. I just found both his whores wrapped up in blankets on the floor and smelling of booze. I wanted our wedding's press release to go flawlessly, but now I have to make sure none of those women will sell his debauchery to the tabloids and overshadow us."

It was on the tip of my tongue to warn him about Colleen, but I stopped myself. A threesome? Fuck. I only saw what happened in my guest room. I guess he had a really, *really* good night.

Joseph stopped shouting when he noticed me. "Oh, I'm so sorry, Vera. I didn't realize you were out here." I bit my tongue and forced myself not to remind Joseph that my mother and I had been enjoying Sunday morning coffee every week for the last eighteen years of my life before he came along. He knew this. He had to know this. He inserted his life into ours and made interrupting us a sport.

"I didn't realize you had a brother," I said, trying to ignore the annoyance I felt in my gut at the sight of my new stepfather.

Conquer, Vera. Adapt.

There was just something off about him. He had never been blatantly rude to me, nor had he given me any reason to distrust him, aside from a few careless moments where he forgot I existed. I just instinctively felt off about Joseph. I wished I could figure out why. It made me feel like a petulant child afraid to share her mother. For fuck's sake, I wasn't a baby.

"That's by design, dear. Hamilton doesn't usually come to family events, and my father works overtime to keep his depravity out of the papers."

I stared at my stepfather for a moment. Was that what he would do to me if I jeopardized the Beauregard reputation? Would I stop being invited to family events? Would I be allowed to know my sibling? The doubts were difficult to digest. I'd always been quiet and studious. I wasn't one to party or make waves. I'd been conditioned from a young age to be mindful of my behavior. I was a direct reflection of my mother's parenting, and the critics were harsher when you were a young mom. This wouldn't be any different, but I wondered when I wouldn't have to worry about my actions directly affecting someone else.

My stepfather was picture-perfect. I never saw a hair out of place. He always had a smile on his face. Joseph was a handsome man. He had dirty blond hair slicked back in a preppy style and bright green eyes. Fashionable and rigid, he held the air of someone superior. He was tall and spent most of his free time looking down his nose at me.

"Darling, you really shouldn't be drinking coffee in your condition," he said to my mother before slowly sliding his eyes over to me in a moderately calculative move. He then paused and grinned sheepishly. "Oops. I just meant she was probably dehydrated," he quickly added.

"I already know about the baby. Congratulations, Joseph." I smiled at him, though the joy didn't quite reach its full potential. I should have been happy about a new baby, right?

He smiled, like he was thoroughly pleased with himself. "You'll have to come visit our new house and see the nursery when we get back from Paris!"

My mother started waving her arms, as if he wasn't supposed to say something. I laughed nervously. "Well, of course I'll come visit. I'm staying with you and commuting to school," I replied. "I thought that was the plan since your new house is so close to campus." Where the fuck else was I going to stay?

Joseph tilted his head to the side and gave me a sympathetic look. Oh no. What did this mean?

"I thought your mother told you?"

"Told me what?" I asked while turning to look at

Mom. She looked like there were crickets in her coffee mug. I watched her lips pucker in annoyance. More secrets. Was this the new norm?

"Jack and Joseph found you an apartment. We figured you would want your own space, you know. It's only thirty minutes from our new house and is right on campus. You can still visit for dinner and attend events. Jack was going to surprise you with it. Your new grandfather thought an apartment would be a fun graduation gift. He's so excited that you're attending Greenwich."

I turned to my stepfather. "Wow. He really didn't have to do that," I said.

Joseph walked over to my mother and bent down to kiss her on the cheek. "We just assumed that you wouldn't want to live with a couple of newlyweds. You're eighteen now. You can get a head start on the college experience. My father even mentioned an internship at his office if you're interested."

I wasn't going to school for politics, but the way Joseph suggested this new opportunity, I got the feeling it wasn't optional. I guess in some ways, politics and social work went hand in hand. The Beauregards were all about their image.

"I'll think about talking to him about it," I replied noncommittally. "Thank you, Joseph. I really appreciate it. But are you sure you don't want me to stay at home, Mom? With a new baby and all, I really don't mind helping." What I meant to say was that I didn't want to miss out, but the words wouldn't form. Maybe most people would be happy to leave their parents and start their journey of independence, but she was all I'd ever known. I wasn't ready.

"She will have more than enough help with me and the nannies I've hired," Joseph replied, ending the conversation.

"I lost my virginity to our nanny," said a smooth voice. I hadn't even noticed Hamilton walking back up the steps toward us. My spine straightened as I glanced his way. Hamilton stalked up the steps with a grimace. Shit. His entire demeanor had changed. He was calm with me, but now I sensed a hardened edge to his presence that bled through his expression.

"Hamilton," Joseph said. "You're such a crude fucker. Be polite while meeting my new family."

Hamilton arched a brow and walked over to shake his brother's hand. "Congrats on the wedding," he said, though it didn't sound at all congratulatory. Hamilton had seemed sweet when it was just us. Something changed, and I wanted to know what.

I eyed both Beauregard brothers, trying to find traces of similarities in their expressions. Hamilton was all shadows and mystery. Cocky mischievousness wrapped up in a sinfully sexy package. Joseph was like polished fine china or bars of gold.

Hamilton sauntered over to us, and I crossed my arms over my chest. "This is my new stepdaughter, Vera," Joseph said while nodding in my direction. Hamilton grinned like a Cheshire cat. I was about to admit that we'd already met, but Hamilton cut me off.

"You look so familiar. Have we met before?" he asked while holding out his hand to shake mine, as if we hadn't just had a conversation on this very porch. As if I hadn't walked in on him last night. As if I didn't know how hard he liked to fuck strangers.

So, this was how he wanted to play it? Great.

"I don't think so. If we had, it must not have been memorable," I replied. I wasn't necessarily mad about our little secret, just amused.

"And this is my new bride, Lilah," Joseph then said with warm affection before placing a possessive hand on my mother's shoulder. Loving the attention,

Mom stood up and patted her hair before reaching out to shake Hamilton's outstretched palm.

"It's nice you finally meet you," Mom greeted.

"The pleasure is all mine," Hamilton purred playfully before bringing my mother's hand up to his lips to place a lingering kiss on her skin. "You're much prettier than my brother. How'd he snag you?"

She blushed. "I had no idea your brother was so charming, Joseph," she said to her husband. I fought the urge to roll my eyes at her comment. I had the feeling Hamilton was the sort of man to make women fall to their knees in front of him.

"I was going to head back to my house, but I left my wallet inside. Since everyone is up, should I go get some champagne for mimosas?" He then snapped his fingers. "Ah. I forgot. You're expecting, yes?"

Did everyone know but me? Or was Hamilton making an educated guess?

"Yes. I'm twelve weeks as of yesterday," Mom rushed out proudly.

Twelve weeks? Twelve fucking weeks? How did she keep this a secret from me for so long? I looked over her body once more. She was so thin.

"Congratulations," Hamilton said with a smile before turning his attention back to me.

"Will you be staying here while the happy couple are honeymooning in Paris?" he asked me while running a hand over his thin white Hanes undershirt. His dark hair was a mess on top of his head, the glossy strands curled in waves. I guess that's what happens when you spend all night fucking anything that moves.

"She's staying here for a week, then she's moving into her new apartment. It's completely furnished. You'll just need your personal effects. I'm so sorry we won't be there to move you in, dear," Joseph answered.

That intense warning in my gut returned. I'd worked hard to go to college. I graduated at the top of my class and signed up for every free extracurricular activity possible that would offer me a scholarship. Hell, I was president of the chess club. This whole ordeal felt cheapened by Joseph's overbearing influence on my college experience.

Now it was ruined. Rushed. A narrative I hadn't planned for.

"I don't mind helping," Hamilton offered.

"Don't you have an oil rig to be on?" Joseph asked.

"I'm off for twenty-one days," Hamilton replied. "I can stop by and get her moved in safe and sound."

"I'd rather hire a moving company," Joseph replied with a frown.

"You'd rather send your new stepdaughter off to her first apartment all alone while you're parading across Paris? How very Jack Beauregard of you," Hamilton said with a grin.

Mom looked completely crestfallen, as if it had just occurred to her that I would be taking on this new adventure alone.

"Maybe we should wait until we get back? Or cut our trip short. I don't like the idea of her moving all alone. This feels a little sudden, yes?" she said, her head turned in Joseph's direction and her index fingernail in her mouth. It was a nervous tic of hers.

"I'm sure Vera will be fine," Joseph replied. "Won't you, sweetheart?"

I didn't want them to end their trip early, and I certainly didn't want Mom to feel badly. "I'll be fine," I replied with a tight smile. "I'm happy for you." The practiced words I'd been using on the journalists and anyone else that asked how I felt about this strange new marriage just fell from my lips. I hadn't even realized I was saying them.

"Are you sure?"

"Yep. I want you to have fun. Don't worry. We can meet up when you get back."

Conquer. Adapt.

Hamilton tipped his head back and laughed before placing an arm around my shoulders. He smelled like scotch and sex. "Look at her! Already fitting in."

Hamilton squeezed me in an awkward side hug. Joseph looked like he wanted to strangle his little brother.

"I'd say it was good to see you, but that would be a lie," my stepfather snapped. It was the first time I'd heard him be so outwardly hostile. I didn't get it.

"Sure thing, daddio." Hamilton let go of me and made his way to the back door. It wasn't until he disappeared inside that I let out the breath I was holding.

What did he mean? And why did I get the feeling that Joseph wanted me out of the picture?

3

*M*y mother and Joseph had been in Paris one long week. I spent the majority of my time at the Beauregard home where Mom and Joseph were married, aside from a few trips to the local bookstore. It was a quiet, luxurious reprieve from the chaos of planning their wedding. I felt uncomfortable at first, staying alone in such a large home. Jack had been in DC for the last six days, lobbying for some bill that was intended to make rich men richer. Despite the distance, Jack dutifully checked in regularly, making sure I had enough food and knew where the car keys to his Aston Martin were, not that I'd ever drive it.

Jack would be home tomorrow, and he agreed to help me move into my new apartment since Mom and Joseph decided not to come home early to see me off. Mom was loving her luxurious tour of Paris. I couldn't even blame her.

"Baby!" she exclaimed over FaceTime, her smile broad. Her calls felt like bittersweet fragments, hollow little reminders that everything had changed. I was sitting on the deck, soaking up some sun in my black bikini and drinking an iced lemonade. "Look! It's the Eiffel Tower!" She turned the camera so I could see the iconic view. The tower was lit up with lights, looking majestic against the dark night sky. Mom was sitting on a balcony in a red dress, about to leave for dinner with Joseph. She looked elegant and polished up, like a pretty china doll.

Mom and I always spoke about traveling together and seeing the world. I was happy she was getting to do this with Joseph, but I selfishly envied him for getting this experience with her.

"It's gorgeous, Mom. I'm glad you're having fun."

"Are you doing okay? How is everything there?

You need anything?" she asked just as Joseph called her name. She twisted her head and held up a finger, wordlessly asking him to wait a moment. I didn't mind ending the call early.

Conquer. Adapt.

"I'm fine, Mom. Go enjoy your dinner. I'm going to spend the rest of my day reading raunchy romances. Everything is perfect. It's like I'm on vacation—promise. Once class starts, I won't have time to read; I'll be too busy studying all the time."

"Okay, baby. I miss you!"

"I miss you too," I replied. I really did miss her. There was still so much left unsaid. I felt unsure about moving into an apartment I hadn't even seen before, and I wanted to know more about the baby. Did she know the gender yet? When was she due? Should I be planning a shower? Each question piled up like the contents of a forgotten junk drawer.

We waved goodbye, and the call ended. I leaned back in my lawn chair, soaking up the midday sun while pushing thoughts of change to the back of my mind. I'd endured upheaval these last few weeks. I just wanted a few moments of solitude and peace. It was nice to sit in the stillness. A slight breeze kissed my cheek as the warm sun danced across my flushed skin. I allowed myself to relax and quiet my mind.

"Enjoying yourself?" a nasally voice asked. I shot up and opened my eyes, twisting in my seat to see who was there. "Sorry. I didn't mean to startle you." My eyes landed on a tall man with blond hair. He wore slacks with suspenders and had a leather messenger bag slung over his shoulder. "Are you Vera Garner?" he asked while taking a step closer. His lanky build somehow made him look more intimidating, like a scrappy street fighter. "Of course you're Vera Garner. You look just like your mother. Beautiful. Delicate."

"Who are you? Why are you on private property?" I asked, my voice a stammer.

"I just had a few questions. Nothing major," he said before reaching into his pocket. I stood up. What the fuck was this guy doing? I managed a step back. "Whoa! No need to be scared." When he smiled, it revealed bright yellow teeth. "I'm perfectly harmless. I just wanted to ask you a few things and get to know you for my exposé."

I eyed the door, but he was blocking my path. "Are you paparazzi? How'd you get past the guard at the gate?"

He wrinkled his freckled nose. "I hate the term *paparazzi*. I prefer the term *investigative journalist*." He revealed his phone and snapped a photo of me.

What the fuck? I wrapped my arms around my body to block his view. I felt vulnerable and exposed under his harsh gaze. This was so fucking intrusive. Deciding it wasn't safe to pass him and go to the door, I grabbed my phone.

"I'll call the cops!" I shouted.

He waved his hand. "I'll be gone before they get here. The name is Saint, by the way. Momma was hopeful when she named me. She had the right idea but the wrong bitch, you know?" He cackled. I dialed 911 with his inquisitive eyes on me. Unbothered, he continued speaking. "Did you know that Jack's wife died in this house? They say she passed peacefully in her sleep—some genetic heart defect no one knew about. But I don't believe that. The woman was depressed as hell. I have a source that says she spent a lot of time in lockdown at the local mental hospital."

I gulped and held the phone up to my ear.

"Nine-one-one, what's your emergency?"

"There is a man that snuck onto the property at Jack Beauregard's residence," I said as Saint adjusted his jacket, revealing a gun holstered to his hip. I swallowed my words and dropped the phone. The loud sound of it thudding on the deck made me wince.

He looked down at his gun and grinned. "Oh, this old thing? No need to fret, pet. I won't shoot you. I use it more for my protection. People don't like good journalism these days."

He stepped toward me. "Election season starts soon. Jack Beauregard pays a lot of money to look good in the papers. Hell, no offense, but your mother's rushed wedding is newsworthy. Beautiful woman traps a wealthy man? It's a tale as old as time. Everyone knows she's a gold digger, but the papers haven't breathed a bad word about her. Do you wonder why that is?"

I swallowed. "You have no right to talk about my mother that way," I choked out.

"Hey," Saint said while holding his hands up. "I respect her hustle. She's married to one of the richest men in the world now. I'm happy for her, truly." Saint patted his chest. "I'm not really here about her. I mean, Lilah isn't really all that interesting. The real story is with Joseph. You see, things just never add up with him. He just gives me bad vibes. When his own mother died, he didn't cry at the funeral. Just stood there silently staring at the casket. In fact, the autopsy reports looked doctored. I think Joseph had something to do with it, and everyone knows Jack has enough money to pay people off. " He thumbed his nose, then looked around at the mansion and manicured lawns surrounding it. "Case in point."

"I don't know what you're talking about," I said while praying the cops would show up soon.

"Of course you don't. Listen, I'm pretty sure there is a story here. And from what I can tell, you don't want your mom dragged into something sinister, right? I mean, she has a baby to think about now, after all." He stared at me, waiting to see if something in my facial expression would reveal the truth about my mother's pregnancy. They hadn't announced it yet, and something told me Saint would run a confirmation in the papers by tomorrow. When I didn't respond, he continued. "Joseph has always had anger problems. And Hamilton is like this mysterious playboy. We never hear about him, aside from when he has an orgy. Then there was the thing about his birth mother. Nothing ever really came of that, though."

Saint took another photo of the house before pocketing his phone and pulling out a business card. Finally, I could hear sirens in the distance. "Here's my email. Let me know if you hear anything. I only have your best interests at heart." He patted his chest again. "And I'll pay handsomely for any information you send my way that's worthwhile."

I gaped at him like a goldfish, too frozen in fear to move. "You're insane," I finally managed to say.

"Nah. Just hungry for knowledge. Toodles!"

And with that, Saint sprinted off the deck, his long legs carrying him down the path and through the woods surrounding the Beauregard home. I collapsed to the ground just as the police swarmed the place, guns drawn. "That way," I said while weakly pointing at the woods. "He went that way." My voice was weak.

What the fuck had just happened?

———

"I'm sure you're shaken up, but this isn't the first time we've been called here for overeager paparazzi," Officer Anders said. I was sitting on the couch, leaning over my legs while biting my nails. I'd found a summer dress to put on over my bathing suit, but I wanted to change into cozy pajamas and cry. "When Mrs. Beauregard died, they were relentless. Remember that, Josie?"

Officer Anders turned to look over his shoulder at his partner. "That was insane," she agreed while staring at a vase on the mantel. "I wasn't an officer yet, but I remember watching it on the news." Officer Anders and Detective Josie had stayed here for a couple of hours to take my statement and make sure that I was okay. Anders was an older man with thinning, gray hair, and he looked like he was nearing retirement. Josie was a petite woman with a snaggle tooth smile and plum lipstick.

"He was crazy. He had a gun," I replied, still pretty shaken up. I tried calling my mother and Joseph, but it was the middle of the night where they were, and no one answered. Jack's assistant assured me that she would have my busy grandfather call me as soon as possible.

I felt forgotten and alone.

"Saint has been harassing the Beauregard family for years. Jack has a protective order against him. We'll find him and arrest him for breaking it."

I nodded. "Will you leave someone here in case he comes back?" I asked while rubbing my arms.

"This neighborhood has guards patrolling the area around the clock. We've made them aware of the situation, and they'll be parking outside of the house. He won't come back, and if he does, you have our number," Detective Josie said while handing me her card. Yeah, this was not instilling a lot of confidence in me.

"Maybe I should get a hotel for the night?" I asked. Joseph and Mom left behind some emergency cash I hadn't touched. Maybe I just needed to... The sound of the front door opening stopped my train of thought.

"Are you expecting anyone?" Officer Anders whispered while blocking me with his body. Detective Josie drew her weapon. Who the hell was here?

"No!" I frantically whispered back. My heart was pumping chilled blood through my veins so hard that I felt like I was going to pass out. Was Saint back? I wasn't used to being so wrapped up in the public eye—or with the dangers associated with it.

"Hello?" a familiar voice called. "Is anyone home? Why are there cops out front?"

"Fuck," I exhaled before relaxing. "It's Jack's younger son," I explained to Officer Anders and Detective Josie. I wasn't sure why I didn't just call Hamilton my uncle. The title still felt strange to me, probably because I couldn't wipe the sight of him fucking Colleen from my mind.

Josie was holstering her Glock when Hamilton rounded the corner and took in the scene. He looked good, with his hair pushed back and a threadbare navy blue shirt stretched across his massive chest. There was a smudge of grease on his cheek, and a single bead of sweat rolled down his temple. "What's going on here?"

He then eyed me, his severe expression softening some. "Vera? Are you okay?"

It felt like I'd swallowed my tongue. Officer Anders answered for me, likely assuming my silence was a result of how traumatizing the day had been for me. "Mr. Beauregard, I'm Officer Anders. We received a distress call from Vera Garner this morning. I'm sure you remember Saint Torrance?"

Hamilton huffed. "Yeah. I know the guy." He then turned to look at me. "He bother you, Vera?"

I nodded while biting my lip. "Yeah," I finally choked out.

"Fuck." Hamilton turned to look at the officers. "Thank you for being here. My father is gone this week, right? Has he been made aware that Saint broke the protection order—again?"

"He's in DC for the week," Detective Josie confirmed. "His assistant said he will call us soon. We were just assuring Miss Garner that she has nothing to worry about."

"I'll stay here to make sure she's safe. I've dealt with Saint before," Hamilton replied.

A few more pleasantries were exchanged, but I simply sat on the edge of my seat, numb to the entire conversation. It wasn't until Officer Anders was wishing me well that I realized I was alone with Hamilton.

"What are you doing here?" I asked Hamilton after he shut the front door.

He froze for a moment, as if my question surprised him. "I sometimes like to stop by if I think Dad is out of town. My mom loved it here, and his whiskey stash is pretty legit."

That made sense. I guess if I had a fancy home at my disposal, I'd also drop in whenever I could. But why wait until his father was gone? "Well. Enjoy the house, I'm going to get a hotel for the night," I said before standing up. I was still pretty shaken up, and I had zero desire to stay here.

Hamilton took a step closer to me. "I can stay here with you tonight? I know it can be pretty overwhelming the first time."

I shook my head in confusion while squinting my eyes. "The first time?"

Hamilton folded his lips between his teeth and

nodded at his father's bar cart. "Want one?" he asked.

"No. I'm good."

I crossed my arms over my chest as I watched him, waiting for an explanation to his words. What did he mean, *first time*? He pulled a bottle of Bacardi out and let out a low whistle before pouring himself a glass. "The first time I realized my life was no longer my own, I was in the second grade," he explained before finding a second glass and pouring a shot in there. Sauntering over to me, he continued his story while holding out a glass for me to take. "You're going to need this. Every Beauregard knows that trauma pairs well with alcohol." I wrapped my fingers around the cool glass and took it from him.

"You were saying?"

He lifted his cup and eyed me over the rim before taking a burning swig. I eyed the steady bob of his Adam's apple. He licked his lips and continued. "My father had just gotten elected to—ah—I think district representative? I can't remember. He's had so many titles and roles over the years. His perfectionist platform gained him a lot of enemies. People like to poke holes in the lies politicians tell. It's human nature."

I swallowed a sip of my drink and let the burning

liquid saturate my throat and warm my chest. "Everyone likes Jack," I murmured.

"Everyone *thinks* they like Jack," he amended. "The first scandal of our family hit. A very young woman came forward claiming she was my real mother. We looked alike. We looked scarily alike. I was at school when the news hit, and the paparazzi swarmed the front lawn. They had to pull me out of class. I spent years dodging their questions. Oddly enough, I didn't hate them, though," he said before spinning around and walking over to a towering set of windows overlooking the yard. "Suppose it's hard to hate someone brave enough to ask the questions I was too afraid to. To this day, I don't know if that woman was telling the truth."

Fuck. I couldn't imagine. "Don't you want to know?" I asked.

Hamilton spun around to face me, wearing a smile that looked a little too scripted, a little too political. Did he get his convincing nature from his father or from years of trying to be something he wasn't?

"It wouldn't make a difference. I have—had—a mother." This was getting pretty deep and fast. I took another sip. "All I'm trying to say is you're going to have to get used to it. The moment Joseph married your mother, your life changed forever. Slowly, Jack is going to ask things of you. Slowly, they're going to polish you up and use you like a prop. The world is intrusive and chronically curious. They thrive on finding your dirty laundry and airing it out to dry."

"I don't have any dirty laundry." That was a lie. My entire existence was the dirtiest of laundry.

Hamilton smiled before stepping closer to me. "Not yet," he whispered.

"Not ever," I gritted.

Hamilton's eyes thinned to slits. He took a step closer. I took a step back. Back. Back. He pressed on until I collided with the wall. A nearby photo frame nailed to the drywall shook at the force of my landing. "All I'm saying is, you're better off getting used to it now." He caged me in, one of his palms landing beside my head. I was overwhelmed with his scent and emboldened by the way his muscles flexed and curled around me. It felt both predatory and freeing.

How dare he. "Is that why you work in an oil rig offshore and show up late to your only brother's wedding?" I asked before looking to my left at the hanging portrait now swaying on its perch. It was a painted depiction of Jack and Joseph. "You aren't even in the family portrait." I clicked my tongue and reached up to brace my palms against his chest.

"I prefer to be all or nothing," he whispered while leaning closer despite my pushes.

"I prefer to stay at a hotel tonight," I replied.

Hamilton smiled, as if my answer was somehow the right thing to say. "Then let's get you a damn hotel room, huh?"

4

*H*amilton was all too happy to take Jack's prized Aston Martin for a spin. He'd driven his motorcycle to Jack's house and didn't have a helmet for me to wear. I was fine with getting an Uber, but he *insisted* on escorting me to a hotel and taking Jack's classic ride. Something told me he just wanted an excuse to get behind the wheel of a three-hundred-thousand-dollar car.

Hamilton kept eyeing me with his dark gaze as

we drove down the winding roads toward the city. Jack's property was in a gated, secluded subdivision about thirty minutes from town, and the scenic road was lined with luxury cars and limos. It felt like the road to wealth, and the subtle divide between classes became clearer the closer we got to the city.

Before we left, Hamilton mentioned that he had a perfect place for me to stay where I'd feel safe from Saint. I didn't really care where I went, I just wanted out of the Beauregard house and away from the terror I'd felt earlier today. There was a time when Mom and I lived in some pretty bad places, but never had I felt so scared. "Did Saint say anything to you?" Hamilton finally asked once we'd gotten to a red light.

It was on the tip of my tongue to tell him what Saint said about my mother's marriage, but I swallowed it. "He asked me if I knew about your mother," I admitted. "He seems to think there's some scandal to uncover about her death."

Hamilton gripped the steering wheel, and he curled his lip. "Everyone loved my mom," he replied, his words careful and somehow calculating. "I've heard plenty of theories surrounding her death over the years. I'm not surprised that he's still fixated on that. People like to cling to conspiracy theories and gossip when someone wealthy dies young."

I leaned against the window while staring at him. "Jack never told me how she died," I replied. "Saint mentioned a heart condition but wasn't very convinced. I just think it's disrespectful to dig up the past like that. Jack is always so sad when he brings her up. I can't imagine losing your mom. He loved her."

Hamilton ran his tongue over his teeth and stared at the road. "He didn't love her. Not really. And you won't have to imagine it," he snapped back. "You'll lose yours soon enough. If my brother has anything to say about it." My words had obviously angered him, because he accelerated a bit harshly once the light turned green. "Fucking heart condition. What a joke." Hamilton's tone was bitter as he weaved in and out of traffic.

"What is that supposed to mean?" I asked. "What do you mean I'll lose her too?" My heart was racing. I grabbed the handle mounted on the door and squeezed my legs together as he went even faster down the road. The yellow lines dividing the street became a blur as we passed buildings, trees, and other cars. "Fuck," I cursed when he narrowly missed a pedestrian. Hamilton didn't even seem bothered.

"I meant exactly that. You're going to lose your mom, too. Not in the same way as I did, but Joseph is a possessive fucker. He won't let anyone in his life who isn't completely devoted to him. And if someone is in the way, he gets rid of them. You're a glaring reminder of imperfection, and the Beauregards like to sweep their imperfections under the rug."

What an ominous statement. Get rid of them? What did that even mean?

Hamilton's words were coming from a place of anger, but they rang true. I felt it in my gut that Joseph was slowly pushing me out and using everything at his disposal to do so. "My mom wouldn't push me away," I argued as he passed a school bus, nearly clipping the side of it.

"He makes it impossible to say no. He buys people. He uses every tool at his disposal to get what he wants."

When Hamilton swerved to cut off a Tesla, I'd had enough. "Can you please stop driving like an asshole?" I asked on a gasp.

He winced, then slowed down. "Right. Sorry," he muttered.

I watched the speedometer for a long moment before speaking again. "You really hate Joseph, huh?" I asked, fishing for more information.

"It's not an easy task, but I do. It's hard to hate family. You feel obligated to love them. Blood can be a curse if you aren't careful."

I swallowed. It was like Hamilton had spoken my greatest fears. I was the family forced on my mother; Joseph and this new baby were the family she'd chosen. In the end, would she have enough room for me?

Hot tears filled my eyes, and I nervously swatted them, praying that Hamilton didn't think I was crazy for crying in the front seat. We barely knew one another.

"Obligatory love is the worst kind of love," I whispered in agreement.

Hamilton turned to me, concern marring his expression. I swatted another tear as he kept glancing at me. "Oh, Vera," he said before turning into a parking lot full of townhomes. "Don't cry."

"I'm fine," I snapped when he patted my leg. It was a tender but quick touch, and I had the sudden urge to grab his hand.

He pulled his hand back and parked before turning off the car. I looked around, not sure where we were. "I thought you were taking me to a hotel. What's this?" I asked, my voice rough with emotion. I wasn't expecting to get so worked up by his comment. It had been such a difficult day. I just wanted to get cozy and go to sleep.

"My house," Hamilton replied with a polite grin before getting out of the car and walking up the sidewalk to a front door painted navy blue. I looked around at the white wood townhomes with manicured lawns. It was a middle-class neighborhood full of starter homes with young kids playing on the street, dogs barking, and trees swaying in the wind. It wasn't exactly what I was expecting of Hamilton. A bachelor pad would have been more appropriate.

I opened the door and grabbed my duffel bag. "This isn't a hotel, Hamilton," I called at his back as he fumbled with his keys and unlocked the door.

"This is safer. Plus, I have ingredients for a killer taco casserole," he replied over his shoulder before going inside. I gaped at him for a moment before sighing and following after him.

No sooner had I walked through the front door than a large gray ball of floof had launched for me. I giggled at the deep, excited bark and dropped to my knees to pet my new friend, all thoughts of Saint and being at Hamilton's house long gone. I loved dogs. Mom never let me get one because they were an "unnecessary expense," but once I was done with school, I was totally getting my own little rescue.

"Oh my goodness, hey there, girl!" I scratched behind her ears. I didn't really know what her breed was. She had dark gray short hair and a wide snout. Her eyes were a deep chocolate color, and her short tail wagged excitedly as I gave her a hug.

"What's your name?" I asked. "I bet it's perfect because you are just the best little buddy ever," I cooed. Hamilton cleared his throat, and I looked up at him. Leaning against the wall with his arms crossed over his chest, he had an amused look on his face.

"Her name is Little Mama. Found her in an alley with four pups. I couldn't leave them. After finding all her babies homes, I decided to keep her for myself. My roommate watches her when I'm on the rig."

"Little Mama," I squealed. Okay, her name was the cutest name ever. "If you ever need a dog sitter, let me know. Mom never let me have a dog," I said with a pout.

Hamilton grabbed a leash hanging on the wall, and Little Mama forgot all about me. He clicked it onto her collar as I stood up. I didn't wait for an invitation to join the two of them on a walk, and the three of us went outside and started exploring the sidewalk. "I might take you up on the dog sitting thing. My roommate got a girlfriend who's supposedly *the love of her life*, and wants to move in with her. This new girlfriend is allergic to dogs, so I'm trying to figure out what I'm going to do with Little Mama while I'm gone."

Hamilton paused as Little Mama sniffed a bush.

"I'm not sure what my new apartment's rules are on dogs. Actually, I've never even seen the apartment. Or my new college." I scowled as Little Mama did her business.

"You're going to Greenwich?" Hamilton asked. I nodded and we kept walking. "I'm about fifteen minutes from campus. Dad—Jack—wanted me to go, but it wasn't really my thing," Hamilton said. I swallowed my questions about why he called his father by his first name. I had no room to talk, I sometimes found myself saying Lilah instead of Mom.

"How long have you worked on the rig?" I asked.

"Jack got me the job when I turned eighteen," Hamilton replied as a jogger passed us by on the sidewalk. His voice was laced with a tone I couldn't quite process. "I wasn't going anywhere in life. I guess you could say it was an offer I couldn't refuse."

Little Mama started pulling us along, practically dragging her nose along the concrete as we went. "It must be hard," I murmured.

"What?"

"Being gone for weeks at a time. Your routine is constantly changing, and you flip between two homes."

Hamilton slowed his steps, and Little Mama whined. He looked me up and down, as if debating on telling me something. "I guess—"

My phone started ringing, cutting him off before he could say anything. "Sorry," I began. "I need to answer this." I pulled my cell out of my purse and tossed him an apologetic smile before answering.

"Vera? Are you okay?" Jack's voice rushed out. "I'm firing my assistant. I can't believe she told you that I would call you back. Where are you? Are you safe? I'll be on the next flight home."

"Jack, I'm fine," I replied, interrupting his rambling. Hamilton nodded his head once before continuing to walk toward a patch of grass for Little Mama. I watched his back while speaking to Jack. "The police arrived and took my statement. Apparently, this isn't the first time?"

Jack cursed. "Vera, I am so sorry. I'll head home now. I'm sure you're shaken up. You don't need to be alone right now..."

"I'm not alone," I whispered. Hamilton bent down to scratch behind Little Mama's ears. He was grinning at her, the hard lines of his face twisting into a playful smirk.

"Oh? Did Joseph and Lilah come home early?"

"Hamilton showed up," I replied. "He just so happened to be in the area and saw the cops out front. He offered to let me stay at his place tonight." The other end of the phone line went silent. After a few awkward moments, I spoke again. "Jack?"

"Yes. Sorry, I'm here. Hamilton was in the area?" Jack's voice sounded oddly emotional. "Was he coming to see me? Does he need anything?"

"He, uh, hasn't mentioned anything."

"Right. Of course."

Jack went silent again, and Hamilton headed back toward me. He mouthed *You okay?* while watching me clutch my cell to my ear.

"I'm going to head home early. You said you're staying with Hamilton?"

"Yeah. We're at his house now."

"Good. Good. Stay there. I'll be there by morning

to get you moved into your new apartment. Can you do me a favor?"

"Of course," I replied.

"Tell Hamilton thank you. And, uh, tell him I'm glad he was in the area. And that he is always welcome home. And that I miss him. Actually, never mind. I'll just text him. Does he seem okay?" Jack asked, his voice quiet. "Does he seem happy?"

I looked Hamilton in the eye. There was something dark hidden in the depths of his charcoal gaze. I couldn't quite put my finger on it, but it wasn't my assumption to make or my story to tell. "Yeah, Jack," I whispered.

"I'll see you in the morning," Jack replied gruffly before hanging up.

———————

HAMILTON'S TOWNHOUSE WAS NICE. IT WAS impersonal, though. Despite the high-end accents and expansive kitchen, there was nothing personal about the place. No pictures hung on the walls. No decor to personalize the space. It was an open concept but a bland execution.

There were, however, some parts of it that told me about Hamilton. There was an overflowing ceramic bowl sitting on the countertop full of seasonal fruits and vegetables. A banged up wooden cooking block with kitchen knives and shears looked well used. The pantry was stocked, and he had a calendar pinned to the oversized stainless steel refrigerator, with meals written down for every day he was home. Hamilton liked to cook. High-end pots and pans hung from a rack on the ceiling, and he hummed while he cooked a simple recipe from memory.

"So where is your roommate?" I asked as we sat down at Hamilton's wooden kitchen table to eat the taco casserole he'd made.

"She'll be home later," Hamilton replied before shoveling food in his mouth. "Jess works late most weekends. She bartends at a local spot. I sometimes try to stay up so I can visit with her when I'm home."

I took a dollop of sour cream and put it on my plate. "How'd you meet?" I asked. I wanted to learn more about Hamilton.

"We both went to school together. I've known her since I was in eighth grade. We were both outcasts in our families. Her father was a wealthy preacher that directed a local mega church. When she came out, it was a whole scandal."

"Ouch," I replied before taking a big bite of food.

Flavor burst on my tongue, and I nearly died from bliss right there in my seat. "Fuck, this is good," I moaned.

Hamilton grinned. "Thank you."

I continued to chew. Little Mama was lying at my feet, and Hamilton had poured me a glass of red wine that I hadn't touched. "So how many years of friendship is that?" I asked, hopefully sounding casual as I asked his age. Hamilton was definitely younger than my stepfather, but he carried himself in a way that felt more mature than most. It was like he'd seen the world. I once read a book that said trauma aged a person. Bad experiences had the power of maturity.

"Is that your way of asking how old I am?" he teased.

"I'm just curious. I'm going to be almost nineteen years older than my younger sibling. You both seem to have a similar age difference."

"I'm twenty-eight," Hamilton answered before taking another bite.

"Not too old," I replied before reaching for my glass of wine. He clicked his tongue and reached over the tabletop to grab the glass before I could. Our fingers brushed in the process.

"I didn't realize you were underaged. Would you

like a juice box? Fuck. I could have gone to prison for the stunt I pulled at the wedding. Thank hell you aren't a high schooler."

"I don't need a juice box," I snapped back.

"A bottle of milk then?" he teased.

"Hilarious." My dry response had Hamilton laughing. Sure enough, he got up and dumped the contents of my glass out and pulled out some cranberry juice from the fridge. I watched him pour some in my glass and shook my head in amusement when he set it in front of me.

"Here. You can pretend to be a big kid now."

"You do realize you gave me whiskey earlier, right?"

"That was before I realized you were barely an adult," he retorted.

"The legal drinking limit is a joke. I can sign up to go to war, but I can't buy a beer?"

"You're too pretty for war," Hamilton whispered before going back to his seat. His lips formed into a slow, building smile as he stared intently at me. I met his gaze head on as he licked his lips. My heart pounded, and he took a sip of his drink. "Besides, I don't take you as much of a drinker."

I shifted my weight on the hard wooden kitchen chair. "I'm not. I never really had time for wild teen acts of rebellion," I admitted before scraping my fork across my plate.

"My entire life has been one big act of rebellion," Hamilton replied with a laugh before leaning back in his chair. "What's the craziest thing you've ever done then, hmm?" His question made me blush. I knew my answer almost immediately. The memory that bombarded me was both intrusive and dirty. I had to fight the smile begging to cross my face. Hamilton's eyebrow arched. "Oh, this is going to be good."

I licked my lips and averted my eyes. "It's nothing, really. Compared to what you've probably done."

Hamilton leaned forward. "It's all relative. Don't compare your wild to someone else's."

"The comparison trap is a slippery slope," I agreed.

Hamilton bit his lip and folded his hands under his chin, as if preparing to listen intently to me. "Now tell me what has those pretty cheeks of yours turning pink. Give me your worst." I let out an exhale and tucked a stray hair behind my ear while looking at the kitchen. I inhaled the smell of our dinner while prolonging the inevitable. "I'm waiting."

"Fine," I replied before dragging my eyes to his. The intensity that met me made me gasp. "I had sex with the quarterback of our high school football team in a science lab. It was my first time, but he was gentle with me. We'd been flirting a lot," I said before stopping to pick at my nails. I hadn't orgasmed, which wasn't a deal breaker in the moment. It was raw and passionate and...quick...

"Naughty," Hamilton replied. "Were you dating?"

"Not really. I was helping him study for our chemistry exam."

"You know, I think I saw a porno like that once," he replied cheekily while running his hands along his thighs.

I ignored his comment. "It was fun. I felt wild and wanton. But then he texted me about it, and Mom went through my phone," I admitted. "She freaked. Made me get Plan B and then grounded me. She said she didn't want me ruining my life like she did." I never told my mother that I hated feeling like her mistake. She took my first time and twisted it into something that made me feel inadequate and wrong. "She also made me look at photos of STDs and threatened me with all kinds of punishments. She told me that my body was like a delicate rose, and every time I slept with someone, I was plucking a petal off."

Hamilton pinched his lips together. "That's kind of toxic," he replied, his face serious, those dark eyes of his wide in disbelief.

"I get why she is the way she is. She wanted me to have all the things she couldn't have. I think when you're coming from a place of resentment and fear, it's hard to say or do the right thing. I just feel like I'm supposed to do everything she missed out on, you know? Anyway, he and I hooked up in secret a couple of times after that when Mom worked late. But it wasn't anything serious. I ended things when the guilt got to be too much."

Hamilton's face twisted into anger, and he stood up, grabbing his plate as he did so that he could put it in the sink. "I guess he wasn't good enough to make you stay, hmm?" Hamilton asked, his face turned away from me. "And I suppose that makes sense. We try to be everything our parents aren't. It's why I'm determined to be happy."

"Happy?" I asked as he rinsed off his plate in the sink.

"It's the one thing Jack Beauregard isn't," Hamilton answered before turning to face me.

"Jack seems plenty happy," I countered.

"*Seems* is the key word, Petal. It's easy to look one thing and be something completely different." I nodded, understanding Hamilton but not quite wanting to believe him. "It's been a long day. Let's get the pull-out couch set up."

I nodded. "Okay. Yeah. Thanks." This conversation was getting heavy.

We made our way to the living room, and Hamilton found some spare sheets and an oversized fuzzy blanket for me to use. I got ready for bed in the spare bathroom and thought over the conversation I'd had with him. I was desperate to figure out the family dynamics. I knew in my gut that their strained relationships started the day his mother died. But why?

Hamilton was setting a glass of water on the coffee table when I made my way back. "I'll be gone in the morning before you leave. Lock up for me, yeah?"

He started walking away, not even giving me a chance to reply. "Thanks for letting me stay!" I called at him. My only answer was the sound of his slamming bedroom door.

What made Hamilton run so hot and cold?

5

I woke up to the sound of Little Mama whining and an unfamiliar voice chastising her. "Hold on, you needy little brat. You've already had three treats today, and if I give you any more, we both know it'll go straight to your hips. Your metabolism isn't what it used to be." I sat up on the couch, my threadbare sleep shirt hanging off my shoulder. I smacked my lips and looked around the dark room, trying to remember where I was.

Hamilton.

"Good. You're up," a raspy voice said. I looked over the edge of the couch and was greeted by a beautiful woman. She was wearing a gray tank top and ripped jeans. There was a lip ring in her plump pout, and her dark skin was smooth. She was tall and toned. "Hamilton left already but explained the situation. I'm Jess."

Hamilton left? I stood up and nervously walked over to her. "Hey. I'm Vera, it's nice to meet you." I held out my hand for her to shake, and she simply raised her pierced eyebrow.

Up close, I could see specks of gold in her brown eyes, and a shaved line in her eyebrow. She had a slim gap between her front teeth and smelled like cigarette smoke. "Sorry, hon. Any family of Hamilton's is an enemy of mine. Feel free to freshen up and see yourself out. Oh. And fuck you."

My brows shot up. I wasn't prepared for such anger this early in the morning from a complete stranger, but at the same time, it spoke volumes about her devotion and loyalty to Hamilton. I shrugged. I wasn't really the type of person to get offended if someone didn't like me.

"Okay, no problem," I replied while holding my hands up. "I'll go get dressed."

Jess squinted at me as I turned around and made my way to the bathroom. I took a quick, hot shower, not bothering to wash my long hair. After brushing my teeth and putting on deodorant, I got dressed in a pair of high-waisted shorts and a black crop top. When I made my way back to the living room, Jess was sitting on the recliner with a cup of coffee in her hands, looking me up and down with scrutiny.

"How are you and Hamilton related again?" she asked. Oh, so now she wanted to know about me?

I started folding the blankets on the couch. "My mom shotgun married his older brother," I admitted. The honesty dripping from my tongue felt good. "I met Hamilton at the wedding. Well, *meet* is a really loose term for our first introduction. I walked in on him fucking the bridesmaid."

Jess broke out into a smile, showing off her bright teeth. "Classic Hamilton."

I, too, grinned. Looking back at it, seeing Hamilton fuck a bridesmaid was fitting for our strange dynamic. "It *was* pretty memorable." I kept replaying what I saw on loop in my mind. I bit my lip while shoving my pajamas in my duffel bag before checking my phone. Jack had sent a text an hour ago saying he was leaving soon.

"I feel bad for your mom. Joseph is a dick," Jess

said before taking a sip. She was testing the waters with me, I could tell. I knew Jess for all of thirty minutes and could already tell that she wasn't discreet, she didn't bury her disdain deep in her chest. She wore her opinions like a badge of honor. It was endearing, and if one of those opinions wasn't hatred of me, we'd probably be friends.

"I don't really know him, and I don't make a habit of judging people I don't know." I gave Jess a pointed stare, letting her know with a single look exactly what I thought of her snap judgment of me.

"Fair enough." Jess seemed soured but still determined. She set her cup down on a side table and crossed her arms over her chest. "Hamilton brought you here, though. I'm trying to decide if it's because of his tragic guilt that seems to dictate every decision he makes, or if there's something special about you."

Tragic guilt? I wanted to know what she meant by that, but I kept my curiosity to myself. "It's probably neither," I answered. "Maybe he just was trying to be nice."

Jess cackled dramatically, her raspy voice wrapping around me like smoke. "Hamilton isn't nice."

"He was nice to me," I admitted.

"Fine. Let's see if you're worthy," Jess said while looking me up and down. "Rapid fire friendship questions. One round. Don't think, just answer. I like to get to the nitty gritty right off the bat. Favorite alcoholic drink?"

What did this have to do with Hamilton? "Not much of a drinker. I don't smoke weed either."

"Perfect. Hamilton has an addictive personality, so you have to be careful. Women's rights?"

"Well, duh. I'm a woman. Of course I want women's rights."

"I love a strong woman. Hamilton needs someone that doesn't accept less than what she deserves." Jess rubbed her hands together before continuing. "If you had to choose between good sex with a bad partner or bad sex with a good partner, what would you choose?"

I swallowed. My first instinct was to say good sex, but then I thought of roses with plucked petals and said something else. "Neither. I don't settle."

"Pro-choice? I volunteer at a woman's center, so I like to make sure the people I surround myself with aren't going to shame me for that."

The answer spilled out of me before I could stop myself. No one had ever really asked me that before. "That's tricky. My mother was fifteen when she had me. I'm thankful she kept me, because I kind of like being alive, but she shouldn't have had to. I'm not sure if it was guilt that made her go through with the pregnancy or if she just didn't have access to the services to terminate. I know she didn't want to be a mother, but she didn't want to give me up for adoption either. I think she was just too young to make those decisions and didn't have someone in her life to help her through the process. She just did what she thought she was supposed to, and we both struggled needlessly." I slammed my lips closed. I'd never admitted that before. Time seemed to stop, and I pressed the pads of my fingers to my mouth. Was that truly how I felt? Did I wish my mother would have gotten an abortion? She was so young. So vulnerable. "Why are you asking me all of this?"

"Because it's fun." Jess shrugged before pressing on. "Who do you love most in the world?"

"My mom."

"Why?"

I opened my mouth, trying to come up with a list of reasons I knew were appropriate. Because she was family. Because she always took care of me. Because loving her was this instinctual thing children were hardwired to do. "I just do. I don't have to explain why I love someone to you."

"Amen to that. Trying to explain to my conservative parents why I loved women was obnoxious. Fuck them." Jess yelped before fist pumping the air. I noticed a tattoo of Ruth Bader Ginsburg on her arm. "If you could eat anything for the rest of your life, what meal would it be?"

"I lived on cheap mac 'n' cheese for a majority of my childhood, so I'd probably pick that."

"When was the first day of your last menstrual period?"

"Excuse me?"

"I like to know if we are in sync."

"I'm not answering that," I snapped.

"Fine. Is it more important to be a good person or be a liked person?"

I scowled. "Good people are generally liked," I replied.

"You're so naïve. It's cute," Jess replied while cocking her head to the side. "Are you religious?"

"I think there's a god up there. I'm not really a churchgoer."

"My dad is a pastor and kind of an asshole," Jess explained. "Are you attracted to Hamilton?"

"He's my uncle," I stammered.

"That isn't what I asked."

I straightened my spine. It was my turn. Ignoring

her question, I then spoke. "If you found someone's wallet on the ground, would you return it to them?" I asked.

Jess tilted her chin. "Of course."

"If you had to give your kidney to one person in the world, who would it be?"

"Hamilton," she replied, squirming. "Definitely Hamilton. But he'd be stupid and not accept my kidney, then make me plan his fucking funeral."

"Would you rather be rich and miserable or poor and happy?"

"I've been both, and I like myself more when I'm poor," she admitted. "Maybe you're not so terrible. You seem like the type of person I could potentially not hate. Down to earth. You aren't chronically privileged like the rest of the Beauregards, too. I volunteer with a few nonprofits. You should check out my blog, *Activist Bitch*."

I eyed Jess. "That's great," I began dryly. "I've benefitted from quite a few nonprofits over the years. Most of the volunteers liked to take photos with my mom and me when we were at our most vulnerable. Then, they'd plaster it all over Facebook so they could brag to their friends about how generous they are." She stared at me with her brow arched. "For the record, I prefer to get to know people organically and not through some really invasive rapid-fire interrogation, but I'm glad we could get the major topics out of the way. Since you want to know all about me, I'll tell you some more."

Jess laughed, but I wasn't trying to be funny. Teen moms were constantly scrutinized, but even more so, people liked to pity their children and judge their successes and failures based on the shortcomings of their parents. I spent my entire life trying to prove that my mother was worthy and good. I couldn't slip up once, because I was a direct representation of her. People already had a lot to say about a fifteen-year-old girl raising a child. I never wanted to add to her problems.

I continued. "I was born in Atlanta and lived on food stamps most of my life. I always lived in the *bad part of town* until we moved here five years ago. I graduated top of my class because until now, my only hopes of attending college were dependent on whether or not I could get a full scholarship. I've got a teen mom who loves me but also kind of resents me." Jess's smile faded a bit, and I continued. "Despite this, I had a really good life. I'm out of my depth here. I feel like everyone is judging my mother and me, which we're both used to. I'm not looking for anyone's approval, least of all some bitch I just met."

"I was kind of shitty, wasn't I?" Jess asked.

"A little? But it doesn't really matter. Jack's about to be here, and I have to move into a new apartment I've never seen, learn about a school I don't want to go to, and deal with the trauma of a home invasion that happened yesterday. But hey. Thanks for giving me a stamp of approval that I never asked for."

Jess rolled her eyes, like my speech was an inconvenience. "Are you done? Give me your phone," she said while holding out her palm.

"Why?"

"Because I'm going to give you my number and we're going to be friends. I might be a little eccentric and a hell of a lot overprotective of Hamilton, but it's with good reason. You know, in the four years we've lived together, he's never once brought someone home? He always fucks at hotels. He has some guy friends, but even they don't come here."

Holy whiplash, Batman.

I pulled my phone out of my pocket and tossed it to her, not caring if she saw the text from Jack. She typed a bit and then called herself so that she could have my number too.

"Jack's here," she said while handing me back my

phone. "Do me a favor and tell him to get fucked for me." She licked her middle finger and grinned playfully.

"I like Jack," I answered.

"Sure you do. Everyone hates him eventually," Jess replied ominously. "I'll call you later. We're going to hang out. I can see why Hamilton is *nice* to you."

"Maybe you shouldn't call me? Yeah?" I asked while throwing my duffel bag over my shoulder.

"Too late. I like you now. I'm going to wear you down," Jess said before grabbing the TV remote and turning on the news. I made my way to the front door, with Little Mama hot on my heels.

I paused before opening the door so I could scratch behind her ears. "See you soon," I promised the perfect pooch. She wagged her entire lower body in excitement.

———

"Morning! Do you want a tour of the campus?" was the first thing Jack asked when I settled in the cool leather passenger seat of his Aston Martin. When did Hamilton bring it back to the house? Jack's tone was giddy as he gripped the steering wheel. Something about his demeanor made me think he was avoiding what had happened yesterday with Saint and our phone call about Hamilton.

"That would be great, Jack," I replied.

"Perfect!"

I was still shaken from all the things that had happened yesterday and today. Saint showing up. Hamilton coming to the rescue. Jess interrogating me. It felt like an earthquake tearing apart my own existence. Shaky ground didn't make for a good foundation, and it felt like my entire world was cracked right down the middle. I had nothing really to hold on to.

Four boxes. Four measly boxes lined the back of Jack Beauregard's Aston Martin. My life summed up in flimsy cardboard stuffed with mementos from a life that now felt foreign to me. Thankfully, Jack had grabbed my belongings from the house and brought them here. I was glad I didn't have to go back to his estate so soon. Even though I was anxious about this new phase of my life, I was glad I didn't have to stay there any longer. Saint really freaked me out, and the more I could distance myself from that, the better. I just wanted to feel normal for a bit.

According to Jack, interior designers had already taken over and moved in brand new top-of-the-line furniture. Expertly tailored outfits for every occasion were also delivered two days ago. It felt like too much, but he assured me that he was happy to do it. "We have a lot of events coming up with my reelection. I want you to feel comfortable and have nice things to wear to them."

Was what I already owned not enough?

I tossed him a polite smile while adjusting the freezing cold air vents off of me. It was only fifteen minutes away from Hamilton's house, and Jack was all too happy to tell me every single detail he could recall about Greenwich University, his alma mater.

The opulent campus was timeless. The sprawling manicured lawns were filled with lounging students wearing preppy designer clothes, even though classes didn't start for another two weeks. I immediately felt out of place at this private university, but Jack proudly boasted how he always felt at home when visiting.

"Over here is the new Beauregard Business Building," he said while pointing at a statue of...holy shit...himself. The bronze statue was tall and imposing.

"Whoa," I said.

"You like? I made sure they shaved some of my stomach off. Didn't want to be eternally fat, you know?" He chuckled at his joke and turned down another street. I didn't even want to think about how much money you had to donate to have a new building named after you and get a statue erected in your honor.

"My wife and I first met outside the chemistry building. She wore a plaid skirt and was clutching a mountain of textbooks to her chest. She dropped them all, and I helped her carry them to her dorm," Jack recalled with a secret grin. "She made me work for a first date but oh, it was worth it. When she died, I had her favorite park bench here moved to the gardens at our summer home."

"I bet you miss her."

"Every day," Jack replied.

I chewed on my lip, not sure what to say. Jack continued his tour, pointing out sentimental spots while groaning about changes to the campus. He was a traditionalist and made it obvious how much he hated the new buildings being built—aside from the one named after him, of course.

"So, you want a degree in social work, yes? What exactly do you want to do?" Jack asked.

"I want to be a child welfare specialist," I replied while looking out the window.

"What made you want to do that?" he asked

while turning down a side street toward a collection of apartment buildings.

I bounced my knee in the car, my fingers tingling as I tried to come up with my answer. "I guess you could say I was born wanting to be an advocate for children," I whispered.

Jack nodded and let out an, "Ahh. Your mother."

I snapped my head to the left to stare at him as he pulled into an unfamiliar parking lot. "What do you mean?"

"I, uh, I just mean I know about your mother. She was in an abusive situation, yes?" I knotted my fingers in my shirt, desperate to get out of the car. Jack must have seen something in my expression, because his eyes widened. "I'm so sorry, honey. It's not my place." I was fiercely protective of my mother, and Jack Beauregard just dropped that bomb as if he was talking about the weather.

"How do you know about that?" I asked.

Jack let out a sigh. "My team did a background check on your family when Joseph announced that they were dating. I didn't mean to be intrusive. The report was very enlightening. I'm shocked your mother managed so much at such a young age."

I scoffed. Didn't mean to be intrusive? What the fuck? "And what exactly did your report tell you?

Did you find out that my father was actually one of my grandmother's boyfriends?"

Jack pulled over, then looked down at his lap. A white-hot anger burned through me. "You both are very tenacious. You've overcome so much. It's honestly impressive how far you've come. I didn't mean to overstep. I'm just protective of my son. You have to understand that. He's wanting to get into politics, and he's going to inherit a lot of money. I didn't want any scandals. I mean, goodness, Joseph mistakenly got her pregnant. I understand why he wanted to do the right thing and marry her, but we had to be smart about it."

I gaped at him. "So how did your people decide to spin it to the papers, hmm? Charity case or a redemption story?"

"Neither. I made sure your mother's abuse was sealed in court records."

"So, a shameful secret," I said softly in disbelief.

Perhaps it was the intensity of the last few days, but I didn't bother holding back. "Thanks for the tour, Jack. I can handle it from here." I unbuckled my seatbelt with a huff of frustration.

"Vera, when you've been in the public eye for as long as I have, you learn that you have to be careful. I'm just trying to protect my family. Joseph impulsively married your mother, and I wanted to know what we were up against. I've never intentionally tried to make you, or your mother, feel like outsiders. But you didn't grow up in this world."

I understood where he was coming from, but it still upset me. I couldn't quite figure out if I was upset because he knew our dirty secret or because it hurt to think about. I blew out a noisy breath and angled my body away from Jack. "You just caught me off guard. You're protective of your sons, right? Well, I'm protective of her. Mom wouldn't want her new father-in-law talking about her trauma so flippantly. She could have been a statistic, but she overcame. She worked hard and protected me. The moment I was born, she got us out of her mother's trailer. She dropped out of school, got her GED, and busted her ass to take care of me. She didn't have to keep me, let alone take care of me, but she did. Please don't let her know that you know. It's bad enough she has to look me in the eye every day of her life and see *him*. She doesn't need to see your pity, too."

Jack sighed. "Most men in my position don't allow their sons to marry for love. We do business arrangements. We set our kids up with someone who will make our fortune grow. Be glad I even allowed it—"

"Allowed?!" I shook my head in disgust. "You think you're so much better than us. I thought you were so kind and welcoming. I had no idea you were looking down your nose at us this entire time."

Jack didn't falter. He had a true politician's soul, because he kept to his views implicitly. "I own some of the largest corporations in the world. I'm the governor of one of the wealthiest states in the country. I've lived my life in the public eye. It's unfair to expect you to seamlessly adapt to a world that molds infants into ruthless billionaires, but you should get used to this."

"Used to what?"

"Every bit of your life will be picked apart from here on out. Your mother married into one of the most well-known families in the world. You see that black car following us? That's my security detail. I'm in the newspaper daily. You're under a microscope, now. I can control what the media knows, but this isn't a fairy tale, Vera. This is your life. I won't apologize for making sure your mother wouldn't ruin the legacy I worked so hard to build. I don't like uncontrollable variables. All I did was look into her past and make sure it wouldn't come back to bite us in the ass. You should be thanking me for handling such a scandal. It's hard to cover up something when there is living, breathing proof. If people knew what you were a product of—"

My heart clenched. My chest felt so tight that I clutched it. "How dare you!" He'd voiced an insecurity that had been plaguing me for years.

"You act like this is a bad thing!" Jack sounded exasperated. "The world is at your fingertips. Your mother could have never hoped to provide you with the sort of opportunities I have access to. She won't have to work three jobs. You won't have to bend over backward for a scholarship at a mediocre school. I don't understand the problem. You're just like Ha—"

Jack chewed on the inside of his cheek.

"Just like Hamilton?" I asked, finishing his statement for him. "The son you sent away?"

"He *wanted* to leave. I gave him an out. He asked for a normal life away from me, and I gave it to him. I can give you the same thing if you'd like. University in Europe. A job at one of my companies. This is a choice—a choice your mother made for the both of you when she got knocked up and trapped Joseph in a marriage. If I weren't running on a platform that prioritizes family values, I wouldn't have even considered it. I have too many corporations relying on the legislation I pass to let anyone ruin my chances for reelection. You can think I'm cruel, but it's just business. I'm just giving you an opportunity to be a part of the family, Vera."

I wasn't sure this was a family I wanted to be a part of. I placed my hand on the door handle, desperate for space from Jack. "Vera," he called after me as I exited his car. I kept walking. "Vera!" I put more distance between Jack and me, mulling over Jess's words as I did.

"Everyone hates him eventually..."

6

*M*om had called me six times in the last two days. I texted her, blaming poor cell service in my new apartment for not answering her call. She was very worried about me. News about Saint breaking into the Beauregard home and accosting me became public, and there was a lot of sympathy surrounding the entire ordeal. I went to the grocery store for some comfort food last night, and someone took photos of me buying ice cream and Coke. The gossip was nauseating. Some said I was eating my feelings. Naturally, there were comments about my weight. Some said I was too skinny. Some said I had gotten fat. There was also gossip that my late-night food run was a product of pregnancy cravings. Now that Mom and Joseph had announced her pregnancy, everyone was curious about our family. Apparently, there was a good portion of the population that believed Mom and I both got pregnant at the same time. They called it the Mother-Daughter Pregnancy Pact.

I hadn't really paid attention to the gossip before, but ever since my talk with Jack, the universe kept throwing it in my face. People called us white trash. Every news organization painted my mother as a gold digger cashing in on an opportunity.

Luckily, Greenwich University was used to catering to the elite, so they had good security on campus. My apartment had guards around the clock, so I felt safe.

But I also felt trapped.

Mom was worried and wanted to hear my voice, but I was too twisted up inside. If she could hear or see me, she'd recognize the anger buried in my tone. I was still livid with Jack, and yet I couldn't blame him, either. My brief brush with this Saint gave me a glimpse into their world. Jack was just trying to protect his legacy, but I was coping with the trauma of where I'd come from. I couldn't figure out if he was conditioned to be heartless and treat the world through such a business-like lens or if he was just that blasé about how he conducted his family's affairs. Either way, it left a really bad taste in my mouth. In my mind, Jack was my sweet, trustworthy grandfather. I really liked him. Was it all an act? And if it was an act, how did he become so good at pretending to care?

Jack just wanted to safeguard his reputation and wealth. I saw the signs. I knew that this rushed wedding and the rumors were true. I just hated that Mom's new beginning was starting off on the wrong foot. She deserved better. It wasn't her fault that her only daughter was a product of rape. And she shouldn't have to hide what happened to her or be bullied for her upbringing. I knew that every single person in the Beauregards' circle would look down their noses at us more than they already were if they knew the truth. In some ways, I was thankful that Jack managed to bury the story to protect Mom. I just hated that he even had to. And more than that, I hated how indifferent he was about the entire thing.

I was sitting on my oversized plush couch,

flipping through help wanted ads online when yet another call came through, but this time it wasn't my mother's name on the caller ID.

I answered the video call, and Jess's face appeared. "Hello there, stranger," she said with a grin. "Hamilton and I are going out tonight, you want to come?" Behind her, Hamilton was shrugging out of a shirt. I couldn't help but stare at the dips of his hard body and the tan skin that stretched over his large muscles. Holy shit. He looked far too beautiful for his own good. "I'm going to take your drool as a yes," Jess teased, snapping me out of my staring. Hamilton turned his head over to us and then looked down at his abs, brushing his fingers along each muscle in a playfully teasing way. He knew exactly what he was doing—and I loved it.

Wait. No, I didn't. Bad, Vera. Very, very bad.

"I'm not drooling," I rushed out. "And where are we going? I'm not even sure I like you, remember?"

Hamilton chuckled and picked up a black shirt before putting it on. "Were you mean to my little rose petal, Jess?" he asked. Rose petal? Why did that make my cheeks feel hot all of a sudden?

Jess's eyes widened. "Yours, huh?" she asked before continuing. "And maybeeee," she replied.

"Come on, *Petal.* Let's go. Don't you want to meet people? You wanted to make friends, right?"

"Where are we going?" I asked, my mind still on the paparazzi that followed me to the grocery store. What if they found Hamilton and me together? It was normal, right? To spend time with my...uncle?

"My girlfriend's band is playing at a local venue. She's really good, and last time she had ten people show up. Tonight, we're hoping for fifteen. Come on. We need all the help we can get."

"What kind of band?" I asked.

"It's kind of a crossover between polka and alternative screamo."

My face twisted up in horror. "That sounds terrible."

Hamilton tossed his head back and laughed. "That's what I said!" he called out.

Jess picked up something and tossed it at his head. "Please! I'm trying to support my girl here, guys!"

I chewed on my lip before responding. "I'm not sure if I should. I had some paparazzi follow me to the grocery store, and I don't want to give them any more ammunition..."

"I've been dodging journalists for years. You're yesterday's news, Petal," Hamilton said, his voice a lazy drawl. "They won't find you there. And if they do, I'll do something scandalous so they'll focus on me and not on you."

"Are you sure? This is all new to me, and I just don't want to—"

"It'll be fine! Promise," Hamilton assured me.

"Are you going to interrogate me more?" I asked Jess, brow arched.

"I solemnly swear not to ask you a million questions again," she promised while holding up her pinky finger for me to see.

"Fine," I began. "Send over the address. What time does it start?"

"I knew I liked you," Jess replied. Liar. "It starts at ten."

"I'll meet you there. I'm still trying to figure out the public transit situation, so I might be a little late."

"I'll come get you," Hamilton called over his shoulder.

"That's okay—"

He marched up to the phone and grabbed it out of Jess's hands. Once he was fully in the frame, I swallowed at the sight of him. God, why did he have to be so hot? Up close, I could see every detail of his perfect face. "I'll come pick you up. See you in thirty minutes. Text Jess your address."

I nodded, unable to say anything because my fucking traitorous throat closed up.

"Do I make you nervous, Petal?" he asked, picking up on my mood.

"No." I straightened my spine to echo my words. I didn't know how to respond. My conversation with Jack had cut deeper than I thought. He was all about his image, and for reasons I was still learning, Hamilton was already an outcast. How would it look if I had a foolish crush on my...uncle? Saint would have a field day with that knowledge. The title made me want to gag. Not that it really mattered. Hamilton wasn't interested in me. I just felt like I was navigating a chessboard and didn't know the rules.

"You feel it, don't you?" He licked his lips, his eyes dark as he cocked his head to the side. "The chemistry between us."

I swallowed; my eyes widened in shock at his assessment. "Do you think we have chemistry, Hamilton?" I asked, unsure why I was hanging onto his answer like it was air and I'd been sitting under water for hours.

"I'm choking on the tension between us, Petal. My cock's been perpetually hard for the last three days just thinking about you," Hamilton mocked with a smile before pulling away. "See you soon. Wear something slutty."

I shook my head. Hamilton gave me whiplash with his mood swings. "What are you, my pervy uncle?"

He tipped his head back and laughed. "I'm the uncle that's going to help you get laid and loosen up a bit. You need your pussy licked. Fuck the rose analogy. Petals are meant to be picked, Watcher."

My throat went dry. Something was different about Hamilton. He was more brazen today.

"I'll wear what I want."

"You tell him, girl," Jess called.

Hamilton hung up the phone.

———

I WAS SMOOTHING THE THREADBARE FABRIC OF MY favorite band shirt when a knock on the door made me pause. I decided to wear a black denim miniskirt with combat boots and my tee tied up at the waist. The outfit showed off a sliver of my tanned, toned stomach, and my long hair fell in waves over my shoulders and down my back. Every bit of my outfit was picked with Hamilton in mind.

I couldn't help but obsess over his words…

Petals are meant to be picked.

I reached up and pressed my index finger to my bottom lip, imagining the feel of his full mouth on mine. Attraction was such a fickle thing. How could something so out of reach—so forbidden—feel so necessary? Ever since Hamilton's gaze clashed with mine, I felt this dirty, filthy need for him. It wasn't right, and I knew that it was risky to spend more time with him. Wanting Hamilton Beauregard was like standing outside in the middle of a lightning storm while holding a tall metal rod in your fist. There was a thrill in the risk of getting struck by lightning. Self-preservation had me wearing rubber boots but still wanting to dance through the storm.

Mom would be disappointed in me. Something told me she wouldn't want me fantasizing about her new husband's younger brother. It was too scandalous. Too taboo. Then, of course, there was the issue of these feelings being unrequited. Hamilton ran hot and cold. Anything between us would be raw, passionate, and *fucking temporary*. I wasn't sure the risk was worth it.

I could do one-night stands, but I knew in my gut that Hamilton would be different. I'd had sex before, but I still allowed my mother's words to dictate the shame I felt about doing it. Every time I fucked, I was so in my own head that I rarely came. I craved physical intimacy. Maybe it was time to stop letting my mother's hang-ups and trauma dictate my own sexual exploration.

But like lightning, Hamilton would ruin me.

He knocked again, and I cleared my throat before moving to answer it.

A light dusting of spicy cologne hit me the moment I saw him. Hamilton looked sexy, with dark jeans and the same black shirt from before. The outline of his muscles could be easily seen through the worn fabric. His dark hair was still wet, as if he'd just showered and rushed over here. The dark strands curled slightly at the ends. In his front pocket, I saw the distinct outline of a pack of cigarettes, but I'd never seen him smoke. He smelled of tobacco and mint gum.

"You took my words to heart," Hamilton said while looking me up and down. I felt embarrassed by his obvious perusal.

I let out an exhale and grabbed my purse hanging on the nearby rack and put my cell phone inside of it. "I have no idea what you're talking about," I quipped. I was about to shut the door and lock it when Hamilton reached out and grabbed my hips, walking me back through the threshold of my apartment before kicking the door shut. "Wh-what are you doing?" I stammered. His hot hands pressed against my exposed skin, teasing me at the waistband of my skirt. I had to fight to keep my eyes open.

"We should probably talk about a couple of things," he whispered, his smirk proud and tempting.

"Oh?" I choked out. "About what?"

"Tonight is a date," he replied. "I just wanted you to know exactly what my intentions are."

"Hamilton...we can't. Where is this coming from?" It's not like he'd acted interested in me leading up to this point.

"I can't stop thinking about how you watched me with your wide, beautiful eyes. I have a theory."

I gulped. "A theory?"

"Part theory, part hypothesis. I wonder if you'll gasp when I slide inside of you. Will your lips part? I don't make a habit of denying myself of life's pleasures, as you can tell. And I decided that we could have a lot of fun, Vera."

"I don't think that's a good idea," I rushed out. "This feels a little sudden."

"Is it though?" Hamilton asked. "Because to me,

this tension between us has been building since the moment I laid eyes on you. I know you feel it, too."

"I don't know what you're talking about."

He ignored me. "You can't wear this," he whispered over my skin. I chewed on my lip, feeling a wave of arousal hitting me in the gut.

"Why not?"

He threaded his finger through my belt loop and tugged me against him. I braced my palms against his chest. "For starters, you have no business looking this fucking delicious."

"You think I look delicious?" I asked. I wasn't expecting him to say that, and I could have kicked myself for being so lame and asking.

He smirked before leaning over to hover his lips over the shell of my ear. I felt his warm tongue run along my neck. My stomach became a flurry of nerves, and he whispered again. "Yes. You do."

"You probably shouldn't do that," I whispered.

"Do what, Petal?" Hamilton asked while reaching up to wrap his fingers around my neck.

"This. It's not right. Don't kiss me," I pleaded when his lips hovered over mine. He was just one mistake away from swallowing my lust whole. He lightly squeezed at my words, and my lips parted on a gasp. I wanted him in that moment. It would have been easy to give in—to strip naked and fuck him on every surface of the apartment his brother was paying for.

But I didn't.

"As you wish," he replied reluctantly before pulling away. "No kisses. But you really should change. I brought the motorcycle. I'm not sure you want to show the entire world your panties on the ride there."

I pulled away to look down at my skirt and inhaled. Fuck. I could choke on the tension. His motorcycle? "Who says I'm wearing panties?" I replied before instantly regretting my statement. Talk about mixed signals. What was it about Hamilton that made me so bold? Maybe I just needed to get laid. Fuck.

Hamilton licked his lips. "You're such a tease," he whispered while brushing the tips of his fingers along my thigh. "I can't kiss you, right? Is touching off the table?" I slammed my weak legs together and pressed my forehead to his chest.

"Stop," I whispered.

"Stop what?" Hamilton asked while lifting higher and higher, running his thumb along my sensitive skin.

"Stop touching me," I said. His other arm wrapped around my waist, and he chuckled.

"I just want to see one more thing," he whispered before pressing at the apex of my thighs and running his hand along the now damp fabric covering me. My skirt had completely risen, and I was thankful we were in the privacy of my apartment. What would people say?

"I want you to stop," I reiterated in a throaty whisper.

"Your thoughts are so fucking loud, Petal," he pressed on before rocking his hand back and forth. I knotted my fingers in his shirt at the hot sensation. "And you're a beautiful little liar."

He withdrew his hand, and the temporary insanity that seemed to take over my body whenever Hamilton touched me faded. My phone started going off, and I stepped away from him. "You're such a fucking pervert," I cursed while grabbing my cell from my purse. Fuck. Mom was calling again.

"You going to answer that?" he asked teasingly.

"No. Let's go." I had zero desire to talk to my mother with Hamilton in the room. Besides, I was still avoiding her.

His brows raised. "You aren't going to change?"

I probably should have, but I was feeling reckless. I shook my head.

"Alright then," he replied before grabbing my hand and leading me back out of the apartment. I locked the door, and we made our way downstairs and to the parking lot. He kept silent as he let go of my hand and continued walking toward his parked motorcycle and mounting it. With a kick of his leg, the engine started roaring.

I debated walking away. The night air was still warm, but a chill traveled over my skin.

What was I doing?

I tugged at my skirt and got on the back of his bike, holding him close so I could use his body to hide my lacy black panties from the rest of the world. Lacy, black, *drenched* panties. I wrapped my arms around his waist and pressed my cheek to his muscular back, breathing in the smell of him while I had an excuse to hold him close. When he pulled out of the parking lot, I almost forgot how wrong it was to want Hamilton Beauregard.

7

The venue was a small café just off campus. The moment I walked through the door, I was hit with the stench of pot and sweat. It wasn't crowded, not in the slightest, but the small stage at the front of the room was overflowing with instruments and wires. It looked like a fire hazard, but no band was on stage yet. Hamilton threaded his fingers through mine. "Come on, let's get a drink," he said while pulling me across the warm hardwood floors toward a small bar manned by a dude wearing a crop top.

"A bottle of Pepsi and a scotch on ice, please," he ordered. I arched my brow, unamused that he'd ordered for me. I absolutely wasn't going to be drinking tonight; I could barely control myself when I was sober, let alone with some alcohol in my veins. It made me think back to our conversation in his kitchen.

"I'm way too young for you," I murmured when the bartender slid the vintage glass bottle of Pepsi my way. I clutched it in my palm and took a long, slow sip. The carbonation bubbled down my throat.

"That you are," Hamilton agreed while taking his glass. "Too young. Too innocent. Too off-limits. I suppose that's part of the appeal," he then admitted.

"Here I thought it was my winning personality that had you all in a tizzy," I replied before crossing my arms over my chest, the cool bottle clutched between my thumb and index finger.

Hamilton slammed some cash on the bar top and guided me toward a far wall with dozens of tiny paintings on it. The eclectic vibe was warm, inviting, and sensual. Soft jazz music was playing through the speakers, and it looked like Jess managed to pull off getting no more than fifteen people into the small space. I people watched for a moment while mulling over Hamilton's words.

I suppose that's part of the appeal...

I felt like a fetish, not a date.

Not that I wanted this to be a date. Hamilton didn't even ask me, he just assumed that this was what we were doing. He leaned over me, his whiskey breath feathering down my neck as he exhaled. "What are you thinking about?"

"This isn't a kink thing, right? No shame, but if you get off on the idea of fucking your younger niece, then I want no part of it."

The words left my mouth before I had a chance to filter them. Thank fuck I was only drinking Pepsi. "Oh," Hamilton replied, a wicked grin on his beautiful face. "So, we've graduated to fucking now. Back at your apartment, you didn't even want a kiss. And I'm pretty sure you're against the idea of this being a date." I opened my mouth to argue, but he placed his index finger against my lips, silently quieting my protests. "But now you're accusing me of fetishizing our dynamic. How *interesting*."

I inhaled deeply, wishing the world would swallow me up so I wouldn't have to see the smug expression on his stupidly perfect face. "I didn't mean—"

"Of course you meant it. You don't say anything you don't mean, do you, Vera? You're particular about the things you say. About the things you do. The things you want." He licked his lips and took a sip of his drink. "Tell me, Vera. Did you develop your sense of self-preservation over time, or did you inherit this fear from your mother?"

"Don't talk about my mother," I snapped.

Hamilton grinned, as if he were pleased with himself for pushing my buttons. "No," he finally relented. "You aren't some kink. I haven't been jacking off to incestual videos on Pornhub while thinking of you. In fact, I don't even consider us family. Your poor mother married my asshole brother, yeah. But it's not like we grew up together. You're just the beautiful woman that watched me violently fuck someone at my brother's wedding." I swallowed at his words, my heart racing with lust and need. "I don't get off on knowing that you're ten fucking years younger than me. You're hot, Vera. I don't need a reason to want you. It's not a kink. It's an attraction that could ruin us both. So, shut up and enjoy the evening before I remember that I'm not supposed to do anything that will harm our family's *precious* reputation."

I needed to say something—anything. Hell, I wanted to lift up on my toes and slam my hungry lips to his. He was right, it was only a matter of time before shit hit the fan. At the end of the day, I made a promise to myself to never do anything that would hurt my mother. One touch could ruin us. One kiss could end our happy little family.

Lilah Beauregard deserved better, and I had worked far too hard to let everything get fucked up over one pretty boy.

One pretty, dangerous boy.

One pretty, dangerous, twisted, tempting man.

"Hamilton?" a small voice said. "Have you seen Jess?"

I turned to look at the woman walking up to us. She had long green hair, fake lashes that looked like spider legs, and a birthmark right above her upper lip. She wore a short dress that was likely to show off her panties if she bent the wrong way, and her tiny nose was so fucking cute that I wanted to bop it with my finger. "Yeah, she was rounding up a few more people for your show and should be here any minute," he answered her.

This must be Jess's girlfriend. She sighed in relief

and turned her eyes to me. "Hi," she began, her voice breathy and high-pitched. "I'm Infinity, Jess's girlfriend."

"Nice to meet you," I replied with a smile. "I'm Vera, Hamilton's...friend."

Friend was okay, right? It sounded better than being his niece. It was definitely safer than calling myself his date. Especially considering I decided fifteen seconds ago that this couldn't be a date, regardless of his caveman declarations.

"I've heard so much about you. Sorry Jess can be kind of a bitch. I don't think she knows how to be anything but overprotective," Infinity admitted. "Hell, my band sucks, but she threatened the owner of this shop to let us play here once a month, and drags everyone she meets to the show."

Hamilton stammered. "No, that's not true. We all want to be here. You're going to be a star," he lied tragically.

"Right. Keep lying, and I'll make you come on stage and dance for one of our sets. You know Jess will make you if I ask."

Hamilton's eyes widened. "I feel like there is no safe way to respond to that. So I'm going to take my niece, who is also my friend, who is also my sexy date for the evening, over to a table to sit down."

Infinity's brows raised, and she quirked a smile.

I could have punched him. "Oh, he's just joking," I stammered as Hamilton placed his hand on the small of my back and guided me to a table with two chairs toward the front. Once we were seated, I gave him an angry look. "Why did you say that?" I hissed. "That's how rumors get started."

"Infinity won't say anything, and I really enjoy watching you squirm. When you called yourself my friend, I knew I had to tease you about it." Hamilton placed his palm on my upper thigh and grinned. The warmth from his touch made every nerve ending in my body tingle. Fuck. He was seriously messing with me. My libido was all out of whack.

"Um," I replied while shoving his hand off of me. He bit his lip and took another drink of his scotch. "When does the show start again?"

"Another thirty minutes. So, tell me, Vera, how did your mom and Joseph meet? You didn't always live here, right?"

I wasn't expecting Hamilton to ask me about her, but it seemed normal enough. He probably just wanted to know more. "We moved to a town about three hours north of here from Atlanta when I was in eighth grade. Mom wanted me to attend a better public school so that I had a better chance of getting a scholarship for college. She found a housekeeping job, and the homeowners let us stay in their converted garage. It was a small apartment, but I was able to go to a really good school. And the hours were awesome, so she also got a night job at a local restaurant that had good tips."

Hamilton stared at me as I spoke. It was an easy enough story. I left out the parts where I felt like an outsider in the pretentious community. Once people learned that my mother was a housekeeper for one of the wealthier families, they treated me like I wasn't good enough to breathe the same air as them. I had to work three times as hard to prove that I was worthy. I stayed focused and only dated a few people casually. It felt like a gigantic *fuck you* when I graduated valedictorian. I'll never forget the way Mom cried when I delivered the class speech.

"I guess Joseph went to eat there while he was visiting a nonprofit in town. They hit it off. He took her on a couple dates and bam."

I shrugged, not really knowing the details. Mom was never the type to share about her dating and personal life with me. One minute she was single and working all the time, the next we were moving here to be with Joseph. Thank God I had graduated before we had to move. I would have been devastated had it ruined my valedictorian status.

"It's just so unlike my brother," Hamilton admitted. "Your mom is beautiful and definitely out of his league, but he's the most calculating, cautious, meticulous person I know. Marrying someone he'd only been dating for a few months is completely out of character for him. I figured he'd marry someone Jack set him up with for sure. Not that I'm mad he went against that. It's just...curious."

I let out a huff of air. "I just want her to be happy." There went that same damn phrase again. The more I said it, the less authentic it felt.

"And what about you?" Hamilton asked.

"What about me?"

"You can be happy too, you know," Hamilton whispered before putting his hand back on my upper thigh. This time, I didn't push him away.

I internally scoffed, though. I was happy. Plenty happy. I was starting school soon. I had a place to live. What more could I possibly need?

"Are you thinking about how happy you are right now?" Hamilton asked.

I sputtered. How the fuck could he read my thoughts? "I am absolutely happy," I promised, though my tone felt forced and my teeth were clenched so tightly I thought my tooth would crack. What the fuck did it matter? I was taken care of. I was successful, right? "You could have been a therapist, you know." I wanted to put the attention back on Hamilton. It was safer that way.

"I've seen enough over the years you could call me an expert." He rubbed my thigh with his thumb, pressing the pad of it against my bare skin. I swallowed. "I found my mother when she o—died."

My shoulders slumped, and I felt myself softening in pity for him. "I'm so sorry—"

"I didn't tell you that for your pity, Petal. My first therapist quit after my eighth session; she told me that I was allowed to be happy and that I didn't have to grieve my dead mother for the rest of my life. I told her to get fucked and jump off a bridge."

My eyes widened. Well holy fuck. "She sounds like a shitty therapist."

Hamilton nodded. "I guess what I'm trying to tell you is, you're allowed to be unhappy. It's easy to give ourselves permission to be happy. Happy is easy. You want to really dig through the trenches of your mind? Let yourself be anything else. I think you'd be hot as fuck while good and angry."

Hamilton leaned in and kissed my neck. His lips tugged on my ear lobe. I squirmed in my seat as his hand drifted higher, and higher, and my eyes scanned the room. Was anyone watching?

"Relax. It's just you and me, Petal. Let's smell the roses a bit," he said before pressing the tip of his middle finger against my heat.

"Please stop," I whimpered, not meaning it at all.

"Kiss me, and I will." Hamilton brushed his lips against mine. It was a soft question, a demand. I chased after the brief touch with my bottom lip, aching to prolong the heated touch. "Tease," he chastised me on a breathy whisper.

"I'm not going to kiss you, Hamilton," I promised. "You and me? We'd be a disaster." I murmured those words painfully close to his perfect mouth before pulling away and straightening my spine.

"I can't wait to break you, Petal."

I picked up my Pepsi and took a sip of it before clearing my throat. "To be honest, I want you, Hamilton," I admitted. "You're attractive. Experienced."

He grinned. "Well, what's stopping you?"

"Have you ever ruined someone's life? I mean genuinely ruined it—whether intentionally or not." His expression turned serious. I waited for him to answer me, but he never did. I continued. "I don't want to draw attention to myself, because I'm a product of the most painful thing to ever happen to my mother. I'm a living, breathing atonement for my existence. I'm a perfectionist and a martyr. Acting on the impulse—and this is an impulse—to kiss you would be too reckless and risky to be worth the reward. Like it or not, you're Joseph's brother. I don't need your orgasms, your heated words, or your temptation, Hamilton. I'm not foolish enough to think that I am anything more than a game of pleasure to you, and I'm not willing to gamble on my mother's shot at happiness."

We exchanged a heated stare once more. Something passed across his expression, a break in the determined flirtatiousness of his behavior that caught me off guard. I broke our eye contact first to look around. Our moment had the power to stop time. I hadn't realized we were in a room full of eyes.

It wasn't until my gaze landed on a familiar, smarmy face that my blood turned cold. "Saint," I whispered before snapping myself away from Hamilton.

"What?" he asked.

"Saint. He's here," I choked out as my heart raced. Hamilton spun around in his seat and cursed. Saint was wearing jeans and a tight shirt. He raised the glass in his hand with a satisfied smirk on his face. Had he taken a picture? Oh shit. Hamilton and I were sitting awfully close.

Hamilton got up just as the band took the stage. Jess intercepted him as I started to hyperventilate. Was Saint going to follow me everywhere? Were Hamilton and I going to make the front page of the newspapers tomorrow? The edges of my vision turned black.

"We're Diet Fun," Infinity said softly into the microphone. "And we're going to rock your socks off."

The drums started playing, and Infinity immediately screamed into the microphone. I tried to look for Saint, but he disappeared down a hallway. Jess was still chatting with an angry-looking Hamilton. My chest felt so fucking tight.

Why was he here?

I stood up and made my way toward the door. No scandals. I couldn't ruin anything. My eyes felt hot with tears. It was such a mistake coming here. "Vera!" Hamilton called at my back, his deep voice raising over the music. I ignored him and exited the café, air hitting my cheeks the moment I made it outside.

Standing on the sidewalk, I called the one person I could trust in this world. "Mom?"

"Finally, you call me! Baby, it's late. What's up?"

"Are you home?"

"Yeah. Our flight got in a few hours ago. What's wrong?"

"Can you come get me?"

8

I was sitting at a McDonald's down the street from the café when my mom pulled up in her brand-new Escalade. She was wearing pajamas and marched up to the door with her hair in curlers. I grinned at the determined look on her face. "Where is he?" she snapped when I got up from my spot at the booth and gave her a hug.

"I don't know. He disappeared when the band

started playing. I got out of there and called you while walking here."

I didn't mention that I was with Hamilton, but I knew it was only a matter of time before Mom found out that I was there with him. "Joseph had to go to the office to work on something for Jack, but he assured me that he would make sure Saint is arrested immediately. I can't believe he's just following you around now."

She let out a huff, and I smiled at her protectiveness. "Can you just take me home?" I asked. It had been a long night, and I wanted nothing more than to lock the deadbolt and curl up under my bed. Maybe I needed to get a dog. The apartment already had a security system, but I'd watched enough crime television to know that a security system wasn't much when up against a crazed person.

"Should we go to the police? I'm just not sure about you going home. Want me to spend the night?"

Letting out a sigh, I wrapped my arms around her tiny body and breathed her in. She smelled like coffee and her cinnamon body wash. "Yeah. That would make me feel a lot better, actually."

We got in the car, and she followed my directions to my new apartment. In my purse, my phone kept ringing. Both Jess and Hamilton had called me numerous times, but I didn't want to talk to either of them. I wasn't sure what to say. I had sent them both a text to let them know I was fine and got a ride home, but they were relentless.

"I just don't understand what this guy's problem is. He's a reporter, right?" Mom rambled as she turned into the parking lot. "Why does he think you have a story, huh?" She looked at me out of the corner of her eye. "Who were you with at this café, baby?"

I swallowed. "Hamilton's roommate invited me. Her girlfriend is in the band that was playing," I explained, hoping she wouldn't question it.

"Hamilton? As in Joseph's brother?" she asked, surprise marring her expression.

"Yeah. You know he was there when Saint first showed up. I met his roommate, and she was really nice. I think they just feel bad that I know no one here. It was probably a pity invite," I explained, though it didn't feel like a pity invite. It felt like a date. It felt like a date that went to hell the moment I saw Saint. I knew I needed to tell my mother the truth. If Saint took a photo of Hamilton and me, I just knew it would look far too suggestive for friendly family members enjoying a concert together. By tomorrow, it would be all over the headlines.

But I didn't want to tell her just yet. I couldn't believe that I fucked everything up.

We got out of the car and made our way inside the building. "Joseph has told me a lot about his brother, you know," she said while tugging at her pajamas. "I'm not sure you should be spending time with him, baby."

I knew she was right. Hamilton was trouble. But something within me broke at her words. I didn't want to stay away. Was I really so lonely that I would risk everything for a one-night stand? Because that's all he would ever give me. One. Night.

"What did Joseph say?" I prodded.

"Just that Hamilton has always been a bit of a wild child. He was really heavy on drugs a few years back. Joseph isn't sure if he still is, but he used to be manic. Would lie all the time—and he was apparently good at it. He could convince anyone of anything."

I swallowed as we made the way to my door. After turning onto the hallway where my apartment was, I abruptly halted when I saw someone leaning against the door. "Fuck," I cursed. There was a single light overhead, casting the person in shadows. Was Saint here?

"Who is that?" Mom hissed while grabbing my arm. At the commotion, the person turned to face us, and we both let out a sigh of relief.

Hamilton.

He jogged down the long hallway toward me, and the moment he was close enough, Hamilton wrapped me in a tight hug. "You scared the shit out of me," he said with a curse. I felt stiff and awkward in his arms, my mother clicking her tongue beside us. "Are you okay? Saint got out of there before I could talk to him. I bet you're really freaked out." He cupped my cheeks and stared me in the eye, making me feel dizzy from all the fucking butterflies in my stomach.

Mom cleared her throat. "Hamilton."

He didn't stop holding me. He didn't even glance at her. We were locked in a stare down. Like Saint *hadn't* interrupted us earlier and my mother *wasn't* standing right next to me.

"Hamilton?" I said.

He pulled away and straightened his shirt. "Hey, Lilah, good to see you again," he said to my mother while wrapping her up in a hug. She patted his back, and he pulled away.

"Wish it could be under better circumstances," Mom replied while looking him up and down. "I didn't realize you and my daughter had grown so close."

Hamilton smiled politely. "Family is very important to me, Lilah."

My stomach flopped at his words. Mom replied while I stood there tongue-tied. "Right. Well, we are fine. Thank you for checking on her, but I've got it from here. Joseph promised me that he would call the police."

"You might want to tell them about this, too," Hamilton said before nodding at my front door. Tell them about what? I looked in the direction of my apartment with my brow furrowed. After seeing something there, my feet had a mind of their own, carrying me to a ripped sheet of paper taped there. My heart pounded. Mom called my name, but I didn't stop. It wasn't until I could see the messy, scrawled note that the terror clicked into place and ice filled my veins.

Vera,
Your secret is safe with me.

For now.

-S

"He was here?" Mom shrieked. "I'm calling the police."

Mom pulled out her cell phone and dialed 911 while I turned to stare at Hamilton. He looked eerily calm, but there was a fiery determination in his gaze. His dark vacant eyes glared at the ominous threat. Fuck. This was too close.

———

HAMILTON AND THE POLICE WERE LONG GONE. BY THE time we gave our statements and they did a sweep of the apartment, it was three a.m. Mom was snoozing peacefully on the mattress next to me, one hand on her stomach, one behind her head. I felt safer knowing she was with me, but I still couldn't fall asleep.

Hamilton disappeared the moment we called Jack to let him know what was going on. Part of me was relieved, but the other part of me felt safer having him around. I wasn't thinking clearly when I ran away from the café. I just wanted to put space between me and the man following me. I was terrified that my strange attraction to Hamilton was going to ruin my mother's new marriage. Not to mention create more speculation. But now, even though there was a cruiser parked outside my apartment building, and my mother was sleeping beside me, I felt terrified. Saint didn't look menacing. He was twisted and creepy and very invasive. It was more the breach of my privacy that freaked me out than his presence. Minus the gun, I could probably beat his scrawny ass if I wanted to. It was his unpredictability and the power he held over me that made him more threatening.

My phone vibrated on the nightstand, alerting me to a text.

Hamilton: Are you okay?

Me: Can't sleep.

The chat bubbles flashed on my screen and disappeared. When his message finally came through, I was surprised by his question.

Hamilton: Why did you run from the café?

I chewed on my lip, trying to find a way to respond that sounded sane.

Me: I guess I was in fight or flight. I got out of there as quickly as I could and called my mom.

Hamilton: It was very reckless. I was really fucking worried about you. If you were here, I'd

bend you over my knee and spank that perfect ass of yours until it was red.

I swallowed and stared at his message, reading it over and over and over again. Slipping out of bed, I made my way to the living room, leaving my snoozing mother to sleep in peace. By the time I had sat down on the leather couch, Hamilton had sent two more messages.

Hamilton: Did I lose you?

Hamilton: Come back, Petal. Don't be afraid.

Me: I'm not afraid of you.

Hamilton: What are you afraid of?

I ran my tongue over my bottom lip while grabbing my throw blanket and tossing it over my bare legs.

Me: Saint. Ruining my mother's new marriage. Not being good enough.

I didn't actually send the last two bits. That was a little too honest, and I wasn't sure Hamilton had earned the truest parts of me yet. We barely knew one another. There was an attraction, yes, but I couldn't honestly say there was any more to it.

Hamilton: Want me to help you think of something else?

Me: What did you have in mind?

Those taunting chat bubble dots blinked a few

CORALEE JUNE

times, and I waited with my breath caught in my throat for Hamilton to reply. Minutes passed, and I had all but given up on him when my phone rang.

"Hello?" I answered, my voice worn with exhaustion.

"What are you wearing?" Hamilton asked in a deep voice. The cliché phrase would have sounded dull coming from anyone else, but not him.

"My comfort shirt," I admitted.

Hamilton chuckled. "Is it a sexy comfort shirt?"

"It's an oversized white T-shirt I've had since I was thirteen. It used to be my mother's."

"Ah, I can see it now. Hits just at mid-thigh. Your nipples poke through the thin material." My breath hitched at his raspy words. "Are you alone?"

I let out a shaky exhale while looking around the living room. "Not really. Mom stayed over.

Hamilton paused for a moment, then spoke. "You don't have to say anything. You don't have to do anything. Just listen to me, okay?"

"Okay," I murmured.

"I'm fucking pissed our night was ruined because I wanted to take you home and taste you, Vera." His words rattled me.

"We can't—"

"Right now, we can do anything we want. It's just

136

talking." I heard the sound of him shifting around. "I can see it now. I'd lay you down on my bed and slip off that sexy black skirt you had on. Your fucking creamy thighs would be trembling, and your pussy would be slick."

My breathing turned ragged, and I touched my neck with my free hand. "You'd probably say some bullshit about how this is a terrible idea. Because you're a good person that doesn't want to hurt the people she loves *and* because you were taught that your body is a delicate little rose better suited for vases on holidays. But..."

My chest constricted. "But?" I asked.

Hamilton laughed. "But I'm a selfish bastard that won't let you talk me out of the best damn feast of my life. Oh, Vera. You'd squirm all over my sheets. I'd hold you down. I'd taste every drop of you. I'd suck on your needy clit until you were grinding my face, pulling my hair and shaking all over."

"Fuck," I cursed.

"I'm going to pluck you to pieces. I'm going to chew on your thorns. I'm going to breathe in your sweet scent, clutch you in my fist and ruin you, Petal."

Why was that the hottest fucking thing anyone

had ever said to me? "Petal, huh? You seem to really like that nickname," I replied.

"I'd really like to fuck you."

I pictured Hamilton lying on a bed with his muscular arm behind his head and his bare chest rising and falling with every breath. He was probably smirking at me, holding the phone up to his ear while waiting for me to moan into the receiver from his heated words.

I looked back at my bedroom door, thinking of my mother and all she'd sacrificed to give me a good life. I could do this one thing. I could stop entertaining Hamilton's advances.

"This doesn't have to mean anything, you know," Hamilton continued. "It's just two people with an insane amount of chemistry, enjoying each other's company. You asked me earlier if I had ever ruined someone's life," Hamilton said, his voice soft.

"And?"

"And I think you and I have more in common than I realized," he admitted. What did that mean?

I let out an exhale. As much fun as that sounded, there was no way in hell Hamilton was worth the risk. "Good night, Hamilton," I whispered.

I wished I could see his face. I pictured him smiling in triumph, as if he could hear the hesitation in my voice. If I was another girl, I probably would have taken an Uber to his place and let him do all the delightfully dirty things he promised.

But I wasn't someone else. I was Vera Garner, the bastard daughter of a victim.

9

"**Y**ou okay, baby?" Mom asked while looking at me over the rim of her cup. She was drinking a decaf latte that was more sugar and milk than anything else. Even with messy hair and the same pajamas from the night before, she looked beautiful. She probably could have modeled if she never had me.

We were sitting in my oversized kitchen and catching up. Mom slept till almost noon, and it wasn't until Joseph called her cell that she got out of bed. We ate cereal at the kitchen island and slowly processed everything that had happened the night before. "You look so tired," she added while sweeping her eyes over my face. She was probably more exhausted than I was. She was jet-lagged from her trip to Paris and had to spend all night taking care of me. A pang of guilt rocked through me.

"I didn't get much sleep last night," I replied, my cheeks turning crimson at my words as thoughts of what kept me up flooded my mind. It wasn't Saint plaguing my mind, though it probably should have been. No. I spent most of my evening thinking about *Hamilton*. True to his word, he got me to stop thinking about the creepy and intrusive journalist who was now stalking me. Instead, I was picturing all the naughty things he spoke about.

His head buried between my thighs.

The scruff of his jaw burning my skin with the coarse movement.

My moans filling the room. His wet tongue lapping me up.

His filthy mouth making me come again and again and...

I swallowed. Mom started talking, jolting me out of thoughts of Hamilton once more. "I can only imagine. This Saint person seems unhinged. What kind of person hounds a family like that?" Mom shook her head and continued speaking. "I'm so sorry that you've had to deal with this. I knew things were going to be different when I married Joseph, but I had no idea the paparazzi would be so intense. The Beauregards are well-known in our community, but Jack's not a fucking Kardashian."

I bit my tongue. It was only going to get worse— much worse. Joseph wanted to be a career politician. He went to Greenwich University for a double major in political science and business and was too patriotic for my tastes. His conservative platform, family business expertise, and his father's legacy had set him up for success. Mom might have been in denial about our future, but I knew with complete certainty that this was only the tip of the iceberg. We had to prepare ourselves to be hounded the rest of our lives. Was Mom really ready to have her past put on display for the world to see? Jack might have had the court records sealed, but people talked. There were plenty of people back in Atlanta who would be happy to sell our sob story to the highest bidder. Not even the Beauregard money could get us out of that. I was surprised it hadn't been exploited already.

Memories of my argument with Jack made my

stomach plummet. Everyone was already gossiping about my mother; it was likely to only get worse as Joseph climbed the political ladder.

I replied, "I'm not surprised, honestly. It's human nature to be curious about public figures. Jack is well-liked in the community, and Joseph wants to have his name on a ballot. We should honestly get used to it." Politics felt like living in a house that was on fire. It wasn't a matter of *if* the flames would scorch you, but when. The Beauregards were sitting in the kitchen while their living room was ablaze. Was this why Hamilton escaped to work offshore?

Mom set her coffee mug down and inhaled deeply. Uh-oh. I knew that look. The corner of her mouth was pressed into a line, and she was looking at me with pity. "Spit it out. You look like you want to say something," I told her, eyebrow raised in question.

Mom rolled her eyes, feigning playfulness despite the heavy tension I could feel in the air. Something was up. "I have a couple of things I would like to say. First, Joseph and Jack would like to get you a personal bodyguard. Last night just further proved that things are getting intense. Joseph was recently offered a job."

I frowned. "What kind of job? I thought he

wanted to run for Congress."

"That was his original plan. The President—yeah, the actual fucking President—wants to appoint Joseph as Secretary of Commerce. It hasn't been announced yet, but it's a really major opportunity. He would be the youngest—"

Holy shit. I wasn't expecting that to come out of her mouth. "Do you have to move to DC?" I snapped.

Mom tried to remain calm, but I could tell my lack of enthusiasm was bothering her. She was probably hoping I would be excited, but my face was twisted in horror. "Should Joseph accept the position, then yes. We got the call while we were in Paris. The reason Joseph didn't come last night is because he flew to DC so he could look at properties."

So, he wasn't at the office. He was in DC? Another fucking lie. This sounded like a done deal. "So, Joseph is going to accept?"

Mom folded her lips in and picked at her sleep shirt. "Yes."

"I thought you were going to move into a new house thirty minutes from campus. So, you're just going to leave? What am I supposed to do? School starts in a week. When are you leaving?"

"We're moving next week," Mom said with a frown. "He's formally accepting the position today. I wanted to tell you before you found out from someone else."

"Like you told me about the baby?" I asked sarcastically. "Or like how I had to move to this apartment by myself when we've been planning for college since I was three?"

"I thought you would like the apartment! It's better than whatever cheap dorm you would have been in without Jack's generosity."

"It's not about the apartment. It's about all these changes happening so soon," I pressed. "I thought my life was one thing, and now I'm having to hide from an aggressive investigative journalist, and I'm attending a school that wasn't even on my radar until you married Joseph." I got up from my spot at the kitchen island and walked over to her. "Mom. Are you sure this is what you want? Our entire lives are going to be plastered everywhere. This is a very public position. It was bad enough with Jack being the Governor, but—"

"But nothing. I'm going to support my husband through this incredible opportunity. We're going to raise our baby in DC, and you can come visit us whenever you want. You're an adult now. You can't keep clinging to me. It's time for you to live on your own."

My eyes widened. I knew she was right. Most people my age left for college without a second thought. But this was more than that. How could I make sure Mom was okay if she was in DC? "It's just a lot of change in a short amount of time," I sputtered. "I'm not trying to be clingy. But you're my best friend—"

"I'm your mother, Vera. And I'll always be your mother. But it's time for us to grow up a little bit, baby."

"I can't believe you would drop this bomb right after what happened to me last night," I croaked. My throat was clogged with emotion.

"Well, this is why I wanted to mention the personal bodyguard. Jack and Joseph think it's a good idea while we are in transition. I want you to be safe. See? I'm not abandoning you."

It sure fucking felt like she was abandoning me. "Right," I chirped sarcastically. "I don't want a bodyguard, Mom. I'm fine."

"But you're not fine," Mom said. "You're spending time with Hamilton, Vera. That in itself is a red flag. I'm not sure how I feel about you being around him. He looks at you like...like he wants to eat you up.

Don't think I didn't notice how he was last night. Is something going on between you two? You're about to start college, you don't need the distraction. And Vera, I don't think I have to tell you how irresponsible that would be. He's technically your new uncle."

My heart raced. My head pounded, and for a moment the only thing I could hear was the whoosh of blood in my ears. Did she want someone to protect me, or did she want someone to report back to them about where I was? "Hamilton is the only friend I have here. I would never do that to you. I can't believe you would even ask me that," I cursed. "He was just being nice to me. It's not like you've been around. Saint really freaked me out."

"I was on my honeymoon, Vera! You can't blame me for finally being happy and in love and seeing the world. I'm sorry some psycho did that, but there wasn't much I could do from Paris. I can't spend every day of my life taking care of you."

Her words felt like a punch to the gut. "I don't need you to take care of me," I whispered, feeling like a small child. "That's not what I meant. I just don't understand why I can't be friends with Hamilton."

"Because Joseph doesn't trust him. I have to stand by my husband now, Vera."

"What about standing by me? Or have you forgotten?"

"How could I ever forget!" Mom screamed, the veins in her neck bulging with anger. "I've spent my life standing by your side. Don't you get it!? It's my turn, Vera. It's my turn to have all the things you stole from me."

Mom's eyes popped open in surprise. She placed her fingers to her lips and gasped as tears streamed down her face. My emotions felt like a water hose. I reached deep in my chest and turned the valve off, praying she didn't see me break. "Baby. I'm so sorry, I didn't mean it."

"It's fine," I replied calmly, stopping her before she could say anything else. "I'm really happy for you and Joseph. You're right. It's selfish of me to get in the way. I want you to go."

"Vera," Mom whimpered. Tears streamed down her slender cheeks. "Vera, I'm so sorry. I didn't mean it."

"Yeah. You did. Please tell Jack and Joseph I don't want a bodyguard. It's hard enough starting at a new school, I don't need to be followed. The police are already doing everything in their power to catch him, and we're installing a new security system here at the apartment. I'll stop talking to Hamilton. I don't want you to piss off your new husband. I'm sure I can make more friends once school starts."

Mom set her coffee cup down and sighed. "I'm going to go," she whispered. "Jack is throwing Joseph a party this weekend to celebrate. Will you be there? I want to see you before I leave." Her voice was hopeful.

"Yep," I replied with a tight smile. "I'll be there." I would always be there. I would always support my mother.

Mom gathered her purse and made her way over to the front door. With her hand lingering on the knob, she turned to look over her shoulder at me. "It's just my turn," she whispered. "I hope you can understand that."

I averted my eyes.

Yeah. I got it.

The moment she was gone, my cell pinged, alerting me to a text.

Hamilton: How are you this morning?

I angrily typed out a response without thinking before blocking his number.

Me: Don't text me again. This is done.

10

_____

 he opulent dining room Jack rented to host the celebration for Joseph was filled to the brim with power and influence. I'd seen some of these people at the wedding, but there were even more elbow-rubbing political influencers vying for Joseph's attention. They had a few journalists scattered about, but I hadn't seen Saint anywhere, thankfully.

An entire week had passed since my mother said

those hurtful words. I spent most of the time in my apartment, moping and getting ready for school starting next week. I wasn't sure if I didn't want to leave my place because I was depressed or because I was still scared to see Saint. I absolutely felt safer in my apartment. It was like the things out to hurt me couldn't see me if I just stayed in my pajamas under my covers.

But I couldn't hide forever.

"You look beautiful, Vera," Jack said while walking up to me. I looked down at the slinky black dress I wore and frowned. I hadn't wanted to wear the expensive Vera Wang evening gown, but mother sent a single text reminding me that I needed to look nice for the evening.

"Thank you, Jack," I replied with a tight smile. We hadn't spoken since our last argument. I didn't particularly want to talk to him now, but I knew that any animosity from me would be a direct representation of my mother. I didn't want to make any more problems for her than I already had. "And thank you for having your personal stylist send this over," I added while looking down at my strappy dress. Around the room, tables set with fine china, crisp white linens, and oversized floral arrangements filled the space. A string quartet played classical pieces in the corner of the room, making everything feel more elegant. The ambiance was rich with affluent touches only money could buy. It was the sort of wealth you couldn't fake. Expensive diamonds dripped from the necks of women in evening gowns who clung to the arms of old men in perfectly tailored suits. They walked the room, scouting. Watching. Networking. Comparing. Gossiping. It felt over-the-top and exactly the sort of thing I wanted nothing to do with.

"I've missed chatting with you, you know. I've debated on calling you this week but wasn't sure if you'd answer. I know my words were abrupt, but I hope we can move past it. It's important that the family shows solidarity right now. This is an exciting time for the Beauregards." I read his meaning loud and clear. Smile. Get over it. Look pretty for the pictures. "I'm really thankful you are here, and I'm so excited for you to start school next week." I wanted to be frigid with Jack, but instead, I let out a slow exhale and said exactly what he wanted to hear.

"I understand why you did what you did. And I know you weren't intentionally trying to be malicious. You were just protecting your family. I don't know this world. I don't know what you've had to do to safeguard your way of life. But I do know that we are stuck with one another. With Mom and Joseph moving to DC, you'll be the only family I have around here."

"Not exactly," a familiar voice said at my back. Jack's eyes widened, and his mouth parted. "I'm on the rig for a couple weeks every month, but I always come back. Like an annoying gnat you can't swat away. Right, Jack?"

"Hamilton?" Jack stammered.

I spun around and nearly toppled over at the sight of Hamilton in a suit. His hair was combed to the side, and his broad shoulders looked impressive in the black jacket he wore. His bright purple tie complimented his tan skin, and his dark eyes glimmered with mischievousness.

"Hello, Vera. You look stunning." He swept his eyes hungrily up and down my body—with his own fucking father standing right next to me. His gaze was hot and needy. Devastatingly tormenting. Wrong. His gaze had the power to start a war within my body. I was a home for need that had nowhere to go.

"Hamilton. You're here. I didn't think you would show up," Jack said while taking a step toward his son. He didn't even seem to care that *said son* was giving me bedroom eyes. Hot bedroom eyes that made me squirm.

"Hey, Jack," Hamilton replied, not moving his eyes from me. "I'm assuming my invitation got lost in the mail again. First the wedding, now this?"

"I told Joseph to—"

"Save it. We both know I'm not welcome, but you can't very well kick me out without making a scene, now can you," Hamilton said, his voice dark. "You're so transparent, Jack."

"Don't be silly, Hamilton. I'm happy you're here. Hell, I invite you to dinner every single time you're home. I've missed you. If your mother were here—"

"Don't talk about my mother," Hamilton snapped, his hand balled up in a fist at his side. "You don't get to talk about her. I'm here for the open bar, the free dinner, and..." Hamilton paused to look at me. "The company. It was nice talking to you, Jack. Now run back to Joseph and focus on him. Like you always do. Like you *prefer* to do."

Jack's shoulders slumped, and for a brief moment, I almost felt bad for him. Jack stared at his son, the skin around his eyes bunched up in pain. He seemed genuinely upset that Hamilton was pushing him away. Jack might be overprotective of his family, but I sensed longing in him where Hamilton was concerned. I couldn't tell if he wanted a relationship with his son or if he wanted him to get in line and obey the standards associated with the Beauregard name. Hamilton was rebellious and an outcast. He didn't hide the fact that he wanted nothing to do with his family. I just couldn't quite put my finger on what Jack wanted. My new grandfather was normally a proud man, but his spine was bent, like he was physically pained from Hamilton's words.

"I love you, son," Jack whispered before giving me a lingering look, his mouth hooked to the side, as if he didn't know what more to say. "Let's chat later, Vera."

Hamilton huffed and wrapped his arm around me protectively. Jack eyed the possessive move, cocking his head to the side with scrutiny. "Bye," Hamilton gritted.

I watched Jack's back as he walked away, noting the defeated slump of his posture. Then, I slowly shrugged out of Hamilton's grip—or at least, I tried to. He held me tight against his hard body, his lips hovering over my ear. "You blocked me, Petal," he whispered. "I've been trying to text you all sorts of naughty things."

"I told you to leave me alone," I gritted before

stomping on his foot. Hamilton let out a guttural groan the moment my stiletto jammed the top of his dress shoes. He let go of me to bite his fist, and I started walking away, grabbing a flute of champagne from a nearby tray as I went. It wasn't long before Hamilton caught up to me, though. I felt his hungry presence at my back, like a wolf stalking his prey.

I didn't turn around to greet him; instead, my eyes turned to the front of the room where Mom was standing with Joseph and greeting some of the guests. She'd given me a polite hello earlier, but the two of them were now too busy schmoozing other important people to really pay attention to me. Taking a sip of my drink, I watched them. Joseph had a bright smile. His chest was puffed out proudly as he shook a diplomat's hand. Mom stood dutifully by his side, her hair tied up in an elegant updo and her gold evening gown brushing the ground. I eyed her stomach, thinking about the baby. Would I really know my younger sibling?

"Is that why you blocked me?" Hamilton asked. His presence at my back sent a shiver up my spine. "Are you trying to please your mom? I suppose I can understand that. If Joseph had his way, he'd send me to hell for half a chance at never seeing me again.

Although, he's had a room booked at the devil's hotel since he was born."

"What does it even matter?" I asked in a low voice while spinning on my heel to face him. "I said I was done. Why are you here?"

Hamilton grinned and grabbed a champagne flute. With his dark eyes on me, he downed it whole. Once his glass was empty, he slammed it down on a nearby table and wiped his plush lips with the back of his hand. "Free booze and a pretty girl."

My brows raised. "*That's* why you're spending time with family you obviously hate?" I asked incredulously.

"Do I need more of a reason?" he asked before invading my personal space. Hamilton was *constantly* invading my personal space.

I glanced over my shoulder at my mother. I was expecting her to be giggling over something Joseph said, but no, she was glaring at me. Her posture was stiff, and the angry rise and fall of her chest made me duck in shame. Beside her, Joseph kept his expression void of emotion, but he was aggressively adjusting his cufflinks. "Please leave me alone," I whispered. I didn't want any trouble. I didn't want to make things more difficult for my mother.

"I can't even talk to you? That's not fair. I have a

job for you that I wanted to discuss," Hamilton pouted.

"What?" A job?

"I'm leaving for the rig tomorrow. They called me back early. Jess officially moved in with Infinity, and I need someone to watch Little Mama while I'm gone. I was wondering—"

No way. I was going to get to dog sit! "Yes. Absolutely yes. Can I come get her tonight? Do you need anything for her? I should get her a bed for my apartment. A kennel? Dog treats. Toys. A leash."

Hamilton grinned. "Whoa. Hold up. I have all of those things. I can bring it over tomorrow, but you're going to have to unblock me. I need to be able to FaceTime Little Mama at least once a day."

I narrowed my eyes at him. "This feels like a trick."

"I'm just using every advantage I have. Blame it on my Beauregard blood," Hamilton replied before reaching out and running his index finger down my arm. I shivered at his touch. I knew if I looked down that my chest would be flushed. Fuck, this was not the time or the place.

"Fine. I'll watch her. But this"—I gestured between us to emphasize my point—"can't happen."

"Sure, it can," Hamilton whispered. "What are

you afraid of?" I looked back at my mother. She was whispering to Joseph, her eyes locked on me.

"Why does Joseph hate you so much?" I asked.

A bit of the playfulness in Hamilton's expression faded. "I've given Joseph plenty of reasons to hate me over the years. Hating someone doesn't make you right and them wrong, it's just an outlet for hurt. There's a lot of hurt in our family, Vera. I'm sure you'll learn all about it soon enough. Does that scare you?"

"A little," I admitted. Hamilton wrapped his large hand around my wrist. The push and pull between us was exhausting.

"Come with me," he whispered before pulling me through the crowd and away from the interrogative eyes of my mother, though I could feel her hard stare on my back.

We exited the ballroom through a side door, then started traveling down a long dark hallway toward another part of the venue. Towering glass windows lined the walls we walked past, and I could see lush gardens outside. It really was a beautiful place. If Joseph wasn't determined to get married at his family home to feel closer to his mother, I bet Mom would have loved to tie the knot here.

"Come on," Hamilton whispered before pulling me into a small storage room.

"What are we doing?" I asked as he slammed the door shut.

"This," Hamilton groaned before cupping my cheeks and slamming his lips to mine.

We collided so beautifully. It was an intense embrace between my body and his. His tongue searched my mouth with white-hot fever. I moaned against his lips, clawing at his back like this wasn't wrong. Like we weren't forbidden. Like this didn't have the power to ruin everything.

Heat traveled up my spine, and my nipples hardened into tight peaks, pressing against the thin fabric of my black dress. My body felt like a carton of fireworks, his fingers like the strike of a match against my skin. He found the helpful slit in my dress, and he roamed his hands over my heated thighs, teasing me, pleasing me, making me pant with need. "Are you going to let me taste you, Petal?" he asked. He ran his thumb along my panties, and I moaned before sinking my teeth into his bottom lip. I felt wild and wanton.

I reached for the zipper at my ribcage and slid the barrier between us down. Hamilton shoved the straps of my dress off my rounded shoulders and shoved the expensive material to the ground. My free breasts pressed against his chest, and he palmed my peaks with his warm hand. I arched my back, pushing him closer. Harder.

"If I wasn't so fucking desperate for you to ride my face, I'd make you drop to your knees and put my dick in that perfectly pouty mouth of yours, gorgeous." His voice fractured as he pulled away. He ran his thumb along my bottom lip, his hooded eyes heavy with arousal. He then licked my neck. My chest. My nipples. My stomach.

Straightening, he pulled me over to the wall and pressed me against it. A loud thud filled the room from the impact of my body against the solid surface, followed by heavy breathing.

Looking like a god in his perfect suit, he dropped to his knees and gently lifted my leg, my foot still studded with my expensive stilettos. He eased my thigh onto his shoulder, then stared at the thin black thong I was wearing. "I have a thing for panties," Hamilton said with a wicked grin. "I want you to come while wearing them, so then I can take home a little souvenir that smells like your needy cunt."

I felt dumbfounded. Too stunned by lust and need to say anything. "Perv," I finally groaned.

"You love it," Hamilton said before leaning

forward and inhaling me. Deeply inhaling. "Tell me I can have your panties when we're done, Petal," he whispered.

"You can have whatever you want. Just touch me, Hamilton," I pleaded. But instead of teasing the bundle of nerves at my core, he simply breathed me in again. It was like he wanted to fill his lungs with my arousal. Then, without warning, his tongue landed on the drenched fabric, and he started tasting me. Pleasure bloomed from my core. It was raw and hard and nasty passion.

"So fucking good. Just like I imagined," Hamilton murmured before pinching the thin fabric covering me and shoving it to the side. "Look at those glistening pussy lips. So hot. So pink. So needy for my tongue."

"P-please," I choked out.

"You want me to make you feel good, Petal?" he asked. "Tell me you want to be ruined, and I'll let you cover my chin with your come."

His words were too much. That was the root of it all, wasn't it? "Ruin me, Hamilton."

With a dark chuckle, he dove for my clit, wrapping his lips around it, and sucked. My trembling legs nearly collapsed beneath me, and he had to reach up with his free hand and press me against the wall at my stomach. I threaded my own hands through his dark, thick hair and tossed my head back as he alternated between sucking on my needy nub and circling his tongue around it.

I climbed that peak of pleasure. He ate me out like a starving man. It was everything I'd ever imagined and more. "Fuck, Hamilton," I cried out as my body tensed from the impending orgasm. He swept his firm tongue over my clit one more time, and my entire body shook from the force of pleasure rocking through me. He rode each wave of my bliss with his mouth taking it in, smiling in triumph as I grinded against his face.

It was one of those rolling orgasms that never seemed to end. On and on. Time stopped. And little aftershocks rocked through me until I was spent. I probably would have collapsed if he wasn't holding me up. "You're a fucking dream, Petal. You have to be," Hamilton murmured.

I calmed my breath. "I think you're the only guy that can make me angry and horny at the same time. I thought I told you this couldn't happen, hmm?" Hamilton eased my leg down and stood up, his filthy mouth still shiny from my pleasure.

"You did say you wanted to be ruined, Petal," he whispered.

"Stop calling me that."

A fresh wave of shame slammed into me. What the fuck was I doing? Was I seriously so starved for sex that I let him...

Oh fuck. This was bad. This was so bad. We shouldn't be here. What if someone saw us walking together? I probably looked thoroughly fucked, and it was only a matter of time before someone noticed that Hamilton and I snuck away. "I'm so fucked. This was a bad idea."

I shoved him to the side and went to grab my dress from the floor, trying to avoid looking at the impressive hard-on tenting the front of his dress pants. I didn't owe him anything. This was a mistake. "Vera?" Hamilton called the moment I picked up the wrinkled fabric off the floor.

"What?" I snapped, suddenly feeling overwhelmed, overstimulated, and just plain over all of this.

"You're forgetting something."

I stepped into my dress and looked him up and down. "I don't owe you an orgasm."

"No," Hamilton began while stalking over to me. His hands reached out to help me put the straps of my dress back in place. "I'm talking about your panties. A deal is a deal."

I huffed. "I don't remember agreeing to anything."

"I think it's fair compensation for a job well done. I'm about to be on a rig with fourteen other men for two weeks. It's the least you can do."

I rolled my eyes. Hamilton smirked. The room was dark, but a small light illuminated his hungry face. One impulse was all it took, and I was boldly reaching under the skirt of my dress and rolling the drenched panties down my still trembling thighs. "So obedient," he teased when I slapped it in his palm. "Pleasure doing business with you, Vera."

The pleasure was all mine.

11

*A*s I walked back through the ballroom with my blushing skin and messy hair, I knew it was only a matter of time before someone guessed what we had done. I was still buzzing from the pleasure Hamilton coaxed from my body. Every step teased me. Every press of my legs together sent an aftershock of need through my body. "Stop fidgeting, you look suspicious," Hamilton whispered with a satisfied grin. He looked way too proud of himself as he licked his lips and followed after me.

Many people were already sitting down, prepared to enjoy their overpriced meals as they gossiped. I'd completely lost my appetite.

"I *am* suspicious," I hissed. "Stop following me." I didn't actually want Hamilton to stop following me. Aside from my mother, he was the only familiar face here. But it was for the best. We'd taken things too far. This was exactly the situation I was trying to avoid. If word got out that I was lusting after Joseph's younger brother, it would be a media shit storm. It was taboo and wrong.

"Who else am I going to talk to? This party is stuffy. Want to leave? I've got a couple of steaks marinating at my house. I'll even break the rules and give you a glass of wine. You really need a fake ID."

I pinched the bridge of my nose and kept walking toward the buffet table. I needed a drink. I needed to go home and wash Hamilton off of my skin.

"You look hot all flustered like that," Hamilton whispered. "It's kind of cute how your cheeks turn red. Are you thinking about it, Vera? Are you thinking about how I still have your taste on my tongue?"

"Stop talking," I pleaded. "It's like you want to be caught."

"What's the worst that could happen? I mean honestly."

"People could talk," I forced out. "It could make my mother look bad."

"I didn't realize you cared what people thought about you. It's a shame. Life is so much more fun when you let go of all the expectations the rest of the world puts on you."

I stared at Hamilton, at his shiny lips, his wild eyes and his ruffled hair. "You don't care what people think of you?"

"No. I care about having fun, feeling good, and doing whatever the fuck I want to do. Life is too short to live by someone else's rules, Vera."

"I feel like I've got a flashing neon sign over my head telling everyone what we just did," I huffed out while fixing the strap of my dress.

"It's kind of hot. Would you be into people watching us sometime?"

I blushed and avoided looking at him. "This was bad. Really bad."

"I thought by the way you screamed my name, it was fucking good, Vera," Hamilton replied in a low voice. "So fucking good that I'm going to be stroking myself to thoughts of you coming in my mouth. You're so sweet."

I let out a slow breath. "Why me? I'm sure you could have anyone."

"Why are you so quick to doubt why someone would want you, hmm?" I thought about his question for a moment. Why was it so difficult for me to wrap my head around the idea of being wanted? Just before I could reply, my mother's voice stopped me in my tracks.

"Vera, baby, where did you disappear to? You missed the toasts."

I snapped my attention to my mother and let out a shaky exhale. "I was just taking a walk. I needed some fresh air. You know how crowds make me anxious," I replied.

She peered at me, and Hamilton being the asshole he was, slung his arm over my shoulders. "Hello again, Lilah. How are you? Congratulations on the move. You're going to love DC. It's a great place to raise kids, too."

My mother glared at Hamilton. The open hostility was unexpected and out of the ordinary. What did Joseph tell her that was so bad? "I'm very proud of my husband," she said in a pleasant tone that felt forced. "He's worked hard to follow in Jack's footsteps. He's got that Beauregard ambition."

"That's such a picky gene. I hear it skips younger siblings," Hamilton replied with a wicked smirk.

"Well, what a coincidence. I heard the very same thing. In fact, I've heard lots of things recently," Mom snapped.

"I'm sure only ninety-nine percent of them are true. Did my brother tell you about the time I bought him strippers for his thirtieth birthday? What a wild time that was," Hamilton replied while cocking his head to the side and looking my mom up and down.

Mom frowned and rolled her eyes. "Vera, let's go stand with Joseph. This is a party celebrating his accomplishments, and you haven't even spoken to him. It looks bad."

I ground my teeth together. If she was worried about appearances, then she was going to be pissed when she heard I let Hamilton eat me out in a storage closet. "Of course." I didn't want to go stand with Joseph. I didn't even want to be at this stupid party, and for the first time in my life, I wanted to get the hell away from my mother. She was like a complete stranger to me.

Hamilton cleared his throat before speaking directly to me. "I'll stop by tomorrow, then."

Mom's eyebrows raised. "Tomorrow? What's tomorrow?"

"I'm leaving for the oil rig. They asked me to come early, and I needed a dog sitter. Vera so graciously volunteered." Hamilton squeezed me tighter to his side. I forgot he was still holding me close. I shrugged out of his grasp.

"I see," Mom replied while tilting her chin up. "And you'll be gone for how long?"

"Two weeks. But I'll be back. I *always* come back," Hamilton promised. There was something ominous about the way he emphasized always.

I looked between them and decided that this was too dramatic for my tastes. "Come on. Let's go see Joseph," I told my mother before grabbing her slender arm and pulling her toward her husband at the head table in the front of the room.

"See you tomorrow, Vera," Hamilton called, loud enough for the neighboring tables to hear. It was like he wanted people to know.

I nodded politely, my lips fixed in a tight smile.

Just before we got to the front table where a positively political Joseph was politely smiling, Mom pulled me off to the side. "Are you trying to punish me? Is that what's going on, Vera?" she asked in a hysterical whisper while side-eyeing the room. "I know that I hurt your delicate feelings last weekend, but I thought you were going to stay away from Hamilton, not disappear with him for forty-five minutes doing God knows what. I raised you better than this. You start college next week. Now is not the time to start going crazy and sleeping around. You cannot seriously be this selfish."

She didn't look at me as she spoke, her gaze too busy watching the room to make sure that no one was eavesdropping on us. "I was doing nothing. I seriously don't understand why you're upset," I lied.

Mom exhaled and parted her mouth, giving me a determined, speculative glare. She then reached up and spun one of my fallen strands of hair on her finger, her expression turning scarily calm. "I wasn't going to tell you this. I know how sensitive you are, dear, but you must know. Hamilton has been trying to ruin this family ever since his mother died." Her voice was a gossipy whisper.

"What?" I sputtered.

"You heard me. He planted drugs in Joseph's locker in high school and got him suspended. He also tries to ruin every public event with some sort of scandal. I mean, he had an orgy at our wedding,

Vera." She looked around. "He's got some sort of vendetta. Joseph thinks he's just jealous. Jack's always been close to Joseph. They have more in common, you know? Hamilton is a selfish, self-absorbed asshole. You need to be careful."

"Why would he try to ruin his family? What did Joseph and Jack do?" I asked.

Mom tilted her chin up and inhaled. "My husband and Jack have done nothing to deserve this behavior." Her haughty tone made me pause. "Apparently poor Jack has spent his entire life covering up Hamilton's mistakes."

I absorbed her words and shook my head absentmindedly. "I don't know. He doesn't seem—"

"You're so naïve, Vera." Mom rolled her eyes, making me cringe. "Maybe I've done you a disservice by protecting you from the evils of the world all these years. I didn't want you to grow up too fast. I wanted you to enjoy being a child, something I wasn't allowed. But you can't live in la la land anymore, baby. Hamilton is bad news. He wants to bring down our family, and he sees you as the weakest link. You don't think he actually likes you, do you? He's ten years older than you, and according to Joseph, he could have any woman he wants. You're just a stepping stone."

There was a lot of cruelty to unpack in her statement. I might not have had a difficult childhood, but that didn't mean I wasn't exposed to the horrors of the world. What about all the times we had to split meals off the dollar menu because we were afraid that we wouldn't make rent? What about Child Services constantly dropping in unexpectedly to check in on us?

And as far as being wanted by Hamilton, that was already an insecurity I was dealing with. I knew in my gut that someone like him couldn't possibly want me. And hearing it from my mother made that wound fester deep in my soul.

"Do not talk to him anymore, Vera. I've asked you nicely, but now I'm telling you. I'm still your mother, and my husband is the one paying for your college. Joseph doesn't like it when we associate with his brother. I mean, gosh, he works on an oil rig. He's going nowhere in life. Jack resents him. Why would you want to spend time with such a loser?"

"Jack invites Hamilton to dinner every week," I replied, my voice too loud. "That doesn't sound like a man who resents his son."

"Jack is too soft," Mom replied. It didn't sound like her, though. It felt like regurgitated words she was brainwashed to repeat.

"Is there a problem here?" Joseph asked. I hadn't even noticed him approach. Mom rolled her shoulders back and held her stomach with her hand, smiling blindingly at him.

"Not at all, honey. Vera and I were just talking about your brother. I just think it would be wise for her to stay away from him, you know?"

Joseph nodded while tugging at the lapels of his jacket. He looked bright and handsome, his green eyes glimmering under the lights of the chandelier. My stepfather was put together, his suit tailored to perfection. But all that perfection didn't feel authentic. It felt like a mask. "Ah. Yes. Hamilton is somewhat of a problem in our family. It's sad, really. But it's not a conversation for right now." Joseph eyed me, his cold gaze sending shivers through my body. "I just want you to be safe. I'm glad your mother told you. Trouble follows Hamilton wherever he goes." I felt it in my gut, that this didn't feel right. It felt like a politician's lie, a tool used to make his opponent look bad. But what was Joseph's platform? What was he fighting for? Joseph let out a shaky exhale, then forced his face into a smile.

"I never got to tell you congratulations, Joseph," I said, changing the subject. Mom beamed, happy to be discussing how fucking wonderful her husband was. I was starting to get a Stepford wives vibe from her, and I was not liking it.

He preened. "Well, thank you. It was too good of an opportunity to pass up. I'm very excited for this new role. I hope I can do it justice. Also, good luck with school next week. I looked at your schedule. I had some of the same professors as you. Be sure to sit in the front row of Doctor Bhavsar's class and she'll love you forever."

"Thanks. I'll keep that in mind." Why the fuck had he been looking at my schedule? It wasn't really his business, was it?

"Also, I used to work at the library. I can put in a good word for you. Dad mentioned you didn't like the internship opportunity," he continued. I pinned my lips shut, thankful that Jack didn't tell Joseph about our argument. "It's a great job to have. I basically got paid to study. You wouldn't imagine the things I saw on the night shift."

I nodded and swallowed. "That would actually be great. I'd like to work for some spending money. I appreciate the apartment and everything else, but I still want to work."

"I knew I liked you," Joseph said with a grin. "You're definitely a Beauregard. You could easily have everything handed to you, and yet you want to work. It's admirable. This country was built by men and women like us."

His words made me feel icky. I couldn't put a finger on it. Maybe I just didn't like politicians.

I knew that I needed to make more of an effort with Joseph. I still had a lot of questions and concerns, but it was important that I try. I took a step forward, my arms stretched open for a congratulatory hug, but Joseph held his hand up. "Hold that thought, can you hug me over there by the flag so we can have a photo taken? It'll look great for the press release."

"Oh. Um. Sure," I whispered before swallowing anxiously. This was the problem with Joseph; his life was a stage, and everyone had a role to play. Something told me that Hamilton was cast as the villain to make Joseph look better. I just couldn't prove it—yet.

12

$\mathcal{I}$ smoothed my skirt and twisted my long hair into a bun. Little Mama was snoring and snoozing in her brand new, plush dog bed in the corner of my bedroom. She liked her beauty sleep early in the morning; otherwise, I would have made her go on a jog with me to work off the anxious energy in my veins. I didn't even like running, but I had all this anxiety with nowhere to go.

Today was the first day of school.

Babysitting Little Mama was good for dulling my nerves. Hamilton ended up catching an earlier flight to work, so Jess brought her by and gave me the rundown on all Little Mama's quirks and needs. I probably took the poor dog on five walks yesterday just so I could get the buzz out of my bones.

I couldn't quite figure out the source of my turmoil. Was it from my mistake with Hamilton in the storage closet, or was it from the fear of not fitting in at my new university?

Something told me it was both.

Everything about Greenwich University contradicted my vision for college. It felt like a fancy prep school with elite expectations.

My morning class was Philosophy, and I kept anxiously checking my messenger bag to make sure I had all the right textbooks for the day. I loved the feel of a fresh start. I loved the idea of being somewhere new and exciting, but this was tainted with the Beauregard legacy. Joseph jokingly reminded me that everyone who was worth knowing was well-informed that a Beauregard was now attending Greenwich. He made it sound like he expected me to wear the privilege like a fine fur coat. I wanted to blend, not be held to standards I didn't understand yet. I was still Vera Garner—not Vera Beauregard. And I wasn't sure I ever wanted to carry the burden of his name.

I laced up my combat boots and tugged at my black skinny jeans. My white shirt was simple and crisp. I tucked it into my jeans and finished off the outfit with a Gucci belt. I tied my hair up in a bun and swiped some mascara and blush on before deciding that it didn't matter how I looked today.

My phone pinged.

Hamilton: Testing. Am I still blocked?

Me: No. I unblocked you this morning.

Hamilton: How is my favorite girl doing?

I blushed and hovered my fingers over the keys.

Me: I'm fine. Nervous about the first day of school.

Hamilton's response was immediate.

Hamilton: I was asking about Little Mama...

I giggled to myself and rolled my eyes as another text came through.

Hamilton: You're going to be amazing.

Hamilton: What are you wearing?

I chewed on the inside of my cheek for a moment while staring at his message. I knew he was just taunting me—distracting me for his own selfish benefit. I turned on the camera and took a quick mirror selfie before sending it to him.

My phone started ringing as soon as my message said delivered.

"You're way too beautiful, you know that?" he said the moment I answered.

"You're way too obnoxious, you know that?" I replied. I was finding it hard not to smile.

"Have you ever genuinely accepted a compliment, Vera?" Hamilton whispered. "I mean really basked in the fact that someone truly found you to be painfully beautiful and wonderful and fucking perfect?"

I thought over his question. "No," I admitted. "I'm not good at compliments."

"Let's practice then, hmm? Vera Garner, you are the most stunning woman I've ever seen. You have the most kissable lips, and I could devour them all day. You just sent me a fully clothed photo, and I'm hard as a rock. You've got me fisting my cock at eight in the morning on a Monday, Petal." I breathed out, too stunned for words. "Now I want you to say thank you. And then go kick today's ass."

"Thank you," I whispered.

"Bye, Petal."

"Goodbye, Hamilton."

I hung up the phone and stared at it for a moment before shaking my head free of the spell Hamilton had put on me. What was it about Hamilton that managed to ease my worries while causing them at the same time?

————

THE LECTURE HALL WAS LARGE AND INTIMIDATING. The moment I strolled through the imposing double doors, my heart felt like it had crawled up my throat.

Greenwich University was very overwhelming. Every person on campus was designer. Designer bag, designer clothes, shoes. Hell, even designer breeding. There wasn't a single flaw. It was like an entire race of supermodel humans roamed the grounds, clutching their expensive cell phones and chatting about taking the private jet to their daddy's private island. Symmetrical faces. Slim bodies. Smooth skin. Many of them looked like they got plastic surgery as a gift for their high school graduation.

I felt so incredibly out of place that it made me sick. Even though Jack's team of personal stylists made sure I looked the part of a Greenwich

University freshman with more money than God, I still felt like an outsider. This wasn't me.

I eyed an open seat at the front of the room and made my way over to it. This was the class Joseph warned me about. Apparently, I wasn't the only one that was informed of Dr. Bhavsar's preference for students who sit in the front, because the last rows in the auditorium were completely empty, and there was barely any room in the first two. It looked like a few students were debating whether or not to sit on the floor at her podium. I was surprised I managed to find a spot at all.

I sat down, then pulled out my journal and a pen before shoving my new designer tote on the floor at my feet. There were still ten minutes before class was set to start, so I took the time to look around. Some groups of students were gossiping. Most were playing on their phone or their laptop. I realized that I was the only person in the room who didn't have a MacBook on their desk. Was it a requirement? I didn't even own a fucking MacBook.

"A traditionalist, yeah?" a smooth masculine voice asked beside me. I twisted in my seat to look at him and licked my lips. He was handsome. Polished. Tall. He barely fit in the auditorium seat, the fold out desk pressing against his muscular thighs. He had to be over six feet tall, though I couldn't really tell since he was sitting down. His torso was long and built. His eyes were a deep blue, and his clean-shaven face was chiseled and strong.

"Huh?" I asked, feeling lame.

"You handwrite your notes? Too cool for modern technology?" he asked.

I chuckled. "No. Just unprepared. I have a desktop at my apartment, but I didn't think to bring a laptop to class. I already get distracted easily, so it hadn't even occurred to me to bring one. I'd probably end up surfing the internet during lecture."

The guy looked around. "What do you think all these people are doing?" he asked before nodding at a guy toward the back. "He's probably looking at porn." He then stared at a girl chewing on the edge of her pencil and scrolling through web pages. "She's shopping with her daddy's credit card for some new shoes—and I don't mean her real daddy. I mean the guy she's fucking."

"Kinky," I replied with a laugh. "And what about you?"

He pulled out his MacBook and opened it up, revealing a Word document. "I'm transcribing the lecture with my dictation tool. This program records the professor's voice and writes the notes for me. I'm in a frat, and a lot of my brothers like to skip class. We sometimes take turns transcribing so we all have the notes. Sometimes this program sucks though because it picks up *everything* that's said. You have to weed through the useless bullshit, but it works well enough."

"Do you sell your notes to your fellow frat brothers?" I asked with a smirk.

"I cannot confirm nor deny that I charge for my services. I'm not necessarily hurting for money, but I do like to make them squirm. Especially around midterm season. I will never understand why they think cramming for a test is going to work."

I grinned before holding out my hand. "I'm Vera," I said with a smile.

He took my hand, and I felt small in his warm grip. "Jared," he replied. "Are you a freshman?"

"Yep. First day of school. It's a little intimidating. I'm not even sure where my next class is."

"Well, lucky for you, I have a weakness for pretty girls that like to handwrite their notes. What's your next class?"

I blushed before tucking a hair behind my ear. Was he flirting with me or just being nice? "Feminism and Social Justice with Dr. Eva Yanukovich." I pulled out my planner to double-check that was actually where I was supposed to go. "I'm going to school for social work," I then quickly explained. My schedule was full of unique classes that I couldn't wait to sink my teeth into. One of my favorite things about college was getting to learn more about the subjects that genuinely interested me, and I *loved* studying people and society.

"Yanukovich also teaches my Paradoxes of War class," Jared replied excitedly. "She's seriously a genius."

My mouth dropped open. "Lucky! I was waitlisted for that class! I swear her thesis on Classical Sociological Theory changed my life."

Jared grinned. "Sociology minor?" he asked.

I shook my head. "Nah. I'm fascinated by sociology, though. I've pretty much filled up all my electives with Yanukovich lectures."

Jared nodded and licked his lips. "I think we're going to get along very well, Vera."

I chewed on the inside of my cheek and shifted in my seat. Jared was handsome and intellectually on my level. It was rare I found someone as excited about class as me. He tossed smoldering looks my way, rendering me nearly speechless.

But I couldn't help the little thought in my mind that he wasn't Hamilton. Not even close.

The front door opened, and in walked a woman wearing kitten heels, a cheetah print skirt, and a button-down black blouse. She had black hair tied up in a bun and round glasses. "Okay, class. Let's get started." She pulled down the projector screen and flipped off the lights. Jared shifted in his seat, brushing his arm against mine. "I'm not going to insult your intelligence by going over the syllabus. You're more than capable of reading the thorough description of my expectations in the packet I emailed last week. We're going to dive right into one of my favorite philosophical topics."

The screen flickered on to a single quote. "You," Dr. Bhavsar said to a slender brunette girl seated four chairs away from me. "Read it."

The girl cleared her throat before speaking. "Those who tell the stories rule society."

"You," Dr. Bhavsar said while nodding at another student. "Tell me what this quote means."

He looked around the room nervously before answering her. "The stories we tell have the power to control our realities," he answered.

"What a beautiful textbook answer. I believe you read that on page fourteen, did you not?" He nervously nodded. "Stories are essential to building perception, ladies and gentlemen. We cannot function as a society without them. And he who tells the story, controls the narrative." She licked her lips and clicked the next slide. "Stories help us make sense of the world around us, but they can also be dangerous. In many ways, stereotypes were created by irresponsible storytelling. Tell me a quality about yourself, and I can tell you a story that the world has assigned you. Most of the time, they aren't even true. But again, *those who tell the stories rule society*. And there are many people in positions of power who profit off irresponsible narratives.

"What makes a credible storyteller? Why do you trust me to stand at this podium and talk to you about people long dead? Is it the multiple degrees hanging in my office? That thesis I spent four years writing? You"—she nodded at Jared beside me —"tell me why you trust me to stand here and teach you."

Jared's eyes widened, and he squirmed in his seat before answering, "You're an educated woman who's dedicated her life's work to studying philosophy."

"You don't know me, though. How can you be certain that I'm not inserting my own bias or beliefs into my lecture? I'm molding the minds of future leaders. The next generation is under my thumb, and if I were persuasive enough, I could convince you that my version of events is correct, could I not?"

"We don't know," I replied, feeling embarrassed for speaking out of turn the moment those words left my lips.

"Oh?" Dr. Bhavsar asked. "So, what do you do? How do we navigate a world of potentially lying storytellers?"

"We tell our own stories," I mumbled. "We research. We question everything, even people in positions of power—especially people in positions of power. Credibility is established over time, through fact checking. We don't allow bias or opinions to shape our realities. We create our own through putting in the work. Those who tell the stories only rule society if society allows it."

Dr. Bhavsar smiled. "Exactly."

———

"I can't believe we live in the same apartment building. Now I'm absolutely going to bother you all the time," Jared said with a grin. Jared had walked me to my classes and even had lunch with me at the dining hall. I wasn't expecting him to spend the day with me, but I wasn't angry about it.

"You don't live at the frat house? By the way, I'm still surprised you're in a frat. Aren't you supposed to be a raging alcoholic that parties all the time? All the nineties college movies I watched to prepare myself for this year really missed the mark."

Jared touched his chest. "I'm really hurt by that stereotype, Vera," he replied. "We aren't all party hard frat daddies with daddy issues." I giggled as we walked toward our apartment building. "But *maybe* your assumptions are partially true. Part of the reason I moved out of the Pike house was because they are slightly disgusting, and I never got any sleep because they were too busy partying all the time. I swear to God the communal showers were coated in a thick layer of cum."

"That sounds disgusting."

"I stay for the cute guys and my parents' approval, but I'm tempted to leave for the same reason. It's a tragedy."

Cute guys? I thought Jared was hitting on me before. I guess—

"I see the cute wheels in your head turning. No worries, I'll happily explain. I'm pansexual," he explained. "I lost my virginity to a woman twice my age in London. Last year, I dated a football player. I spent last month in New York hooking up with a beautiful trans woman. *Last night*, in the psychology building, I sucked a mediocre dick belonging to a very confused fraternity president. And right now, I'm really hoping you'll let me take you on a date."

"Oh. I..." I wasn't expecting him to ask me out. It wasn't his sexual preferences that had me pausing. It was thoughts of Hamilton. I was just about to explain that I wasn't looking for a date when my phone started ringing. It was a FaceTime call from Hamilton. "Excuse me, I have to answer this," I whispered. One of the stipulations of watching Little Mama was that I answer whenever he called, as long as I wasn't in class. He was a needy bastard.

I held the phone up and smiled before clicking accept for the call. Hamilton was lying on his bed in what looked like a small dark room. His hair was a mess, and there was a smudge of grease on his cheek. "Thank fuck you answered. I swear my dick has been hard all day just thinking about you."

I coughed and Jared grinned beside me before looking over my shoulder to stare at the screen. I tried to angle the phone away. Even though there was no possible way for Jared to know that Hamilton was my uncle, it was only a matter of time before he did.

"I'm guessing that date is a no then, hmm?" Jared asked quietly.

"Who the fuck is that?" Hamilton asked while sitting up on his mattress and leaning closer to the screen for a better look.

"It doesn't matter. If you're calling to check on your dog, I'll be home in just a few minutes so you can see her," I said.

"Were you bringing this guy home?" Hamilton asked.

"No. He lives in the same building as me. Why are you acting jealous?"

"Maybe I had a taste and I don't want to share." Jared shamelessly hovered over me, listening to my conversation with Hamilton and grinning at the camera. "You look familiar," Hamilton then said to Jared. "Have we met before?"

"Can't say we have. I would have remembered you," Jared replied with a smirk.

Hamilton's eyes thinned to small slits. "I don't like you."

"You barely know me," Jared countered before chuckling.

"I'm a pretty good judge of character. Doesn't take much. Stay away from Vera."

At that statement, I decided to interject. "I told

you. This is not happening. And I'm not having this conversation in front of my new friend. Did you need anything, Hamilton?" I asked.

"Just you. I need you right now, Petal."

"Petal?" Jared asked. My heart rate picked up.

"I'll call you later, Hamilton," I choked out before hanging up the phone.

Jared started laughing hysterically. "Now you *have* to go on a date with me. Mostly just to piss him off."

I scowled. "I was going to tell you before I was so rudely interrupted that I'm not looking to date anyone right now. I really am just trying to settle in and make some friends."

"I get it. And who wants to date when you have someone like that ready to eat you up?"

I let out a shaky exhale and continued walking. The shaded sidewalk had arched trees covering the path, and expensive cars drove past us. "It's complicated," I admitted.

"Complicated how?" I debated on telling Jared what was going on. I hadn't really had anyone to talk about this with. The moment Hamilton steamrolled into my life, I struggled with my strange fascination-slash-attraction to him. It might be nice to have someone to talk to about it all who wasn't my mother or a Beauregard.

"He's technically my uncle?" I offered.

Jared stopped walking. He blinked twice. "Come again?"

"My mom married his older brother a month ago," I rushed out in explanation.

"Here I was thinking you're all straitlaced, and then you drop a taboo bomb like that in my lap?" Jared shivered delightfully. "I'm so impressed. And a little turned on."

"That's not weird at all..."

"Come on," Jared said. "We're going to your apartment, and you're going to tell me everything. Don't you dare leave any information out."

13

"Gosh, you're so cute. I wish I were home so I could cuddle you," Hamilton said over FaceTime. I rolled my eyes while swiping blush along my cheeks. Little Mama was wagging her tail as Hamilton spoke to her. "Is Vera giving you plenty of treats? Is she scratching behind your ears? You just say the word and I'll spank Vera if she isn't treating you right. I'll have her ass red in no time."

I picked up the phone off the floor and arched

my brow at Hamilton. "Is that really necessary?" I asked.

"I'm following your rules!" he playfully exclaimed. "No flirty, dirty, naughty, or possessive talk. I'm not allowed to talk about how much I wish you were riding my face right now or ask if your pussy is soaked from thinking of me. I'm *absolutely* not allowed to ask where the fuck you're going tonight looking sexy as hell in that tight skirt. Your tits are about to spill out of that top, and I want to catch them with my mouth, beautiful." My breath hitched, and he grinned wickedly while angling the phone ever so slightly so I could see his hard, shirtless torso. Fuck. "But if I were allowed to ask these things, I'd also tell that fucker Jared to keep his hands to himself."

I fought a grin. Hamilton made me feel sexy. Desired. Part of the reason why I liked him so much was because he made me feel good about myself. It wasn't a feeling I was used to. "Is that all I am to you? A warm body?" I boldly asked. We hadn't connected on an emotional level, but boy did we collide physically.

"I bet if you let me get to know you better, we'd like each other. But again, I'm following the rules.

We have chemistry, Petal. I'm not afraid to act on that. And you know what I think?" he asked.

"What?"

"I think you like being pursued. I think it makes you feel powerful. And I like seeing your confident smile. Just don't let Jared reap the benefits of my hard work, Petal."

I set the phone down on my vanity and continued to get ready. I wasn't ready to end the phone call, but Little Mama was already snoozing on my bed. I picked up some red lipstick and started applying it. "Fuck," Hamilton whispered. I glanced at his hooded eyes and parted lips before returning to my reflection.

"If we were getting to know one another, what would be something you'd tell me? What's your story, Hamilton?"

"I don't really have a story," he replied in a soft voice.

"Everyone has a story," I countered before putting my lipstick down and grabbing some finishing powder.

Hamilton let out a lingering, long sigh before speaking to me again. "Mom and Jack were much older when I was born. They were a happy family of three up to that point. Jack was in the height of his career. Mom was in the height of her depression. It wasn't until the news broke that Jack knocked up some coed and had me that shit went south. I guess Mom had been cool with raising me as long as the world didn't know her husband was a cheating cunt. I was born a mistake. I'll probably die one, too," he said, his voice even, despite the painful words.

"That's...awful."

"Joseph liked to remind me every day of my goddamn life how I ruined everything. I used to think it was his only child syndrome, but now I think it's more. When Mom died...it got worse. Jack let Joseph push me around because he wanted me to suffer for existing, but was too much of a coward to do it himself."

Jack confused me. He was callous and pretentious, but he cared about Hamilton in a way that felt authentic. I didn't have all the facts, so I didn't feel like I had a right to pass judgment. Hamilton was raised by them. His feelings were valid. Still, I wanted to figure out Jack's perspective since he seemed to genuinely want a relationship with his son, despite Joseph's blatant hatred.

"Have you ever wanted to meet your real mom?" I asked.

"I had a real mom. Her name was Nikki

Beauregard. She was smart. Tenacious. She loved me even when she didn't have to. She fought through mental health issues. Have you ever wondered if your mother resented you?"

I frowned. "Why would you ask something like that?"

"We're sharing things about our lives, are we not? It's why you're so obedient. You think you have to be perfect to make up for the fact that you exist."

My eyes burned hot with emotion. "That's not true," I choked out.

"Isn't it though? I should know. I lived that way until the day Mom died. What is it going to take for you to live for yourself?"

"I am living for myself."

"You're cute when you lie." I shook my head and swallowed the thick ball of emotions in my throat. "Have fun tonight. If Jared touches you, I'll break every bone in his hand while you watch. I know you like possessive fuckers. I'm not one to normally be exclusive, but I'm starting to see the appeal."

"You haven't even taken me on a date!" I exclaimed.

"Keep fighting this, baby. It makes me hard."

I rolled my eyes and ended the call. Fucking Hamilton.

———

JARED DROVE A TESLA. HE ZIPPED US AROUND TOWN while excitedly talking about a lecture series coming up that he wanted us to go to. I listened and interjected at the right times, but still felt off from my conversation with Hamilton. "You're going to love this bar. It's the best kept secret in Greenwich. The craft drinks are strong, and the vibe is legit. It's painfully ordinary. Cheap drinks. Beer-soaked floors. You don't have to be a trust fund baby to get in. It's totally your style."

I didn't know what a *legit vibe* was, but I was humored by Jared's enthusiasm. We'd been going to school for a week, and he spent nearly every day with me. I liked spending time with him. He was smart, compassionate, funny, and a good study partner. I struggled at first with his constant flirting, but eventually I just realized that it was who he was as a person. He hadn't pressured me into dating him anymore, but sometimes I'd catch him staring at me with his heavy, heated gaze.

"Are you going to dance with me?"

"I'm not very good at dancing," I admitted with a grin as he pulled into an old parking lot with potholes and cars filling nearly every available space. Jared carelessly parked his Tesla up on the curb. He said this was the best kept secret in Greenwich, but this place wasn't a secret at all. Everyone in town was here. Maybe the people of Greenwich liked the *painfully ordinary* more than they let on.

"Everyone is good at dancing," Jared insisted.

We got out of the car and walked through the door. I stepped onto the scuffed floor and nearly crashed into a drunk girl dancing by herself. Jared laughed and grabbed me around the waist, easily maneuvering me out of the way. "Let's go to the bar, gorgeous," he whispered in my ear before easing me over to a barstool.

The bar was eclectic and cozy. Waiters serving drinks walked around the room with their trays in their hands. A couple in a corner booth was making out, the two women were devouring each other whole. Spit was flying. Trembling hands were groping one another. A man sitting by himself was taking shot after shot after motherfucking shot, and a table of fraternity guys waved at Jared the moment I sat down. "Can you stay right here for a minute? I'm going to say hello to my friends. Be right back. Order whatever you want."

I nodded at his back as he walked away. It was

kind of curious that he didn't want to introduce me, but maybe he didn't want us to lose our seats. I placed my purse on his stool and stared at his back as he said his hellos. After a few bro hugs, some of them turned to face me while whispering to Jared. I wondered what they were saying.

"This is why I don't date men. What an *asshole*," Jess said. Wait. Jess? She was on the other side of the bar top, wiping it down with a rag and glaring at Jared. "He just left you here to go say hello to his frat assholes. Why didn't he introduce you?" The fact that she was saying my thoughts out loud validated them.

"You work here?" I asked.

"I do. Rich college kids tip surprisingly well when they're wasted. And they like feeling like they're slumming it at a local spot. Makes them feel superior."

I raised my brows. "How's Infinity and the new apartment?" I asked.

"It's good. Though we need a place with a garage. Her band practices in the living room, and I love her, but that music gets old after a while."

I smiled. "Sorry I left her show."

Jess pulled out a glass with ice and poured some Sprite into it before handing it to me. "No worries.

Hamilton explained what's up. Fucking paparazzi. They've been hounding him since we were teens."

I nodded. "Because of his birth mom, right?" I asked.

Jess quirked her brow. "Are you digging for information?"

"Would you tell me anything if I was?" I asked.

Jess leaned over the worn bar top. Her black tank was stretched thin across her chest, and she had a bead of sweat on her temple. "Hamilton is a good man. He's sometimes a bit of a whore. I don't think the man can go a week without sticking his dick in something, so if you like him, you should probably be aware of that going into this." I swallowed. I knew this. Of course I knew this. But hearing it from Hamilton's best friend was a reality check I hadn't prepared for. It didn't matter anyway though. I wasn't going to act on these feelings, right?

"I never said I liked him," I argued.

"You didn't have to, *Petallll*." Ugh. When was I going to stop lying to myself? I wanted Hamilton. Jess continued. "He's probably the only decent person in that family, aside from his dead mother. He's a bit tortured, but I think all the pretty men are. He has this weird desire to piss his family off and please them all at the same time. It's weird. It's tragic.

I'm not a therapist, but he's really fucked up in the head about them. And don't get me started on Joseph. He's a sick bastard. The kind to kick puppies, you feel me?"

"Should I be worried about my mother?" I asked in a timid voice.

Jess chewed on the inside of her lip. "Joseph takes care of his toys. It's the people who try to take his toys from him that you should worry about."

I was about to ask her what that meant when Jared settled on the stool beside me. "What did I miss?" he asked before looking at Jess. "I'll have a Jack and Coke please."

Jess nodded and wordlessly made his drink. "Jared, this is my friend Jess. I didn't realize she worked here."

"Oh! Sorry." Jared wiped his hand on his pants before reaching out to shake hers. "My name is Jared, it's a pleasure to meet you."

Jess stared at his outstretched hand before handing him his drink. "I'll be around if you need anything, Vera," she said. "Watch your drink around this one. I keep a Glock under the bar, pretty boy." She squinted at him before moving on to the next customer.

"Did I say something wrong?" Jared asked, his

eyes wide. I couldn't tell if it was shock or amusement.

"No. She just doesn't like people in general," I replied with a forced laugh. "You're lucky she didn't start interrogating you."

"Sounds like my kind of woman."

I took a sip of my drink, happy to enjoy something nonalcoholic. I'd never been out with Jared before and wasn't sure what to expect. Was he a party hard frat boy? He was driven and smart, but I still wanted to be safe. "We can go sit with your friends if you'd like?" I offered while looking over my shoulder. The table of frat boys were now doing shots and getting a bit rowdy. I had zero desire to sit with them, but I didn't want to be rude.

"And risk one of them wooing you? Absolutely not," Jared teased, though his lighthearted tone seemed forced. "I brought you out tonight because I wanted to spend time with you."

I tipped my head back and laughed. "You've spent time with me all week! You practically live at my apartment. I'm going to start making you pay for groceries if I'm going to be cooking for us every night."

"I'll happily pay for groceries if it means getting to have dinner and Netflix with you every night."

I rolled my eyes. "See? We spent all week together."

"Yeah, but not on a date."

"Oh, so this is a date?" I asked, brows raised as I looked at Jared. He was handsome, in a classic boy-next-door sort of way. He could probably have anyone he wanted. He came from a good family. His father was a businessman and dabbled in politics. His mother ran one of the largest nonprofits in the world.

He reached out and placed his hand on my thigh. A shiver traveled up my spine. Maybe...

"I would have taken you somewhere nicer, but I had a feeling you would have freaked out and bailed on me. I know you have a hang up for your..." He leaned forward and dropped his voice. "Your *fucking* uncle. But I think we could be good together. I think you might like me. And if you want to call me Daddy in bed to get your taboo rocks off, I'll let you. Family strokes isn't usually my thing, but I'm always willing to try something at least once. There's a huge market for stepbrother porn." I giggled at his words as he brushed his lips along my neck.

I turned to face him, and my mouth was barely a breath away from his. I could feel his hot breath. It smelled like whiskey. "I'm not looking for anything serious," I said in a low voice.

"I'm not a serious guy," Jared murmured. His blue eyes found my lips, and he stared hungrily at them. My throat became suddenly dry and my breathing more labored. Jared leaned closer, his determination making me grow hot.

This felt like a decision I couldn't go back from. Once I kissed Jared, shit would be way more complicated. I leaned closer, closer, closer...

"Vera," Jess's voice boomed. I jumped back, shaking my head in confusion. Jared cursed. "Someone on the phone for you," she said as my eyes focused on her. She was smiling mischievously, her head tilted to the side. I took the phone from her outstretched palm and watched as she literally snarled and bared her teeth at Jared like a feral wolf.

I gave Jared an apologetic look before holding the phone up to my ear. "Hello?"

"Petal," Hamilton rasped, his tone breathy and laced with anger. My heart thundered. "Did you let him kiss you?" I snapped my eyes to Jess who was full-on laughing now.

"Who is on the phone?" Jared asked. I ignored him.

"No," I replied in a shaky voice. "I was about to,

though." My honesty felt like a lie. I wasn't telling Hamilton because I wanted to come clean, I was telling him because I wanted to piss him off.

Hamilton let out a long exhale. It was hard to hear him over the crowd. "Excuse yourself to the bathroom and call me, Petal. Now." Hamilton hung up the phone, and I winced at the abrupt end of our call.

I handed the phone back to Jess. I could have ignored his demands. Hamilton was miles away offshore, and I was here. *Jared* was here. But...

"Who was that?" Jared asked.

"A mutual friend," I choked out. "Sorry, I'm going to the bathroom. Be right back."

I hopped off the stool and pushed through the crowd toward the bathroom, my purse clutched close to my side. What the hell was I doing? And why was there a spike of thrill shooting through every nerve ending in my body?

I went into the individual bathroom and slammed the door shut, locking it the moment I was inside. Then, I leaned against the wooden door before pulling out my cell and FaceTiming Hamilton. He answered immediately.

"Touch yourself," he demanded the moment our call connected.

"What?" I whispered with a blush, looking around the single bathroom like someone was going to pop out of the sink and call me out for Hamilton's naughty request.

"You let him touch what's mine," Hamilton croaked. He was shirtless and biting his lip. "So now you're going to rub your needy little clit in a public bathroom while I watch. If you're lucky, I'll show you how hard you make my cock."

"Fuck," I rasped. "I can't."

"Yes, you can. You want to be kissed, Petal? You want to be touched? You call me. I don't care what I'm doing. I don't care where I am. I'll take care of my girl. You don't have to find relief somewhere else."

"I'm not your girl, Hamilton. When are we going to stop this?"

He let out a sigh. "You still don't get it. Stop telling me you aren't mine before I hop on a plane and show you how much you are. Put your finger in your mouth. Get it good and wet for me, Petal. Suck it hard." I couldn't see what he was doing because the camera cut off at his bare abs, but I noticed the subtle rocking movement of his arm as if he was stroking himself.

Fuck. What was I doing? There was no one here. This wasn't hurting anyone, was it?

I looked around again before reluctantly obeying him. My plump lips wrapped around my finger, and he smiled when my cheeks hollowed out as I sucked. I watched him with hungry eyes for a moment before pulling out with a pop.

"When I get home, you're going to wrap those lips around my cock, Vera," he said with a grunt. "Now touch yourself. Let me see you fall apart. Let me see how much you're mine. Your mind might not know it yet, but your pussy sure as fuck does."

I inhaled deeply before slipping my hand behind the elastic waistband of my skirt. I was already soaked from Hamilton's words, my panties a damp mess as I sank into my heat and started swirling the pad of my finger around my sensitive nub. I twitched; my lips parted as I stared at Hamilton.

"You're so fucking gorgeous, Vera. Look how hard you make me." He eased the camera downward, and I gasped at the sight of his thick, veiny cock. His fist barely closed around it. He stroked it leisurely, and I licked my lips, imagining what he tasted like as I pinched my clit and moaned. "That's right, baby. *I'm* the one that can get you off from the other side of the country. *I'm* the one you can't seem to stop thinking about. *I'm* the one that's got you feeling selfish for the first time in your goddamn life. No one else is here, baby. It's just you and me. Your pretty pussy and my words. Your furious little fingers working that clit because I commanded it. Not some fuckboy you think you should be with. Me. Me. Me. *Me.*"

Fuck. I exhaled and an orgasm tore through me just as loud knocks pounded on the door. "Vera? You still in there?" Jared's voice called out. Hamilton grinned wickedly before pumping himself harder. I watched him shamelessly while biting my lip and falling down from my high. His cum erupted in thick, creamy ropes, coating his palm as he tossed his head back, groaning my name. The name he'd given me. *Petal. Petal. Petal.*

I didn't care about the line forming outside, Jared's furious knocks, or the heated blush coating my cheeks. I wanted Hamilton, and I was done denying myself of the things I wanted.

14

"We have our first test next week. You should already be on chapter four in the textbook," Dr. Bhavsar said while pulling down the projector screen. Her hair was up in a tight bun today, and the kitten heels strapped to her feet were a bright fire-engine red. Her class was quickly becoming my favorite out of all of them. I loved the way she viewed the world.

I tucked my smooth hair behind my ear and adjusted my sweater over my shoulder. These auditoriums got cold. Pretty soon the Connecticut fall would be in full swing, and I couldn't wait for the cooler weather.

"Want to have a study session this weekend? I'll order some takeout?" Jared offered. We had an awkward twenty-four hours after the bathroom incident, but he showed up the next morning with a box of donuts, undeterred. He had to have known what I did in there. When Hamilton and I were done, I opened the bathroom door with my shaking legs, flushed face, and racing heart. Jared was standing on the other side with his arms crossed over his chest. He hadn't pressured me to explain what had happened, but I didn't have to. At least he hadn't pushed for another date. I knew with complete certainty that Jared and I were only meant to be friends. I couldn't be seduced by his determined politeness or the playful press of his leg against mine as we watched Netflix on the floor of my living room. I couldn't be swayed by his compliments, his gifts, his thoughtfulness, or his unwavering niceties. Jared was like Tylenol, dulling the slight ache to my pounding restlessness. Hamilton was opium—bad for me and addictive.

Jared still flirted all the same, it was in his nature to do so. But he'd absolutely reined it in since our almost kiss at the bar. I was thankful that he had backed off, because while he was reestablishing himself as a friend, Hamilton was staking himself as...well, I wasn't quite sure.

Hamilton and I spoke daily. About nothing. About everything. He talked about his job on the rig, and I told him about my classes. I was oddly comfortable with him, but it constantly felt like the other shoe was about to drop. Every time I saw his name pop up on my phone, my stomach fluttered, and I didn't even bother to play it cool. I answered every time, pushing the guilt down as far as it would go, all while telling myself that this would be the last time.

I'd lie on my back, hidden in the shadows of three a.m. as he spoke in his signature deep voice to me.

Wet.

With a secret smile on my lips as he spoke dirty promises. Every night, I fell asleep with the rumble of need deep in my gut. I felt like a pretty thing on Hamilton's shelf. He was waiting to take me down, polish me, and throw me the fuck away.

Mom called me once to check on classes, but it

was a surface-level conversation. Hamilton was slowly becoming a big part of my life, and it was hard to talk to someone who would disapprove of that. I knew it was wrong. I knew that a lot of people wouldn't understand our relationship. This was bound to upset her new husband, but I was starting not to care.

"Miss Garner, I'd like you to summarize your response for the writing exercise I asked each of you to complete." I had been daydreaming and twirling my hair on my finger. Dr. Bhavsar's voice made me startle.

I cleared my throat. "Of course," my squeaky voice chirped as I pulled out my printed paper. Dr. Bhavsar made it a habit to call on me. Despite the full auditorium, her lectures and attention made me feel like the only person in the room. Even though she was hard on me, I felt like she only did it to the students she liked, and it made me that much more prepared for class every day. "I decided to focus on a teaching from Lao Tzu, specifically his quote that states, 'The usefulness of a pot comes from its emptiness.'"

"Interesting," Dr. Bhavsar said with a smirk. "I had a feeling most of the class would choose the popular philosopher's quote, 'This too shall pass.'

I'm thrilled you picked something original, Miss Garner."

I tried not to outwardly preen from her compliment, but the impulse was difficult. I didn't want to admit it, but Mom just sort of expected good grades from me. She was proud, sure, but she never complimented me for working hard and giving up my adolescence in exchange for good grades and obedience. It felt nice to be recognized by this woman.

I cleared my throat before continuing. "You have to empty your mind before you can let anything else in. Lao Tzu is talking about preconceived notions or opinions. How can we listen to another person's point of view if our head is already full of bias? Usefulness could be another word for growth or humanity's ability to effectively adapt and learn."

"And do you agree with this statement?" Dr. Bhavsar asked.

"I do," I replied simply.

"I think you're absolutely right. But we could take this a step further. Sometimes a full pot can hold us back from getting the things we truly want. It's almost like the cliché of bringing baggage into a new relationship. Are you familiar with it?"

"I am. We bring our experiences and worldview

to every new relationship we form," I answered as Jared shifted in his seat.

Dr. Bhavsar continued. "I think there is a difference between carrying our experiences with us wherever we go and burdening ourselves with a full suitcase—or as Lao Tzu likes to say, a full pot. There's no room for anything else. You could be missing out on new experiences because you're too busy clinging to something else."

Someone in the row behind me interjected. "So, are we supposed to just constantly treat each day like a clean slate? Many philosophers challenge us to use every experience in our arsenal to make meaning of the world and learn. What's the point of filling our pot, so to speak, if we're just going to keep emptying it for something else?"

Dr. Bhavsar smiled. "That's a very good observation, Mr. Shine. What do you think, Miss Garner?"

I swallowed while thinking of how to answer. "The pot isn't a metaphor for our full experience as humans. I think it doesn't have to be complicated. I think it's a pot's *ability* to empty itself of burdens that are no longer useful or beneficial that gives it meaning. Willingness to pour out the old makes all the difference. Perhaps a better metaphor would have been a fountain or a river? Ever changing but still of the same source."

"I'd like to fill you up," a dumbass guy in the back row said under his breath. I rolled my eyes. Dr. Bhavsar continued.

"Well done, Vera. I personally think you could learn a lot with this lesson. You've been holding back a bit. I want you to really dig deep into the nitty gritty of these assignments." Dr. Bhavsar turned to face the auditorium, now speaking to everyone. "Most of you simply discuss the concept without applying it to your own human experience. Your next assignment, I'd like for you to reference yourself when exploring these concepts. Philosophy only has meaning when we apply it."

Class continued and I scribbled notes. Jared teased me for not having a laptop, but I liked handwriting my work. The information stuck better. The ninety-minute class flew by, and my fingers were cramping from the information overload by the end of it. "Wanna grab lunch?" Jared asked as we packed up.

"Yeah. I skipped breakfast this morning because I overslept," I groaned.

"Were you up late having dirty conversations with your uncle again?" he asked teasingly, though there was a hard edge to his tone. I rolled my eyes and shoved my notebook into my bag. "What!" he exclaimed. "We're friends. We can discuss it. Nothing to be ashamed of. Except for the fact that he's technically you're uncle. And like ten years older. And he's gone half the year."

I chewed on my lip. "You sound bitter."

"Can you blame me? I'm just curious what he has that I don't."

The urge to say he had *me* struck me, but I kept my mouth pinned shut. "I don't know. I thought we were over this, Jared. If you're going to keep pressuring me, then I'm—"

"I'm sorry," he interrupted. "Let's go grab lunch, okay? I won't bring it up again. But you can bet your ass, the second he messes up, I'm swooping in."

I let out a slow exhale while thinking back on Jess's words.

He's kind of a whore.

How long until the thrill of chasing after me wore off? I knew it was only a matter of time before he found something else to obsess over. Hamilton didn't seem like the person to stay long.

"I want pizza today," I said, changing the subject.

"Good deal. Let's go."

We made our way out of the building and started walking through the quad. It seemed everywhere we went, someone knew Jared. People were constantly waving, inviting him to parties, and offering him bro hugs. It was weird because he didn't seem like a huge socialite. He spent all his time these last two weeks with me. If anything, I sort of wished that he would give me some breathing room, but I wasn't willing to risk upsetting the only friend I had in this place.

"Jared, my man! You coming to the party tonight?" someone asked.

"I got a hot date, sorry," he replied teasingly before wrapping his arm around my shoulders and guiding me in the direction of the dining hall.

"You know you can go, right?" I said in a soft voice. "You don't have to spend every night with me. Parties aren't really my thing, but you can go, Jared."

"And miss out on dinner and a Netflix marathon with you? No thanks. Maybe parties aren't really my thing either, hmm? Have you ever considered that?"

"I'm just saying—"

"Do you want me to go to the party, Vera?" Jared asked.

I stopped walking to face him. "I'm just saying you don't have to spend every night with me. You can go see your other friends."

"You're my friend," he countered.

"We can still be friends and have lives outside of one another. I love spending time with you, but—"

"But what? Do you not want me around? I don't get it."

"Of course I enjoy spending time with you. I'm just saying it's okay if you do other things too. I don't want you to feel obligated—"

"Who hurt you? Who made you feel like an obligation? Every five seconds, you're pushing me away. Is it him? Is it your uncle?"

"N-no. You're misunderstanding me—"

"You want me to go see them," he said, his teeth clenched in anger. "You know what? I'm going to have lunch with one of my other friends. Give you some space. I don't understand it..."

He ran a hand through his hair and stared at me, his eyes lingering on my mouth for a slow, uncomfortable moment. "Jared? I'm sorry, okay. I was just—"

"Talk to you later, Vera," he snapped before spinning on his heels and stalking away. Fuck. I should have felt bad. I should have felt sad that I'd hurt him, but all I could do was breathe a sigh of relief. I was actually looking forward to a day alone, and that said a lot about how I felt about Jared. I needed to be firmer about setting boundaries.

I continued my trek to the dining hall while smiling to myself.

"I was wondering when you'd ditch him. He's a clingy fucker, yeah?" My blood turned cold. That voice. I knew that voice.

Saint.

"What are you doing here?" I choked out while taking a step back. I'd gotten too comfortable. Saint hadn't bothered me these last couple of weeks, so I'd gotten complacent. He was standing by the door of the dining hall, his hair slicked back and his eyes raking up and down my body. He was wearing black skinny jeans and a loose button-down Hawaiian shirt.

"I was hoping to get a comment about the latest headlines involving your stepfather and mother?" Saint asked while producing his phone. I saw him hit record for a video, and I took another step back. Students walked past me, not seeming to notice or care that Saint was stalking closer and closer.

"What news? I'm confused," I stammered while reaching for my phone.

"Oh! You haven't heard yet. Your mother lied about her pregnancy. I sold the story last night. Seems she faked the doctor appointments, the ultrasounds, *everything.*" No. Certainly he was wrong. Mom wouldn't have done that.

"You're lying," I whispered.

"Nope. That would be your mother. My source is legit. Her doctor? Not so much. Had his license revoked years ago. She's a fraud. It's quite the scandal. I think Joseph might leave her. Do you think your grandfather will still pay for your school? Sorry, I'm tossing a lot at you, but I'm curious."

I started breathing heavily. Saint stalked closer. My thudding pulse pounded as my phone started to ring. "You need to leave. I got a protective order against you."

Saint tipped his head back and laughed. "I think you should get a protective order against Joseph and Jack. They're going to be so mad, don't you think? I mean, it's kind of cliché. The poor waitress seduces the politician. Pretends to get knocked up. The story practically writes itself. I mean, seriously, it's beautiful."

My phone stopped ringing. My throat was closing. Why was he so determined to ruin my family? "You don't look so good, Vera. Do you need to sit? I can wait for your comment."

I looked around me. Some students were starting to stare. I reached for my phone. Two missed calls from Mom. One from Hamilton. "Please leave," I pleaded.

"Please don't call the cops. It's so tedious. Don't you think you have bigger things to worry about, Vera?"

The way Saint said my name made me feel like snakes were crawling over my skin. I felt like I was going to puke. "Help," I choked out. The panic I felt was tangible. My throat was closing up, and I couldn't breathe.

"Did you know she was lying? It's no secret you couldn't have gotten into this university without the Beauregard help. You and your mom are close, right? I mean, you had to have known."

"I didn't. I never—"

"Back the fuck off," Jared yelled before surging forward. He put both hands on Saint's chest and shoved him backward, sending Saint to the ground with a thud.

"That's assault, buddy," Saint growled while helping himself up.

"You're fucking with my girl, dipshit. Get the fuck out of here. Now."

Saint smiled and dusted off his hands before cocking his head to the side. "You sure are protective. I didn't realize you had a bodyguard." Saint looked Jared up and down, his thin lips pressed into an angry line. "I'll leave you be. I think I have enough information for my follow-up interview. I hope you don't get too comfortable here, Vera."

I continued to hyperventilate as Jared wrapped me in his arms. What the fuck just happened? "Come on. Let's get you home."

"I need to call my mom," I murmured. My anxiety was so bad I felt like I was going to pass out.

"You can't do anything until you sit down and calm your breathing. I'm grabbing us an Uber. I don't want you walking like this."

Jared guided me to a nearby bench, but I was on full alert, worried Saint would appear out of nowhere again and antagonize me. Jared rubbed my back. "You're going to be okay. I'm here. He can't hurt you."

"How did you know to come see me?" I asked in a shaky voice.

"I felt bad for storming off. I saw that guy

bothering you and ran over. I'm so sorry, Vera. I should have never left."

"I really need to call my mom," I whispered again. Faked a pregnancy? How? Darkness crept around my vision. I felt like I couldn't get a full breath. Heaving in and out, I watched as Jared stared at me, concern in his gaze. "Can I call her? I really. I really need to call..."

15

I grabbed the cup of tea in front of me with shaky hands. I needed to figure out why Saint was so obsessed with my family. Today, he'd taken things too far. This wasn't just *investigative journalism* as he so eloquently put it. Saint had a vendetta, and I was determined to figure out what it was.

After taking a slow sip of the calming chamomile, I called my mother for what felt like the fiftieth time. I expected it to go straight to voicemail like it had before. After reading the scathing report of her faked pregnancy, I couldn't even blame her for wanting to hide from the world. Saint didn't hold back any punches. He dug deep into our family, picking at our poverty like it was an old scab to make us look like a duo of gold diggers. He even played up my genius, making it sound like I was the brains behind her stupid plan, and she was the hussy executing it.

"Hello?" Mom's worn voice answered.

"Mom," I exclaimed. "What is going on? Why are they lying about you in the papers?" She let out a huff of air. Time stretched. My chest squeezed with every second that she didn't respond. "They are lying, right?" I asked.

"It's not a lie, baby. I'm not pregnant."

I nearly dropped the phone from shock. "What?" I asked, certain I hadn't heard her correctly.

"I had a scare. I was a month late, and I told Joseph. He proposed the next day, and I couldn't say no. This was our chance, baby. Our chance to finally be taken care of. I got my fucking period a week later. Of course, when I *want* to be pregnant, the world has to take a shit on my plans."

I ignored her statement, though it felt like she'd

stabbed me in the chest. "So, you've been lying all this time?" I asked in disbelief. "I-I saw the test, Mom. In the bathroom."

"I bought it off eBay. I took them regularly to throw Joseph off. I told him I just liked checking because I was scared to lose the baby. I then left them in places he would see so he didn't question it."

Diabolical. "What about your doctor?" I asked.

"I found a guy still practicing that had his license revoked. I threatened to tell the board if he didn't help me. It was easy enough."

"Fuck, Mom. You did all of this? I don't get it. Why?"

Mom snorted. "Do you honestly think that a man like Joseph would marry a woman like me without reason? I'm the girl you fuck for fun, not the girl you marry. I barely graduated high school with my GED. I saw an opportunity, and I went for it. I love him, baby, I do. But he needed an extra push to be with me. When we met, our chemistry was off the charts. It wasn't hard to help him forget a condom."

"What did Joseph say?"

Mom choked out a muffled sob, and my heart squeezed. This was such a stupid idea, but I still felt sorry for her. Why would she go to such lengths? Did she honestly love Joseph so much that she was afraid to lose him, or was it something else? "He's mad, but he thinks we should do a press release stating I had a miscarriage. He wants to blame the paper for being insensitive during this difficult time. He just started this job, you know? The timing couldn't be worse."

I twisted my face into a scowl. Was she seriously just going to lie to everyone? I guess she didn't have a choice, not if they both wanted to save face, but what did this mean for their marriage?

"Mom. Are you okay?"

"Joseph is mad, but he will get over it. We're married. He can't leave me," she said softly, her voice distant. "It would look bad if he left me. Vera, we have to do good. We can't give him any more reason to distrust us, okay? I'm serious. Are you still talking to Hamilton?"

I blinked twice. "You can't be serious right now. You lied about the baby, and you want to talk about *my* behavior?"

"I did this for you, Vera! How else were we going to pay for your schooling, huh?" I couldn't believe her right now. She was turning this on me? I had school covered. I busted my ass to get a scholarship. I would have had a full ride to any public school had Jack not insisted I attend his alma mater.

"I could have gotten a scholarship," I countered.

"But you didn't. You got into the top Ivy League school in the country. You're living in a nice apartment—nicer than anything we ever had. You're just as deep in this as I am."

"But I didn't lie!" I yelled.

"But you exist, Vera! You fucking exist, and I'm not going to let you ruin this for me. The pregnancy might be a sham, but I will fight tooth and nail to save this marriage. Right now, Joseph is at some strip club fucking his way through every hot piece of ass he can find. And I'm going to keep my mouth shut like a good little wife. You're going to be a good student and stay out of trouble. And we're both going to fix this."

Hot tears sank down my cheeks. "I didn't ask for this. I didn't ask to exist. I didn't ask for you to lie to Joseph. I was going to do it, Mom. I had been applying for scholarships, I didn't want to go to Greenwich University. I didn't want this fucking apartment. And I sure as fuck didn't ask to be a constant reminder of the trauma you endured. I love you, Mom, but I can't feel guilty for the rest of my life because you feel like I'm the reason you can't have a happily ever after. You ruined things with Joseph by lying—not me."

"I swear to God, Vera, do not ruin this. You read the article. People already think we planned this together. They're calling you the brains of this operation. If I hear you're talking to Hamilton again—"

"You'll what? What will you do?"

"If I'm going down, I'm dragging you down with me. You can forget college. And good luck finding a scholarship after getting kicked out of Greenwich."

I swallowed and lifted my chin, staring at the blank wall in front of me. "Well, then I guess we'd be even then. I ruined your future, you'll ruin mine."

Mom took a steadying breath. "Vera. I know you're upset. We both are. Let's just calm down. Think rationally about this. You love school, don't you? Greenwich is an amazing university. I did this for us, baby. I did this because being a Beauregard comes with a lot of benefits. Think about how good our life could be if we just fixed this. How good my life could be. For the first time in eighteen years, I don't have to work three jobs. Joseph is talking about me getting my degree online. I could finally do all the things we talked about, Vera. I'm sorry I took it out on you, but I just want this so bad."

"Even if you don't love him?" I asked. "Even if he cheats on you?" I had to know.

"He's hurting right now but, baby, I love him so much. I know he loves me too. He just needed a little shove in the right direction. I don't mean to make you upset. You've always been my good girl. Always did the right thing. I just need you to do that again for me, baby. For us. I don't think I could handle losing the love of my life. I messed up, I did. But I know we can fix this."

I let out a sigh. "Fine. I'll do whatever I can," I choked out, though the words pained me. It didn't feel authentic to my true needs. I trusted my mom to be honest about her feelings for Joseph. I wanted their marriage to work because he genuinely seemed to make her happy. She was misguided, but...

"Oh thank you, baby. Maybe I'll come and visit soon, yeah?"

"Okay," I replied. "That would be great."

Mom went on to ramble for a bit more, talking about her new house as if we hadn't just had a huge fight. As if she hadn't just asked me to compromise my morals and happiness for hers. As if she hadn't just broken my heart—again.

"I love you, baby," she cooed.

"Love you too."

I hung up the phone and tossed it on the couch cushion beside me before cradling my head in my hands. How could she possibly do this? Why? Maybe I needed to drop out now and find a new place to live. I could still apply for scholarships. It might have been too late to switch now, but if I applied now, then maybe next semester I could go somewhere else. I needed to prepare for the worst. I couldn't rely on the Beauregards' generosity. Especially since Mom lied.

My phone started ringing, and I half expected to see my mom's name on the screen, but instead, it was Hamilton. I'd never called him back earlier.

"Hello?" I croaked.

"Are you okay? I heard about the article, and my phone has been ringing nonstop for comment."

I tried to be strong. I really did. "Hamilton?"

"Yeah, beautiful. Talk to me."

"You don't think I lied, do you? You don't think I planned this with my mother..." My voice trailed off as I became overwhelmed with emotion. It suddenly occurred to me that Jack was right all along. He was right to look into my mother's past and question her motives. It made me sick to my stomach to think about.

"I don't think you have a fucking malicious bone in your body. Don't cry. I don't do good with the emotion shit."

I started crying harder. Fuck, what was wrong with me? And why was I leaning on Hamilton? "When are you coming home?" I asked before quickly correcting myself. "Um. Little Mama misses you."

I could hear his smile through his voice. "Oh, she does, does she?"

"Yeah. I suppose I wouldn't mind seeing you either."

"Two more days. You think Little Mama can handle two more days?"

I sniffled. "Yeah. I think so. I can't believe Saint came to campus and hounded me. I'm really freaked out."

"Wait," Hamilton growled. "What? He came to your school?"

I clutched my phone. "Yeah. He just showed up and started asking me questions. He's so gross. Jared scared him off, but—"

"What did he ask you?"

Hamilton's abrupt question caught me off guard. "He asked if I knew," I replied with a sigh. "He said a lot of shit."

"Can you remember anything specific?" Hamilton asked.

"No. It was like he just wanted to taunt me." I

listened to the sound of ruffling on the other side of the phone. "Hamilton?" I asked.

"I'm coming home. Do not leave your apartment unless you have Little Mama, Jess, or—fuck—that asshole Jared with you. Okay? I don't like that this bastard is hounding you. What about Joseph or Jack? Have they called? What are they doing about Saint?"

"I think they're too busy dealing with my mom's fake pregnancy. Hell, I'm sure Jack is going to call any minute and evict me from the apartment." My stomach dropped. I knew all of this was too good to be true. "Shit. Where am I going to stay?" More tears started streaming down my cheek.

"Jack is not going to kick you out. I think he actually likes you in his own weird egomaniac way. You're smart and ambitious. He lives for that shit. And if he does, Jess and I both have perfectly good couches for you to sleep on, unless of course you want to sleep in my bed. Actually, that sounds preferrable." I started laughing, even though I didn't feel amused. "Your door is locked, right? Is Jared with you?"

"I sent him home," I replied while getting up to check my door again. I'd already made sure it was locked three times since coming home. I was thankful I had Little Mama here with me. "We kind of got into a fight before all of this, and I just needed some space."

"Shit, Petal. You've had a terrible day."

"Yeah. Combined with my mother threatening my tuition if I *fuck everything up for her by spending time with you*, it's been a doozy."

"She said that?" Hamilton asked, his voice deep and angry.

"Yep. Her marriage is hanging by a thread."

"I'm calling my supervisor. Lock up. Don't leave unless someone is with you, okay? I'll see you soon."

"Hamilton," I breathed before unlocking and locking the door again. "You honestly don't have to—"

"Shut up or I'll bend you over my knee and spank your ass when I get home. You're alone. Your mom is a total cunt. You've had a shitty day, and I don't think you've ever had anyone that genuinely has taken care of you in your entire goddamn life, Vera. And if I'm being honest, I've never been the person someone called. Let me do this, okay? I'm freaking the fuck out right now. I don't like that you're scared. I don't like that Jared was the one to save the day today. I don't like feeling helpless. I care, okay? I care about you, and it's twisting me up inside, so don't argue. Just unlock the door when I show up, and let me hold you."

My mouth popped open in shock. "Okay," I whispered. "I'll see you soon."

"See you soon, Petal."

16

$\mathcal{H}$amilton looked completely and utterly fucked, his hair glossy from traveling all day, and a shadow of facial hair covered his jaw. He was leaning against the doorjamb when I peered through the peephole to make sure that it was him on the other side.

"Open up, Petal. It's me."

Little Mama was wagging her tail at my side and

whining to see Hamilton. With a steadying breath, I unlocked the door and twisted the knob.

"Fuckkkk," he rasped at the sight of me. I was wearing tattered leggings and a cropped sweatshirt that showed off a sliver of my stomach. My hair was a mess of tangles and was still damp from the long shower I indulged in earlier.

"I'm literally in my pajamas. Stop acting like I answered the door in lingerie," I said with a slow roll of my eyes before looking him up and down once more. His shirt was wrinkled. His jeans were tight. The scuffed boots on his feet looked masculine and eclectic.

"I'll stop undressing you with my eyes when you stop undressing me with yours," he teased before dropping his duffel bag and wrapping me up in a bone-crushing hug.

I hadn't realized how much I needed this. The moment his arms wrapped around me, I felt some of the ice in my veins melt with white-hot emotion. My eyes burned with unshed tears. He felt like safety. I nuzzled against his chest while holding on to him for dear life. My body trembled from the warmth rolling off of him. I'd never been hugged like this before. "I'm so sorry, Vera. I didn't want this for you."

I shook my head and reluctantly pulled away. "Why are you apologizing?" I asked. "It's not your fault."

Hamilton swallowed and picked up his duffel bag before walking inside. Little Mama waddled after him with the cutest grin. She whined and wiggled as he crouched down to pet and cuddle with her. Watching them together made my heart warm. "Has anyone bothered you?" Hamilton asked me before standing.

"Other than the ten calls from my mother and Jared's constant knocking on my door, no."

I let out a sigh and walked up to Hamilton. Being around him was like taking a straight shot of serotonin and adrenaline. I tried. I really tried to hate him. I should have probably felt awkward with him. I wasn't expecting him to come to my rescue—a shining knight on a red-eye flight, with whiskey on his breath. There was something about Hamilton that just made me feel comfortable. When I wasn't ridiculously turned on by him, I was enjoying the ease we had with one another. It was like he just understood me. It was a feeling I hadn't ever experienced with anyone before.

But these moments of genuine connection felt

fragile—as if they were written on lined paper easily ripped out of one's journal. Torn to shreds. Burned to ash.

"What are we doing, Hamilton?" I asked while crossing my arms over my chest and leaning against my kitchen island. He smiled at me, as if expecting my question.

"Well. For starters, I'm going to make myself a cup of coffee because I'm running on about three hours of sleep on a shitty, crowded plane."

I nodded. Not exactly where I was going with this, but Hamilton liked to dance around things. His playful and carefree persona ate up all the air in the room. I felt wound up while waiting for the crash. "And then what?"

"Then I'm going to double-check your locks. I'm going to call the police to see if they have any leads on Saint. I'm going to take my dog on a walk and unpack."

"Unpack?"

For the first time since arriving, he looked unsure. I had started to catch his little nuances now. The casual way he averted his gaze when he wasn't sure what to say. He coughed back whatever truth he wanted to spill. "Yeah. Apparently, you've made my dog love you more than me. I figure the only way we can share custody is if I stay here for a little bit."

I smiled as he sauntered over to me, his own mouth curved playfully into a smirk. "I see," I whispered.

"And I want you to feel safe, Vera," he whispered. "And I want to spend time with you. Is that okay? I'm not moving in, so don't start writing my name next to yours in your diary, okay?"

I shook my head playfully. "*The* Hamilton Beauregard doesn't do relationships, huh?"

He cupped my chin. I wore exhaustion like a second skin. The dark circles under my eyes didn't deter him, though. He then spoke. "*The* Hamilton Beauregard cares only about himself about ninety-nine percent of the time. He's selfish. Abrasive. Static. Detached. He breaks hearts without a single fuck and takes what he wants."

I stared up at him as he spoke so poorly about himself. I thought about his best friend, Jess. I thought about the dog he rescued. I thought about Jack, a confusing man who craved a relationship with his son. I thought about his long trip here to comfort a girl he was just starting to know.

"Whatever you say," I replied with a shake of my

head. I was too tired to argue with him, and his perceptions of himself were deep-rooted. I didn't know if he was trying to convince himself that he was bad news or me, but either way, I didn't care.

"I'm serious, Vera."

"So am I, Hamilton," I replied before casually wrapping my arms around his neck and lifting up on my toes to kiss his jaw. The tender and light brush of my lips on his rough skin sent shivers down my spine. Having him here, I almost forgot about my mother's lies and the pressures of being a Beauregard. We were all alone. No one was here to tell me that this was wrong. Saint wasn't lurking in the corners of my apartment, looking for a story.

He cleared his throat and licked his lips, his tongue clipping my cheek in the process. Another shiver passed through me as I curled my body against his, aching to be closer. "I should get that coffee, huh?" he questioned.

"Get whatever you want," I whispered back before running my hand through his hair and breathing him in.

He gripped my ass and pulled me closer, his movements slow and tentative. I'd never experienced this side of Hamilton. It was like something now was holding him back. I didn't understand it. Was he uninterested now because there wasn't a chase? Did he only like things that run?

"I'm going to get that coffee and shower. I want you, Vera, but not while my dick smells like airport. And you need to rest. I came here to take care of you."

I pulled away, my eyes heavy as I licked my lips. "And why is that? If you're as selfish and detached as you claim, why are you here?" I boldly questioned him.

He let out a sigh and averted his dark gaze from mine. "I don't know."

He finally pushed away from me and went to make himself a pot of coffee. I watched his back, with Little Mama at my feet as he went through my cabinets, searching for coffee filters. "I'm going to try and sleep," I whispered. We weren't going to get anywhere at this time. He was here, though. He was really here. That had to mean something. All of this had to mean fucking *something*.

"Good. You look like shit, Vera. Seriously. You need some rest."

I rolled my eyes. "Keys are hanging by the door if you leave. The couch pulls out into a bed."

I padded away from him and to my door, pausing

when I heard him curse under his breath. I turned to see what had him worked up and frowned when he pulled out his cell phone and angrily answered it.

"Stop calling me. I'm done." He ended the call and slammed his palm down on the counter.

What the fuck was that about?

———

I COULDN'T SLEEP. MY PHONE KEPT GOING OFF WITH texts from my mother, and knowing Hamilton was in my apartment but so emotionally distant created a dissonance in my mind. There was so much against us. Our families. Public opinion. My desire to do right by my mom. His own issues with relationships. At first, it was easy to put him into a category of chemistry and physical needs. It's easy to justify something if it's just carnal acts to get off to.

But he showed up today. He kept showing up.

I heard my door open. My heart raced. The mattress dipped beside me. Warmth slipped under the duvet covers, and strong arms wrapped around me. "You done pretending to be asleep?" Hamilton asked. He smelled like my citrus shower gel. It was oddly feminine on his impossibly masculine body.

"Are you done pretending you're selfish and that this is only fucking?" I asked.

"Oh, so we're fucking now?" Hamilton asked in a whisper, his lips hovering over my ear as he shifted his hand and moved to cup my breasts. I let out a gasp when he pinched my nipple and lightly twisted it. Arching my back, I pressed my ass against his groin.

"You know what I mean," I choked out.

"I don't think I do, Petal. Tell me."

I reached behind me and grabbed his hard cock through his sweats. His bare chest pressed harder against my back as he let out a startled hiss as my long fingers wrapped around his girth. I felt powerful in that moment. I had him by the dick. "We have chemistry," I said before stroking him. He continued to knead my breast while kissing my neck. "I want you, Hamilton. We could fuck right now. Get the tension out of the air and go back to living our individual lives."

He stopped kissing me and grabbed my wrist, pulling me away from his hard cock. I waited for him to say something, but instead, he flipped me on my back and straddled me. I looked up at his sharp expression, like a knife cutting through the tension. He grabbed both my wrists and pinned them to the mattress above my head. "You think we can just fuck each other out of our systems, Petal?" he asked, his voice a dangerous, low timbre.

"Isn't that what you want?"

He leaned over and scraped his teeth along my collarbone. "Why do we have to be anything, hmm?"

"Because I could very well lose my only family if we cross this line."

"So, what? You want me to fuck you and leave?"

"I want you to be worth it, Hamilton," I whispered. He stalled and shot up to stare at me.

"You don't think I'm worth it?" There it was. The crack. The break. The thing that kept Hamilton trying. That tragic need for approval from the people we cared about buried deep in our souls.

"I know you have the potential to be more than worth it, Hamilton. If we're doing this, don't half ass it. Don't just make it some bullshit one-night stand where we both have fun, but it ends there. I want something real. Don't catch a last-minute flight here to make sure I'm okay, then push me away. Don't hurt me, Hamilton."

He lifted the edge of my shirt up, pulling it over my head. I sank my teeth into my bottom lip while watching him take in the sight of me. Fuck. "I won't half ass this," he whispered before taking my heavy breast in his mouth and swirling his tongue around my nipple. I practically lifted off the bed. My body was completely fucking wrecked. Heat traveled through my limbs. Sticky wet need coated my thighs. He pulled away and gripped the band of my leggings. "This won't be a one-night stand."

He jerked my pants down, taking my pink thong with them. A rush of cold air flooded my exposed skin before he was there. Licking. Sucking. Tasting. I moaned and writhed on the bed. I cried out his name.

I came.

Hamilton wiped his lips with my inner thigh as little aftershocks rocked through me. He sat up. "This can be real, Petal. I won't push you away."

He undressed slowly. I watched his movements. I watched him dig in the pockets of his gray sweats and pull out a condom. Did he know it would lead to this? Did he know I ached for him?

He rolled on the rubber. He climbed on top of me. He spread my legs. I felt stripped bare as he positioned himself at my entrance and tugged on the loose strands of my hair. His hand clamped around my neck, then his body surged forward and impaled me with his cock. I stretched. I screamed. I slowly eased into the fullness that was Hamilton Fucking Beauregard.

"You're so goddamn tight. You okay, Petal?"

I gripped his forearm with one hand and grabbed his hip with the other, urging him to move. I couldn't tell him I was alright. I wasn't exactly sure if I was.

Hamilton made me feel fucking dirty.

And I treasured it.

In and out. He pounded into me. I was a writhing puddle of need. Crashing. Falling.

Breaking. I was breaking.

Sweat clung to his brow. My nightlight, meant to illuminate my fears, cast shadows on his glistening skin.

We didn't inch toward completion. No.

We raced to that finish line with our muscles spent, our bodies exploding from the tension. I came hard and raw and with everything I had.

Hamilton stared at me, his eyes wide with wonder as I fell apart. Thrusting. Thirsting. Fucking. Pumping. *Something close to loving*—but not quite.

He collapsed on top of me. Orgasms had the power to clear a person's mind. I wasn't thinking about the what ifs. I wasn't worried about what people were going to say. I just felt him growing soft inside me. Breathing on top of me. Kissing my skin with wordless thank yous.

But my subconscious was whispering something. Something I wanted to ignore.

He never said he wouldn't hurt you.

17

*H*ot breath feathered down my neck. Sweat dripped at my hairline. Warm limbs tangled up. Salty soft skin. Light snores. Bliss.

A hard knock on my door made my eyes shoot open. "Who the fuck is here?" Hamilton groaned. I was too exhausted. We spent all night twisted up in one another, working through this fatal attraction we shared. Even now, as I lay naked in my bed, with his dried cum between my thighs and a hickey on my neck, I craved him again.

"Ignore them," I mumbled.

His hand was wrapped around my stomach, the tip of his fingers edging toward my pussy. He moved them lower—slower. The touch was slightly teasing but also calculative and full of promise.

Even in his sleepy state, Hamilton moved with intention.

The knocking continued. "For fuck's sake," Hamilton growled before pulling his hand back. *No!*

With one move, he shoved the warm duvet off of his side of the bed, and a rush of air fluttered over my skin. He sat up and rolled out of bed before stomping out of my room. It took me another moment to realize he was buck naked and headed toward my front door. I shot out of bed and grabbed some clothes just as Jared's voice boomed. "What the fuck are you doing here?"

Shit. I wasn't in the mood for a confrontation first thing in the morning, especially when I was so close to having yet *another* orgasm to start my day. Hamilton liked tossing out pleasure like it was candy on Halloween.

I tripped while putting on my sweatpants and ran toward my front door with my thin, oversized green shirt slipping off my shoulder and my wild brown hair bouncing with every step. "Can you just get the fuck out of here already? We were sleeping, man. Who comes over at nine a.m. on a Saturday?"

"Yeah. I can fucking see that you both were *sleeping*," Jared growled. "How old are you even, bro? Thirty? Isn't Vera a bit young for you? Or is that part of this whole kink?" I frowned when I saw them both in the entryway. Hamilton was as naked as the day he was born, not even bothering to cup his junk. Bruises in the shape of my lips covered his body. Scratches ran down his back. His glossy skin looked angry and red.

And his fists were clenched.

Jared was the complete opposite, with his freshly showered hair slicked back. His polo tucked into his khaki pants. He looked crisp and clean. "Vera," he breathed out. Disappointment dripped from his tone. I forced a smile.

"Hamilton, why don't you go get some clothes on?" I asked.

"Nah, I'm good," he snapped. "Jared here was just asking me about my kinks. Should we tell him how you begged me to bend you over the edge of the mattress? I pounded your pussy until you nearly blacked out from your tenth orgasm, didn't I, Petal?"

He turned to Jared once more and sarcastically shrugged before placing his index finger to his plump lip. "I mean. Since you want to talk about my kinks, I like choking her, Jared. Do you know how to make a woman come when she's on the brink of passing out? Do you know the right amount of pressure? Do you know how her creamy ass looks when it's marked up with my handprint?" Hamilton was on a roll today. I guess he wanted to have a dick measuring contest. Fucking hell.

"Don't disrespect her like that!" Jared yelled.

"Jared, it's fine," I said softly.

"It's not fine, Vera. I just wanted to make sure you're okay. I didn't realize he was coming over. *Or* staying the night." Jared shuffled on his feet. I had just realized he was holding something. "I got us bagels. Figured we could go to the park and decompress? The article was taken down."

"What?" Hamilton asked.

Jared ignored him and continued to speak directly to me. "I guess your grandfather had the piece removed. People aren't really talking about it. It's like everyone has been told not to."

Hamilton ran his fingers through his hair and let out a huff. "Yeah. I'm going to go put some clothes on," he murmured before raising his voice.

"Keep your dainty little hands to yourself, lover boy."

Hamilton stalked off, his abrupt departure making me wince. What was he upset about? I hadn't asked Jared to come over, and it wasn't like we were dating or anything. I'd made it very clear that Jared was just a friend. An annoying friend that I seriously needed to establish better boundaries with. "So, the article is gone?"

"Gone. I asked the building manager and campus security to keep an eye out for Saint. If they see him on campus, they'll arrest him on the spot."

"Wow, Jared. Thank you for checking up on all of that for me," I whispered before looking down at my toes. This was awkward. Very awkward. "I'll call you later—"

"Did you really fuck him?" Jared asked. "Or was he just saying that to rattle me?"

The question caught me off guard. "What? You're going to make me say it out loud?" Couldn't Jared see? I mean Hamilton answered the door stark naked.

"Did you fuck your uncle, Vera?"

I gaped at him. "Yeah. She did," Hamilton answered for me while walking back into the room. He was shirtless, and the jogging pants he wore were slung low on his hips. Beside him, Little Mama was wiggling and whining to go outside. "Do you want the dirty details, you kinky fucker?"

"No, I just want to know if she realizes how bad this will look for her family," Jared replied. "I've grown up in this world. I know what the media is like. I've been on the receiving end of their bias and prejudice more times than I care to count."

"And you think I don't know?" Hamilton replied lazily while grabbing Little Mama's leash. The poor pit mix looked like she was going to pee on my tile.

"I think you don't care," Jared scoffed.

"You're probably right," Hamilton replied. My heart sank. The world cracked open and swallowed me up. He doesn't care? Care about what? Me? "I don't care what the media thinks. I need to walk my dog. I'd like for you to be gone by the time I get back." Hamilton grabbed a sweatshirt and shrugged it on before slipping on some shoes and walking over to me. With one hand on Little Mama's leash, he grabbed the back of my head with the other and smashed his lips to mine in a possessive display of power and heat. His tongue surged past my parted mouth. His groans filled the kitchen, and as quickly as our kiss began, it ended when he tore his hot lips from mine.

"This is so fucked," Jared cursed.

"Be right back, Petal," he whispered before taking Little Mama on her morning walk.

It wasn't until the front door shut that Jared spoke again. "You know this won't last, right?"

His question rang true in my heart. "Yes," I answered honestly. This couldn't last. There was never any guarantee that anything ever lasted, was there? "Let's not talk about this, okay? Give me a bagel, I'm famished."

Jared snorted. "I bet you are. I saw the bite marks and scratches all over him, wildcat. Jesus. This is bad. For the record, I do not support this."

I snatched the bag out of his hand and made my way over to the island where I pulled out a stool and sat down. "Why do you care so much? It doesn't affect you," I said before pulling out the everything bagel and sinking my teeth into it. It was like heaven on my tongue. Carbs were nirvana. "In fact, we still sort of barely know one another, Jared. Who I fuck has no bearing on our friendship. If you're worried about being seen with me, then—"

"It's not that. I care about you, Vera. How many times do I have to say it?" he asked before sitting beside me and pulling out his breakfast. "Do you think your stepdad is going to be mad? What about your mom? Jack seems like the kind of guy to want to keep his image clean, too."

"They're not going to be anything because they're never going to find out," I replied. "Again, why do you care?"

"You fucked your uncle, Vera. That's some Wattpad taboo shit. You're an unclefucker."

"He's not my real uncle!" I exclaimed with a full mouth. "And do you read fanfic on Wattpad?"

Jared took a bite of his food. I still didn't understand why this was such a big ordeal to him. I was the one who would have to cope with the consequences. I was the one who was risking my relationship with my mother. I was the one who would get her heart broken when the excitement wore off and Hamilton left. "It won't last," I whispered.

"It won't," Jared agreed. "So why put yourself through this? Why risk it?" I turned on my stool to face Jared. He reached up and swiped his thumb along my bottom lip, making me blush. "Sorry. There was a crumb."

"Do you ever just feel an undeniable connection with someone? The chemistry is unavoidable."

Jared swallowed. "Yeah. I have." The meaningful

look in his eyes was filled to the brim with promise, and I wanted nothing to do with it.

Clearing my throat, I continued before he could once again admit his feelings for me. "I've lived my life according to my mother's rules and opinions. I just want this one thing."

Jared cleared his throat and turned his attention forward. "Right. Well, I better get going. Enjoy the rest of your bagel. If your asshole uncle hasn't left by tonight, invite him out to Throwback Bar, okay? We can all get some drinks and try to be civil."

I raised my brow. "You'll hang out with Hamilton?" I asked.

"Only if he promises not to be a total dick. And at least that way I can make sure he's treating you right." Jared got off his stool and paused for a moment. "You deserve better than a whim, Vera. Better than a secret single thing."

I bit my lip as he let himself out. I wished I could like Jared, I really did. But I was a tragic romantic. I craved what would ruin me.

Hamilton walked through the front door just as I finished my bagel. "Little Mama loves the dog park in your complex," he said with a chuckle before looking at me. I must not have been hiding my feelings well because his playful expression slipped. "What's wrong?"

I didn't want to be that girl. The one that demanded labels and clarification of the relationship after a single night. I knew what this was. I knew we were taking it a second at a time. The nasty unsettled feeling churning in my gut demanded to make its presence known, though. "Jared just ruined my morning glow," I replied with a shrug and a half smile. "He called me an unclefucker."

"We should absolutely get you a shirt that says that," Hamilton replied, trying to lighten the mood. "Do you have plans today?"

"Nope. Jared invited us to Throwback Bar tonight, though. But I wasn't sure if that was a thing we were doing," I rushed out.

"What do you mean?"

"Us things. Like going places as an us, or a we, or a th-they. Plurals. Are we doing the plurals, Hamilton?" Sonofabitch, I was rambling.

Hamilton grinned at me, like my uncomfortable behavior was amusing to him. "I have to go see a friend today for a few, but afterward, I really want to do all sorts of plural things with you, Petal."

My ears perked up. "You do?" I asked, my voice a squeak.

He grabbed my hips and pulled me closer to him. "I want to do us things privately. Publicly. I want to kiss you in front of Jared and see him rage. I want to put you up on this counter, spread your legs and lick your clit until your entire body shakes. I'm all for *us things*." His lips found my temple, and he left a trail of heated kisses there, leading down along my jaw.

"Let's do the plurals then, Hamilton," I replied before pulling at the waistband of his pants and letting him do exactly as he described.

18

I didn't have time to really get ready, mostly because Hamilton and I were insatiable. We barely made it out the door, my wild hair spun up in a messy bun on top of my head and our clothes wrinkled from sitting in a pile on the floor by my bed. Hamilton invited Jess and Infinity to go out with us, and I was looking forward to seeing them again.

"So, Jared legitimately invited us, hmm?" Hamilton asked while turning into the parking lot of the bar. He had one hand on the steering wheel and one on my upper thigh, his thumb massaging me lightly as he drove. Ever since he got here, he had to be touching me somehow. "He must be up to something."

"Why do I find your jealousy so sexy?" I murmured mostly to myself.

Hamilton pulled into a spot and turned off the car. "Because you've never had someone fight for you before, Petal," he whispered while leaning over the center console and kissing me on the mouth.

A palm slamming against the hood of his car made me jump. Jess and Infinity were standing outside, both wearing identical smirks. I blushed. Jess already knew something was up between Hamilton and me, but I still felt that instinctive need to keep this *thing* a secret.

We got out of the car, and Jess immediately hugged Hamilton. She was in black skinny jeans that were ripped at the knee and a bright red flannel shirt. He wore a genuine smile as she squeezed him tightly, then punched him on the arm. "Now I know why you aren't replying to any of my texts. I invite you to breakfast at our local spot and don't hear from you for hours." Jess smirked at me before looking at her best friend once more. "Then, you tell me we're going to this damn pretentious bar. I saw a man wearing a suit go inside, Hamilton. A suit!" Jess scowled for effect.

Hamilton chuckled. "Don't blame me! Vera's boyfriend invited all of us out. You know I'm more about kickbacks at the house than overpriced beer with overpriced clientele." I didn't like that Hamilton was calling Jared my boyfriend. Was my friendship with him bothering Hamilton more than he let on? His possessiveness and jealousy was hot, but it seemed to run deeper.

"I thought you dumped that dude when Hamilton got you off in the bathroom?" Jess asked.

At that question, Infinity elbowed her girlfriend in the ribs with a huff. She was wearing jeans and a see-through flowy blouse. Luckily, Infinity changed the subject efficiently, with her ethereal voice and soft smile. "Sooo, how have you been, Vera? It's so good to see you again!"

I swallowed and blushed, still thrown off from Jess's question. Hamilton wrapped his arm around me and kissed me on the temple while I tried to come up with an answer. Jess and Infinity stared at the subtle display of affection, their mouths parted in shock as they stared at me.

"I've been really great," I answered before looking at Hamilton. He met my stare with a heated intensity that made me waiver.

The smoldering moment was short-lived. "Oh, girl, we are so discussing this later," Jess interrupted with a squeal before grabbing my wrist and looping her arm through mine. Infinity grabbed my other arm, and the three of us started walking inside, Hamilton chuckling as he followed behind us. There was a line to get into the club.

"Did you see that?" Infinity asked Jess in a whisper. "That was genuine affection."

"Totally genuine affection," Jess echoed.

"I can still hear you. And I'm capable of *genuine affection*, you know," Hamilton called at my back. "Also, can I have my girl back? This is worse than when I told you I slept with our history teacher senior year. Gossipy hen."

Jess stopped to gag. "I still can't believe you slept with Miss Gladde. She was engaged to the football coach! Doggy style behind the bleachers, no less."

I looked over my shoulder, feeling a bit out of my element as we got in line to enter the bar. Hamilton had a sheepish grin on his face. "I'd do it again. She was hot."

A gust of wind blew through my hair. "Not as bad as the time you fucked your nanny," Jess added while side-eyeing me, as if trying to gauge how I'd react to their ribbing.

"That was just embarrassing. I came after like three pumps." Hamilton winced at the memory. I winced for a completely different reason.

Infinity giggled before interjecting. "Don't forget that the two of you had quite the affair," the soft-spoken girl said while gesturing between Jess and Hamilton.

My brows shot up. Jess rolled her eyes before speaking. "One time. One time! We were drunk, and I was curious what all the fuss was about. I had whiskey clit and didn't even come—not for lack of trying. It only counts if you come."

"You and Hamilton?" I asked incredulously.

"There was lots of alcohol involved," she grumbled. "Never again."

"Oh, come on. We were great together, baby," Hamilton purred playfully.

"I puked on you!" Jess exclaimed, making the person in front of us in line turn to look over their shoulder.

"You're the only lesbian I've ever slept with that also puked on my dick. It was good for my ego," Hamilton replied dryly. "I mean, it wasn't the worst sexcapade I've ever had, though. It was better than those twins I once fucked in my mother's garden."

I pulled away from Jess and Infinity to rub the back of my neck and look around. Where was Jared? Hamilton definitely had experience. I knew that I needed to hear an unfiltered account of Hamilton's whoring around. Even though this entire conversation was making me uncomfortable, it helped to remind me that Hamilton wasn't the sort of man to do forever. He was good in bed, but he wasn't good for my heart. "Oh, I forgot about them," Jess replied. "Didn't one of them poke holes in the condom?"

"I had to pay her to take Plan B," Hamilton replied with a shiver.

I chewed on the inside of my cheek. This was fine. I knew that Hamilton was a fuckboy. This felt like a test somehow. He'd worn a condom every time we fucked, and I had been on the pill for the last two years, but we needed to be careful. "You okay, Vera?" Infinity asked while giving her girlfriend and Hamilton a pointed stare.

"I'm great," I replied with a fake smile before

inching up to the bouncer. Hamilton cursed softly, but I ignored it.

"My name is Vera," I told the bouncer when he asked for a name. Thank goodness we were here so we could stop talking about Hamilton's sex life.

"Ah. With Jared?" he said after typing something on his iPad.

"That's me."

"Welcome to Throwback." He removed the velvet rope, and we filed inside. I really wanted to get tonight over with. Things were easier when we were just fucking. At least I could pretend this meant something when Hamilton was worshiping me with his mouth.

Jess and Infinity stepped in front of us, then maneuvered through the crowd toward an empty table. This bar was definitely swankier than what I was expecting. Jess was right. Guys in suits lined the stools, and students I recognized from some of my classes were sipping martinis and gossiping in low voices. We stood out like a sore thumb.

I scanned the room, looking for Jared, but he wasn't here yet. Hamilton grabbed my elbow, stopping me from following after Jess and Infinity. "You're upset," he whispered while pulling me in for a hug. "Tell me what's wrong, Petal."

"I don't know what you're talking about," I replied before pulling away. "You can talk about all the women you've fucked. You can even leave here tonight with someone if you'd like. We aren't exclusive by any means." I was pushing it a little far, but I needed to believe what I was saying if I was going to escape this with my heart intact. Plenty of people did casual romps. I wasn't sure I could do this with Hamilton.

Hamilton smirked. "So, if I were to leave with…" He scanned the room and stopped when his eyes landed on a beautiful blonde woman sitting at the bar. She had a short skirt and curled hair down to the middle of her back. Her lips were unnaturally plump, matching her large breasts. "Her," Hamilton finished. "You wouldn't mind?"

"Have at it," I replied, my voice harsh.

"What if I wanted to fuck her, then come over to your house? Would you let me use you up while my skin still smells like her Chanel No. 5 perfume?"

I raged. Cruel words tumbled out of my mouth without my consent. "I might have to kick Jared out of my bed first, but sure."

Hamilton scowled. "Good to know we're both on the same page then."

"Right? Jess told me what to expect going into this."

"She did, huh?" Hamilton asked. "What exactly did she tell you?"

I looked over at the table where Jess and Infinity were sitting and staring at us. "She just said you're a whore, and I shouldn't get my hopes up."

My insecurities were a sharp shovel digging me a hole. Deeper and deeper. "Oh, I'm a whore, sweetheart," Hamilton whispered before grabbing my hips and jerking me forward. "I like to fuck. Hard. Raw. I'd bend you over one of the tables in front of everyone and not think twice about it." My breath hitched at his words. I could feel his hard length pressing against me. We were surrounded by people, and I could feel their eyes on me. "But right now, I'm only a whore for you, okay?"

Hamilton chewed on his lip, as if debating what else to say. "Jess likes you. She's also the most opinionated person I know. Jess speaks her mind, and she doesn't know what to make of this, because she's never seen me like this. She's not me, though. You worried about me fucking other girls while we're doing this *plural* thing, you talk to me about it, okay? Don't end us before we get our fill.

"Jess likes to tease me, but that's not the whole

truth. Miss Gladde? She was in an abusive relationship. I helped her escape. I saw the bruises and walked in on Coach slapping her across the face. I helped convince her to leave and got my dad to find her a job at a boarding school overseas."

Wow. I wasn't expecting Hamilton to say that. "And in the interest of transparency, I was in love with Jess when we were teens. It was a drunk pity fuck because she knew she'd never love me that way." My brows shot up, a million questions filling my mind at once. "I don't love her anymore—at least not like that," Hamilton added. "And the twins? That was just fun. My nanny was a pedophile. We laugh about it because the truth isn't nearly as fun. I use humor to cope, I suppose."

"Oh," I replied because I didn't know what else to say.

"If you want me to write up a list of all the people I've fucked, I can. But you should know that none of them compare to you. I'm not spitting bullshit to make you feel good. It's terrifying, Petal. I want you. Only you. For right now, have faith in that, okay? I won't go fucking some cheap looking blond if you promise to never joke about Jared being in your bed again. I don't trust him. Something is off about that guy. I'm putting up with this because I like making you happy."

I looked over at Jess and Infinity. They were giving us quizzical looks. "Okay," I replied. Hamilton smiled and kissed me on the mouth before wrapping his hand around my wrist and dragging me toward the table.

When we sat down, Hamilton scooted my stool as close to his as possible, and he put his arm around the back of my chair. I felt wired and weirded out. I was still consumed with thoughts of Jess and Hamilton.

Hamilton cleared his throat, then grabbed my hand to kiss it. Jess stared at the move. She and Infinity had already ordered drinks and were sipping on them while staring at us. "So, is this serious?" Jess asked while nodding at the two of us. Her eyes were sparkling with mischief.

"Very," Hamilton replied easily.

"How serious?" Jess asked. "I thought this was—"

"Sycamore Tree, Jess," Hamilton replied gruffly. Was he embarrassed? What did that even mean?

"Sycamore Tree?" Jess let out a long, low whistle. "Wow, Hamilton."

"What does that mean?" I asked while looking

between them. It felt weird to be talked about so openly.

Infinity waved her hand. "It's some code word they've had since they were teens. They had this tree in the park between their houses that they'd meet at."

"Our safe haven," Jess replied. "My parents were assholes. They thought they could beat the disobedience out of me." She cleared her throat before continuing. My heart broke for her. "Hamilton was my only friend. He always protected me. I just had to text him Sycamore Tree and he'd drop everything to be there for me. It kind of became a code of sorts, but it's hard to explain. I guess you'd have to experience it. Remember when you threatened my dad?" Jess took a sip of her drink. Infinity gave her a side hug.

"Your dad is a dick." Hamilton didn't go into detail about their past, he just eyed me and grabbed my hand again.

"Affirmative," Jess replied.

I filed this information away. There was so much about Hamilton that didn't fit my original assumptions about him. He was the kind of man that helped out his history teacher. He dropped everything for his friends. He was serious. Poetic.

Devoted. Physical and unapologetic. He had a rough childhood. Each layer of his personality added something else for me to obsess over.

We started talking about lighter subjects, thankfully. I liked Jess's zero fucks attitude. She wasn't afraid to poke and prod for answers, but I needed a break from the seriousness. She and Infinity started to get a buzz and were kissing when Hamilton turned to me. "I hate the dude, but Jared is smart," Hamilton said in a low voice. "He picked a place known for their discreetness."

I furrowed my brow. "What do you mean?"

Hamilton nodded at a nearby table. "Over there is an heir to one of the largest corporations in the country," he said. I followed his gaze and stared at the slender man tossing back shots. He looked about my age. I was about to ask what the point of all of this was, when an elderly man with deep wrinkles, a limp, and dentures sat next to him and started kissing the younger man's neck.

"This is the sort of establishment that doesn't allow cameras and doesn't ask questions."

"Ah," I replied before shifting in my seat. Why did Jared know about this place? Was it just one of those common knowledge things, or did he need a secret place to hang out with his friends?

"You're nervous," Hamilton stated. It wasn't a question. He just knew.

"Things were easier when we were just fucking at my apartment," I replied. Jess snorted.

Hamilton grabbed my thigh and kissed me on the temple again. He had started doing that a lot lately. It was such a tender and authentic gesture.

"Hey!" Jared's voice boomed. I got out of my chair to give him a hug. In typical Jared fashion, he was wearing tailored slacks, a button up shirt, and a suit jacket that cost more than my rent. His blond hair was slicked to the side, and the Chapstick on his lips made his mouth shine. He wrapped me up in a large hug, picking me up off the floor a bit. I could feel Hamilton's hard eyes on us. "I'm glad you could make it."

"Yeah. Thanks for the invite. This place is..."

"Pretentious as fuck?" Jared finished for me.

"Exactly," Jess replied.

"It's not my usual hang out, but I figured you'd like some privacy, you know, since you're fucking your uncle now." Infinity choked on her drink. Hamilton curled his fist. Jared and I sat down, and my skin suddenly grew hot. With an angry Hamilton on one side of me and an overly affectionate Jared on the other, I felt sandwiched. "If

I'm hooking up with someone not ready to come out of the closet, I'll bring them here." Jared looked down at the empty table in front of me. "Want me to get you a drink? I know how you love gin and tonics."

"That would be gr—"

"I got it," Hamilton replied before waving down one of the cocktail waitresses. Within minutes, we all had drinks and had settled into an awkward silence. I had hoped that maybe this would bring us together, but it just made things more uncomfortable. A buzzed Jess and Infinity disappeared to the bathroom ten minutes ago and still hadn't come back. I was desperate for a buffer, but something told me they'd be a while.

"So, what are you going to school for?" Hamilton asked while curling his hand around my leg, his reach dangerously close to the apex of my thigh.

"Ethics and Politics," Jared replied. "Did you go to school?"

"Nah. I started working as soon as I graduated. Why politics?"

Jared shifted in his seat. "I've just always been interested in it. I grew up in it."

It seemed like everyone in Greenwich had a political background. I tried to remember what Jared told me about his family. I knew his mother owned a nonprofit.

"Family business?" Hamilton asked. "I just can't get over this feeling like I know you from somewhere."

Jared cleared his throat and smiled politely, but I sensed an unease about him. "Can't say we've ever met."

Hamilton tossed back his drink and grinned. "Are you sure? I just really feel like you're familiar to me."

Jared cleared his throat again and rubbed the back of his neck. "Nope. I don't know you, aside from what Vera has told me."

"I bet she's told you all about me, hmm?" Hamilton said before grabbing my hand from where it was resting in my lap, and kissing the inside of my wrist. My breath hitched. "What was your last name again?"

I watched them speak to one another like it was a tennis match. "Anders."

Hamilton grinned before clapping hands together. "That's where I know you. You interned for Joseph last year, didn't you? I'm not usually so involved in the family business. But you have one of those faces you just can't forget. You were at the holiday party. I remember because I saw you when I snuck off with one of the servers for a quicky."

I snapped my head to Jared. "You worked for Joseph?" I sputtered.

Jared licked his lips. "I was going to tell you—"

"Wait. Wait." I pushed Hamilton's hand away before standing up. "You worked for Joseph? Are you still working for him?"

"Your parents just wanted to make sure you'd be safe while here. Joseph promised me a job after graduation if I—"

I shook my head. "You asshole! I thought you were clingy, but really you've been my bodyguard. Was asking me out part of that agreement, too?" My voice was shrill, but I didn't care who heard me.

"Your mother hoped that if we got together, you'd stop this ridiculous thing with Hamilton," Jared explained. "But I promise I like you, Vera. It started as a job but—"

"Stop. Just stop." I massaged my temples. "Have you been reporting back to my mother? Did you tell her about Hamilton and me?" Jared averted his eyes and looked at the ground. Motherfucker. I reared back and slapped him without thought just as a ruffled Jess and Infinity emerged from the bathroom. "You dick! Don't talk to me. Don't fucking look at me." I turned to look at Hamilton, who looked annoyingly pleased with himself. "Let's go."

"Happily, darling," he said before smirking at a red-faced Jared. I stormed out of the bar and walked toward the car with Hamilton trailing behind me.

"Fuck, I wish I could have caught that on camera," he rasped.

"This isn't a joke, Hamilton. My mother knows about us!"

He pushed me against the car and cupped my cheeks. "So what?" he asked.

"So, she's going to be mad."

"So what?" Hamilton repeated.

"Jared has been feeding information to them," I whined.

"So. Fucking. What."

Hamilton kissed me hard and rough against the car door. Jess and Infinity laughed while heading to where they parked. I think they told us they'd call later, but I was too lost in my kiss with Hamilton to make sense of their words. On and on it went. His tongue surged past my lips and lapped me up. I arched my back and grabbed his shirt. I trembled with every stroke of his talented mouth against mine. He tore away from me with a smile. "So. What."

I let out a shaky exhale. "So what," I echoed before pressing my forehead against his chest. "Let's go home," I whispered before pausing. "Oh my God. He's my neighbor. Do you think Joseph coordinated that?"

"Want to go to my place?" Hamilton asked.

I reached up to kiss him on the jaw. "Yeah. Let's go."

19

I woke up to my phone ringing—again. The shrill sound reverberated off my skull and was a high-pitched annoyance that made my body tense up. Her calls were constant. Jared and my mother were desperate to get a hold of me. I didn't have to look at the caller ID to know that it was my mother once again, trying to track me down and stop me from ruining her happy little family. Part of me wished she would get on a plane and have this conversation in person. I wanted her to look me in the eye and tell me that her sham of a marriage with Joseph was more important than my happiness.

I hated this limbo. I was stuck between avoiding her and wanting to confront her, and the longer I ignored her texts, the cruder and pushier they became. It was a side of her that I knew well but was seeing with fresh eyes. I always just assumed her ambitions and selfishness were a result of constantly fighting to survive. Now it felt...different. Darker. I loved my mother. I knew she loved me. But I also didn't think she understood what healthy love looked like.

Mom: What are you doing?

Mom: Where are you?

Mom: Jared called me. You can't seriously be angry at us for wanting to make sure you were safe. You had a stalker, Vera.

Mom: Jared is a nice guy! You'd do well to date a man like him. He comes from a good family. I met his mother at a banquet.

Mom: Why are you mad at me for this?

Mom: Jared said you aren't home. Where are you staying, Vera? Joseph wants to talk to you.

Mom: Vera. Jack is calling now. We seriously

need to talk about this. You can't date Hamilton. I know you're with him.

Mom: This is getting ridiculous.

Mom: Call me right now!

Mom: You're so fucking selfish, Vera. I can't believe that you're willing to toss away our family just so you can get laid. I always knew you were a little slut.

I was scrolling through messages when Hamilton plucked my cell out of my hands with a huff. "No more reading texts for the day. Your mother is seriously going to piss me off. I'm starting to think that she and Joseph are perfect for one another. Toxic motherfuckers." Hamilton groaned while tossing my phone on his nightstand before pulling me closer to him. He was spooning me in bed, wrapping his arms around my middle and breathing in my scent while nuzzling my neck. It was cozy. Comfortable. Intense.

We spent all Sunday at his place, fucking, talking, and eating his delicious cooking. He let me vent and spent most of the time reminding me that it didn't matter what anyone thought. We weren't hurting anyone, not really. We were just testing the stormy waters. I didn't bring up my college tuition problems. It was too late now. I had a feeling that pretty soon my mother would inform me via text message that The Beauregards weren't going to pay for my schooling anymore. She'd already threatened it. She made it very clear that if she was going down, she'd drag me with her. It wasn't Hamilton's fault or responsibility. I was the one who got myself in this mess. I knew the risks, and I still dove headfirst into this messy relationship with Hamilton.

"You have class today, right?"

"Yeah, I do." Might as well attend whatever I could. There was no telling when they'd pull the plug on my education and the apartment I was staying in. I needed to find a job. I needed to find a place to stay.

"What are you thinking about?"

I swallowed. "Nothing," I quickly replied. "Just thinking about all the homework I've been avoiding." I didn't want Hamilton to feel responsible for my mother's fucked up ultimatum, and more so, I didn't want him to feel obligated to help me.

"Get ready," he whispered before kissing me. "I'll make you some breakfast and drive you to school. You get out at three, right? I can pick you up then."

"You know my schedule?" I asked, brow raised. It was little moments like this that reminded me how much Hamilton legitimately cared. Last night he made me strawberry shortcake for dessert because I mentioned it in passing that I used to eat it every year for my birthday. When I borrowed a shirt to sleep in, he also tossed me a pair of socks because he knew how much I hated when my toes were cold at night. It wasn't grand gestures that made me feel safe with Hamilton, it was all the little ways he made me feel heard.

"I do. And I figured you'd like one more day to pretend that shit hasn't hit the fan. Your mom is calling again," he murmured before grabbing my cell and ignoring the call for me. I rolled over and rested my head against his chest, running the pad of my index finger along his abs.

"I need more than a day to pretend. Can I have a year or two? By the way, when do you have to go back to the rig?"

Hamilton softly ran his hand down my arm before replying. "Two weeks. We have plenty of time," he whispered. "And I happen to like your avoidance tactics. The shower sex last night was—" Hamilton stopped to kiss his fingers like a chef.

"Whatever," I replied before sitting up and shuffling out of his bed. Cool air washed over my skin as I made my way to his bathroom to shower and get ready for class. Shower sex actually sounded pretty nice, but I had a big day ahead of me. I'd have to see Jared in Dr. Bhavsar's class, and I wasn't ready for that confrontation. Not even a little bit. I was likely to punch him in the gut, especially after the texts from my mother this morning. I hadn't even bothered to open the messages from him. I didn't see the point. Everything he said was lies, lies, lies. Even though we only knew each other for a little bit, I was still overwhelmed by his betrayal. I thought Jared was a friend, but he was really just bribed into being in my life.

Deciding to look good for class, I showered and blow-dried my hair. I got dressed in a plaid skirt, black tights, my favorite boots and a black, crop top, knit sweater. When I made it into the kitchen, Hamilton was flipping an omelet and humming to himself, still wearing nothing but his boxers as he made breakfast. When he saw me, he licked his lips.

"Shit, you look good."

"Thank you," I replied with a blush. My phone was sitting on the counter and went off again. I eyed it warily. "Do you think they'll file a missing person's report if I don't answer that soon?"

Hamilton looked at my phone, then back at me. "It's possible. But you're an adult, and they all know where you are. Jack called me last night."

Jack had called? Shit. Jack had been honest about the lengths he'd go to when it came to protecting his family's image. He'd looked into my mother's background and was very likely regretting welcoming her into the family now. "What did he say?"

"I don't know. I never answer his calls." Hamilton turned off the stovetop and put my omelet on a paper plate and brought it over to me with a cup of coffee.

"And why is that, exactly?"

"Sometimes people don't deserve forgiveness, Vera," Hamilton replied before changing the subject. "What are you going to say when you finally talk to your mother?" Hamilton asked while handing me a fork and sitting down beside me. "We can practice. Want me to call you a crazy unclefucker to really set the scene?"

Rolling my eyes, I replied with a snappy, "No." In a way, I was glad that Hamilton made this somewhat of a joke. Laughing about the entire situation was better than obsessing over it. "I'm not sure what I'm going to say to her. I suppose I'll ask why she hired Jared and how much of his friendship and attention was her instruction and how much was him. I never wanted to date Jared, but it makes me feel cheap. He didn't actually like me. I was just a means to an end. Our whole friendship was fake. He was clingy and annoying, but he was my first friend here. I just don't like feeling so used."

Hamilton looked at my plate, nodding. "That makes sense. I'm not defending him, but what if he genuinely developed feelings for you? Would it make a difference?"

"No. Our entire friendship was a lie," I immediately replied before stabbing my omelet with my fork. "I'm just glad we didn't do anything. I don't think I'd be able to stomach it if I fucked him. He probably didn't give two shits about me. He just wanted the job. I'm so fucking stupid."

"You aren't stupid, Vera. I think he's a major asshole, and I'd like to kick him off the edge of a cliff, but I can recognize when a man wants someone. He looked at you like you were a snack. A delicious, mouth-watering snack. I bet he took the job thinking it would just be an easy path to his dream job. He probably wasn't planning to want you—let alone care about you. And for the record, this is really fucking annoying for me to say because the idea of anyone wanting what's mine pisses me the fuck right off."

I smiled to myself, then shook my head. "This

isn't the first time my mother has interfered like this, you know..."

I squeezed my eyes shut, trying to force the memory down. "What do you mean?" Hamilton asked, his voice holding a dangerous edge to it.

"The family she worked as a housekeeper for? The dad made me uncomfortable. He would look at me..."

Hamilton reached out and grabbed my leg. "What happened?"

"She encouraged it. She would send me over to pick up things randomly or ask me to deliver messages to him when he was alone in his office. I told her that he was leering at my ass one day, but she shrugged. It took me a while to realize what she was doing. He was married and more than twice my age. My mother wanted him to flirt with me—to pressure me. She told me to let it happen. I think she saw it as an opportunity. I was seventeen..."

"That's really fucked up, Vera."

"He never did anything, though," I quickly added. "I know Jared isn't the same, but it feels opportunistic. He comes from a good family. I'm sure she was all too happy to force us to spend time together." Hamilton went quiet for a long moment, and I quietly ate my food while thinking over what happened. "She always wanted this, you know. Joseph is the perfect kind of man for my mother. I just don't know if she'll ever let me live my own life. She feels like I owe her, as if my existence is a debt I'll never be able to repay."

"You don't owe her a damn thing, Petal," Hamilton growled. "You don't owe her shit. Okay? Fuck. I can't believe she did that to you."

"She didn't do anything really; she just encouraged his attention. He was harmless." Until he wasn't. There was one night where he grabbed my ass and whispered dirty words into my ear, calling me a tease. If his wife hadn't shown up and knocked on the door, I don't want to know what would have happened. Calling the entire experience harmless was probably not a healthy way to look at it, but I'd always struggled with seeing the more sinister parts of my mother's motivations.

"She was trying to pimp her fucking daughter out. Don't you see what's wrong with that? Did he touch you? What was his name?"

I swallowed my bite of food before leaning over the table to kiss him on the cheek. "He never touched me," I lied. "He just looked. He just... lingered." Leered. Licked his lips. Dropped things on the floor and asked me to pick them up.

"And your mother has the fucking audacity to get angry about me?" Hamilton huffed. "She doesn't care about your wellbeing; she cares about money and her image. She's a nasty opportunist, Vera. Can't you see it?"

I always thought it was strange that Mom was willing to sacrifice me, when she was a victim herself. I often wondered if she did it because she didn't know any better or because her morals and rigid views about sex and roses and mistakes had a gray area when it benefitted her.

"I don't want to talk about this," I snapped before getting up and putting my fork in the sink. My trembling fingers could barely hold my silverware. I knew deep down that Hamilton was right. My mother was determined. The fact that she lied about being pregnant and went to such lengths to hide it was proof enough of that.

"I'm sorry if I upset you, I just don't understand your loyalty to her."

I spun around and leaned against the counter. Crossing my arms over my chest, I spoke. "Have you ever loved someone destructive? Someone that had something really shitty happen to them. Someone that had a good reason for being the way that they were. It kills you to watch them ruin their lives, but you understand it. You've seen their trauma firsthand. You've held them during their most vulnerable moments. You've suffered because they suffered."

Hamilton stared at me, his eyes full of emotion but his expression vacant. "Yeah. I have." I wanted to know about the person Hamilton loved who was destructive, but I didn't ask. Letting out a sigh, I wrung my hands through my skirt before responding. How could I possibly explain my mother to Hamilton? To an outsider, her behavior didn't make sense.

I was willing to love a person for what they were capable of. Just because my mother was ruined by abuse and shouldered with the responsibility of raising a baby while barely a teen herself, didn't mean that she wasn't capable of loving. She just didn't know how to do things the right way. You can't blame someone for their ignorance. "She's just a damaged woman. She's struggled with her mental health all my life. Even though she didn't let me see a lot of it, I knew it was there. I know that, at some point, we all are responsible for our actions. We can't always blame our trauma for the bad things we do. But what if the person simply doesn't know any better? What if her only perception of love came from a child she didn't want and a mother who abused her? I guess it may seem like I should challenge my mother to do better, but it's not that easy. She is a product of her upbringing. She's driven by her desire to feel secure. It's not a crime to want a better life. I just want her to be happy."

Hamilton thrust his hands through his hair and looked down at the ground. "I get it," he whispered. "I really get it. My mother was an addict, Vera. Started taking pills after I was born."

I wasn't expecting Hamilton to admit that, and waited patiently for him to continue, though on the inside I was thankful that he was opening up to me —really opening up. It made our relationship feel more real. He popped his knuckles. I knew in my gut that Hamilton had to reconcile with his story on his own terms. He'd only share what he was comfortable with, and if he wanted to tell me more, he would.

"When I was young, I didn't get it, but as I got older and the news about my birth mother broke, it all suddenly made sense." Hamilton stood up and started cleaning up the kitchen, keeping his hands busy as he worked. "I was just a kid. I just wanted her to love me like she loved Joseph. But she was broken by Jack's betrayal. The drugs got harder. The hate got heavier. The burden of her depression became too much, but I wanted to carry it all. I felt responsible for her sadness, you know."

I wanted to wrap Hamilton up in a hug. It broke my heart to hear him talk about his mother. "I've never had normal relationships. I just wanted to be accepted. But I understood her pain. I wanted to take it all from her. And then she ended her life."

I gasped. "Oh, Hamilton, that is terrible," I whispered, emotion clogging my throat. I pushed myself off the counter and went to him, wrapping my arms around his waist and pressing my cheek against his back. He patted my hand awkwardly and remained tense, but after a few minutes, he slowly relaxed into my embrace, curling his shoulders forward and letting out little hums of appreciation.

He pulled away, turned around, and kissed my forehead before speaking. "We're conditioned to think that our parents are invincible heroes. We want the best for them. And slowly their humanity seeps through the cracks, you know? Sometimes they just aren't capable of getting better—of changing. But at what point do we stop letting their issues ruin our lives?"

I didn't have an answer to Hamilton's question. I was still letting my mother call all the shots in my life. Even now, though I was with Hamilton, it was taking every ounce of control that I had not to run to her and ask for permission and forgiveness. I wanted to fix this. I hated disappointing her. That impulse to bend over backward and fix everything was ingrained in my soul.

"Let's get going. Don't want you to be late," Hamilton said, changing the subject.

"Okay," I replied. I was starting to understand Hamilton's cues. When he wanted to end a conversation, when it was getting too close for comfort, he simply ended it.

Ended. It.

20

*J*ared was pacing the hallway outside the auditorium when I walked up. I clutched my textbook to my chest, treating it like armor as I walked up to him. Hamilton offered to go with me, but I needed to do this on my own. Jared had hurt me. If it weren't for Hamilton calling him out, I probably wouldn't have known that he was working for my stepfather. I had to start meeting my problems head on. No more hiding from them.

The moment Jared's cerulean eyes landed on me, he practically sprinted my direction, a mixture of relief and anticipation on his porcelain expression. "Vera! Thank fuck you're here. Joseph has been calling me nonstop—"

Of course Joseph had been calling him. My stepfather was such a prick. I kept walking, avoiding Jared's gaze and heading toward the door despite his bulky frame blocking my path. "I don't want to talk to you about my family and how they hired you to be my friend," I snapped.

Jared grabbed my shoulders, forcing me to stop. "Vera, stop being dramatic. It's a good thing I've been here. For fuck's sake, Saint showed up on campus last week and threatened you. I was just making sure you were safe. I don't get why it's such a big deal."

I looked up and clenched my teeth for a moment before replying. Jared at least had the decency to look completely fucked. His hair was wild, and his normally finely pressed suit was wrinkled. "Right. That was the same day you stormed off because I wouldn't date you. Did you even like me? You were just trying to pressure me into something to make my mother happy. And for the record, it's a big deal, because everything I told you—in confidence—you reported back to my mother! I trusted you, Jared."

Some students walked by, eyeing us curiously. I knew we were making quite a scene, but I didn't really care. "Look, honestly, I'm not a huge fan of your mother. She's a major cunt, and the dating thing was her idea. I get why she wanted to avoid a scandal with the whole unclefucker thing, but she was really pushing a relationship between us hard. Not that it was a hardship. You're hot, Vera."

At least Jared was being honest with me now. Even though it kind of hurt my pride. "Did you like me at all? Not just romantically but as a friend?"

Jared let out a huff. "You're a cool chick, Vera. You're a little boring, and I wish you went out more, but I did enjoy our time together. And you're totally fuckable. But does it even matter what I think? You've really just dived off the deep end with Hamilton there. Your mother wanted me to drag you out of his house, but I'm not trying to catch a case here."

My brow dipped in confusion. Now that all of Jared's lies were out in the open, it was like talking to a completely different person. He was every bit the frat boy fucker I initially thought he was.

"I'm so sorry that my sex life is ruining your future career aspirations."

Jared rolled his eyes. "Dude. I'm not pressed. But you seriously need to get your shit together. I don't know what it is about Hamilton that makes Joseph rage, but he's been shitting a brick ever since I told them about the two of you. Do you know why they hate one another? I mean, damn, Joseph really hates his little brother. There's got to be a reason, right? I don't think Hamilton's being completely honest with you."

"That's rich coming from you. God, I fucking hate you," I growled. "Hamilton has been honest with me from day one. If you want to know why Joseph hates Hamilton, then ask him yourself since you're so fucking close. Why, Jared? It's not like you're hurting for money or a job. Why?"

"See, that's the thing," Jared said while lowering his voice and taking a step closer. "I *am* hurting for money. Dad is close to filing for bankruptcy. I have a scholarship for class, but Joseph paid for my apartment. I actually do need this job. You of all people should understand that."

"What is that supposed to mean?" I asked in a shrill voice.

"I just mean, you and your mom know what it's

like to be willing to do anything to get ahead. I can't rely on my trust fund or my dad's connections anymore. This job with Joseph was a godsend, and I'm not going to apologize for jumping on the opportunity, especially since hanging out with you wasn't much of a hardship."

I was stunned. "I'm going to ignore your statement about getting ahead. My mother married Joseph under false pretenses, not me. I didn't ask for this. I didn't ask for any of this. What's ironic is that my mother is under the impression that you're rich. She keeps pushing me to date you because she seems to think it would be good for me. Fucking joke."

"Yeah, she has the right idea but the wrong dude. I'm broke as hell. Which is why I'm going to politely ask you to stop fucking your uncle and let me go back to working with you. I really need this, dude."

I gaped at him. "You're kidding me."

"Not at all. It's my senior year, Vera. I just need to get a fucking piece of paper and get out of here. Please consider it. I just really don't think Hamilton is worth it. I get the impression that he doesn't have your best interest at heart."

"And you do?" I asked incredulously while crossing my arms over my chest. "You're such a dick."

Jared threw his hands up in mock surrender. "Hey. I just figured I owed you one. I legit think Hamilton is on some next level shit. Something is not right about him. Also, you're really hot when you're mad. Come on, sweetheart, we could be really good together. It doesn't all have to be work, you know." He winked at me. Jared fucking winked.

"You lying, opportunistic bastard!" I yelled, not caring who heard me. "Thank fuck I learned who you really were in time." I poked Jared in the chest and pressed my lips into a thin line before speaking again. "Don't look at me. Don't talk to me. I want absolutely nothing to do with you. Hell, I don't even know you. Leave me alone. Your money issues are not my problem."

"And what am I supposed to tell Joseph?" Jared growled while throwing his hands up.

"Tell him you failed. Tell him to call me. Tell him to get fucked for all I care. Bye."

I left Jared standing there with his shoulders slumped before making my way into the classroom. Deciding to avoid Jared, I took a seat on the fourth row and angrily got out my notepad.

Jared filed into his seat just before Dr. Bhavsar arrived. Her eyes scanned the room, pausing when they landed on me in my new seat. "Good morning, class. Your syllabus says we're going to talk about Ralph Waldo Emerson, the father of the transcendentalist movement. Can someone please tell me what the transcendentalist movement is?"

Someone a few seats down from me spoke up. "It's an idealistic system of thought. It says that humanity is innately good. It also focuses on the supremacy of insight over logic and suggests that experience leads to the revelation of one's deepest truths."

"Congratulations, you can read a textbook," Dr. Bhavsar said dryly before pulling up a powerpoint and continuing. "Ralph Waldo Emerson was a champion of individualism. He rejected the pressures of society and shared his views through essays, poetry, and lectures. He believed in intuition and imagination. He believed that people could be their own authority when deciding what is right."

Dr. Bhavsar clicked the powerpoint and smiled at me. "Have you ever trusted your intuition more than logic, Vera?"

I swallowed. Yes. Yes, I had. Logic was telling me that Hamilton was a train wreck about to destroy me. "Yes," I admitted.

In the front row, Jared snorted. "*I wouldn't call*

being horny intuition," he said under his breath but still loud enough for me to hear.

Fucking prick. Dr. Bhavsar cleared her throat while scowling at Jared. "Emerson believed that our potential was limitless. Do you think that humans are capable of determining what is right without the influence of authority figures, organized religion, government, social institutions, and industrialization? Does a man who lives alone in the woods know not to murder if he's never taught that it is wrong?" she asked. "Emerson believed we should radically seek answers through our own experiences. We stop ourselves from finding our higher selves if we allow outside influences to make our decisions for us."

"We can't just throw out logic for feeling," Jared scoffed. "What if our thoughts are skewed? What if we make a mistake? Just because something feels right, doesn't mean it *is* right."

Dr. Bhavsar looked like she was trying to remain calm. "I'm not here to tell you what school of thought to follow. I'm just here to teach you different philosophies and how they shape the world we live in. Emerson challenged many antiquated views. He was a supporter of women's rights and was an abolitionist, too. Sometimes you have to challenge the rules and follow your own intuition of right and wrong. It's what leads to change. If we all allowed the powers that be to dictate our goodness, we could end up stagnant in a morally bankrupt society. An individual isn't as easily corrupted as a group. Emerson's entire platform was to look within for the answer."

"Sounds like some hippie shit," a frathole beside me said.

The rest of the lecture continued, with less class interaction, but I continued to think about what Dr. Bhavsar had said. I had to stop thinking about how a relationship with Hamilton would affect my mother or how it would look to the rest of the world. I knew that what we shared had the potential to be great. It felt right. *He* felt right.

When class ended, I practically sprinted to the parking lot where Hamilton was parked. I circled his car and ripped open the driver's side door, greeting his surprised face before motioning for him to stand outside.

The leaves were beginning to fall around me. Cars swerving through the parking lot honked at us. A brisk chill traveled down my spine. I'd never felt so utterly present in my entire life. "Are you okay?" Hamilton asked while unbuckling and standing up. I wrapped my arms around his neck, and his eyebrows shot up. I brazenly pressed my lips to his. He wrapped his arms around my trembling body and deepened the kiss. Tongues tasting. Hands roaming. Moaning. The wind picked up my hair as I lifted up on my toes and arched my back to get closer to him. On and on it went until finally, Hamilton pulled away and cupped my cheeks. "What was that for?"

I licked my lips, tasting traces of mint. "Just following my gut," I replied with a smile before wrapping him up in a huge hug and pressing my cheek against his chest.

"Oh? And what does your gut say?"

Pulling away, I looked up at Hamilton. My gut was telling me that this thing between us would be great. It was telling me that he was worth it. That he wouldn't hurt me. That if I allowed myself, I could fall for him.

But I wasn't ready to tell him all of this just yet. "Oh, nothing," I replied before lifting up on my toes and kissing his jaw once more. "Let's go back to your place, yeah?"

Hamilton nodded. "Okay, Petal."

21

*I*t was scary how easily we settled into a routine. We hadn't talked about the fact that I kept clothes at his place and a toothbrush in his bathroom. It didn't feel like domestic bliss—an intimate step forward in our relationship where our spaces merged in tune with our souls. It felt like a vacation. A blissful escape from my mother's texts, which had become more and more sparse. It was a reprieve from Jared's judgmental looks and my own insecurities. I was following my gut, and my gut led us through five days of peace.

Last night, Hamilton seemed off, though. We still fucked like our lives depended on it, and he spent a majority of the evening holding me close. But something was off. It was like a shift in energy—a change in dynamic I couldn't quite put my finger on. Something was up, but I didn't know what.

"I'm taking you on a date tonight," Hamilton said the moment I got into his car. He had made a habit of dropping me off and picking me up from class daily. On Fridays, I just had an hour long eight a.m. workshop, so I was looking forward to going back to his house and napping.

"Where to?" I asked with a grin.

"One of my favorite restaurants in the area," Hamilton replied vaguely. "I thought since you're practically living with me and fucking my brains out every night, the polite thing to do would be to take you on an actual date."

I gulped. "I'm not living with you," I teased nervously.

"Does it sound like I'm complaining?" Hamilton countered. "Between your mother, my family, and

Saint wanting to hassle you, I'm more than happy to have you under my roof...and in my bed...and under me." Hamilton's voice trailed off as he leaned over the center console to kiss me deeply. I smiled against his mouth. A car honked. He grabbed my breast and kneaded it over my knit sweater.

"Fuck, you're addictive," he rasped while pulling away, his lips shining from the gloss on my lips.

I was in a daze, my eyes lidded from lust as I sat back in my seat and pressed my thighs together. "What does one wear to your favorite restaurants in the area?"

"Something short and sexy. Also, panties aren't allowed. I want to be able to reach up your skirt and feel your needy cunt at all times."

Fuck. Hamilton was so good at dirty talk. It was ridiculous how easily his words had my pussy weeping for him. I wiggled in my seat, making a satisfactory smile break out on his face. "No panties, hmm?" I asked as we drove down the road toward his townhouse. The leaves on the trees lining the street were turning a golden hue.

"None. I'll even wear a suit, if you'd like. Maybe after, we can go to this bar I like? Stay up all night and watch the sun rise." I dipped my brow. "Actually, we have all day. We should call Jess. Go do something crazy. What if we drove to California? Yeah. We could do that."

"Whoa. You're planning a lot. I have class tomorrow, we can't just go on a random road trip," I said with a giggle while shifting in my seat to get a better look at Hamilton. Now that I wasn't riddled with lust, I noticed a slight tic in his jaw. His strong hands were gripping the steering wheel, and his spine was so rigid that it looked uncomfortable. "Are you okay?"

"Of course I'm okay. I'm better than okay. Do you want to go get ice cream? I really want some ice cream. And maybe some sex. Can I eat you out when we get home?"

Hamilton seemed manic and like he was avoiding something. "Did something happen this morning, Hamilton?" I asked. I was only gone an hour, but he was very fidgety.

He turned onto his street and let out a sigh. "No. Nothing happened."

"Then why are you acting so..."

"I don't want to sit still today," Hamilton murmured softly while parking. Once the car was off, he pressed his forehead to the steering wheel and breathed in deeply.

"Why not?" I asked before reaching out to massage his neck.

"Because when I sit still, I think. And when I think, I see her face."

"Who?"

Hamilton sat up and stared at his hands for a long moment. "It's the anniversary of my mother's death. I just need to do something or—"

I quickly unbuckled and reached across to hold him. Hamilton trembled a bit, and I felt his pain like it was my own. Hamilton was usually so cocky, mischievous, and playful. He walked around like he owned the world. Nothing could tear him down.

But not right now. Right now, he was like a shattered piece of glass, the shards cutting at my skin with painful clarity. I hated this for him.

"I saw her that day. I was the one that found her, you know," he whispered. "I just don't want to see her, Vera."

"I know," I replied while stroking his back. But honestly, I didn't know. I didn't know what the right thing to say in this moment was. I was at a loss. Hamilton needed help right now, but I didn't know how to give it to him.

A knock on the window made me pull away, and Jess stood there with a forced grin. She was decked out in black armor, with goggles pushed up on top of her head. Strapped to her thigh was a paintball gun. Hamilton wiped his eyes and rolled the window down. "Hey there, asshole. We're going paintballing. I also found a monster of a hike to go on. Then rock climbing. Racquetball at the gym. I've got every minute planned for the next twenty-four hours, so you better suit up so I can kick your ass." Jess turned to look at me and winked. "I know we usually go to the strip club and get baked on the day we shall not name, but I'm thinking Vera can't handle that. Infinity will stab me in the clit if I go."

Hamilton let out an exhale, and the tension seemed to escape his shoulders. "Fuck yeah," Hamilton exclaimed. "That sounds like an epic day. I did promise Vera I'd take her to dinner though."

Jess arched a brow. "Oh? Where to?"

Hamilton swallowed and looked out the windshield, avoiding both of our gazes. "Romero's Italian Restaurant."

Jess went quiet. "Your mom's favorite place," she murmured. "You sure? You want me to go too?"

Hamilton reached out to grab my hand. "Nah. I think this will be really good."

An awkward silence settled over the three of us for a few seconds, but Hamilton ended it with a clap of his hands. "I better go get my gear then, huh? Winner has to buy drinks later." Jess whooped. I felt like I had whiplash. How could Hamilton go from falling apart to talking about paintball so quickly? We got out of the car, and Hamilton ran up to the front door. "Be right back."

I stood on the sidewalk next to Jess, a million questions running through my mind. "Every year on the anniversary of her death, Hamilton gets antsy. Sometimes it can be a tad destructive, but most of the time you just have to plan out the entire day with him. He's like a toddler. You have to wear him out so he won't think about shit," Jess explained casually, though her stance was anything but.

I nodded. Jess had been doing this for him every year? "The fact that he wants to take you to Romero's is a big deal, Vera. He hasn't eaten there since..."

I turned to face Jess. "Do you think keeping him busy until he passes out every year is healthy? He seemed manic almost..."

She scowled. "I think you don't get to tell people how to handle their trauma. If my best friend wants to do crazy shit all day to feel better, then I'm going to do it." I nodded. It wasn't my place to tell them how to handle this. They'd been doing this for years. Jess cared about Hamilton, and I knew she wouldn't do anything that was harmful to him. She was blunt to the point of painful. Running from a conversation or an issue wasn't her thing, so if she was willing to go to these lengths to help him avoid shit, then it must be serious.

"You're right. So how can I help?"

Her brows shot up. "No offense, but you don't look like the type to do extreme sports. Did you hear what I said? Rock climbing. Hiking. Paintball. And that's just half of it. I usually need a week after to recover. He does one thing, then runs off to the next. It's exhausting."

"Do you not want me to come?" I asked.

Jess paused. "What? No. I'm just saying that you'll probably hate it. I've been doing this for him every year since I found out. Hamilton hurts himself if I don't. One time I was busy with work, and he drank himself stupid—nearly wrecked his car. I'm always there for him when he gets like this. His family doesn't give a shit. They never give a shit. He sometimes would wake up screaming from a nightmare... And yeah, maybe avoiding everything isn't the healthiest way to handle it, but I care about him and—"

I wrapped Jess in a large hug. I don't even think she realized how her voice trembled. "You're a good friend, Jess," I murmured to her. She melted into my hug and some of the gruff determination she'd been carrying seemed to fade. "He's lucky to have you."

She sniffled and pulled away. "He's just always been there for me. When my parents kicked me out, he was the one that helped me. I have one day in the year where he lets me return the favor. And I'm damn good at my one day, too. He doesn't ever let me do shit for him. He doesn't talk about his feelings. He doesn't open up. But this is something I can do."

"That's a lot of pressure to put on yourself, Jess. Have you ever considered that just being you helps him? You're best friends. He loves you, Jess."

"Hamilton is my bro, you know? This is my thing. Our thing..."

"Look, if you want me to stay home, I will. But you don't have to do this alone. You don't have to feel like your entire friendship depends on one day."

"Do you ever just feel like you owe someone your life?" Jess asked quietly. She'd curled her arms around herself and was staring at the concrete. I knew exactly what she meant. Every day I woke up, I felt like I owed my mother. "I wasn't always this confident, gorgeous bitch that had her shit together. I once struggled. Really bad. Hamilton stopped me from—" Jess grabbed her chest and rubbed it, like the pain in her words was stewing there. "Hamilton is a good man. A tortured man, but still good. This is the one day a year where he shows his vulnerabilities, and it's also the one day a year I can pay him back for saving my life."

Her words were powerful, landing like a punch straight to my chest.

I wanted to hug her. Reassure her. Shoulder some of the burdens she'd been carrying, but before I could, the front door opened, and Hamilton came jogging out. Jess wiped a stray tear and smiled. "You ready to have your ass handed to you?" she asked, her cocky façade flooding her tone.

"I seem to recall beating your ass last year?" Hamilton replied while Jess shook her head. They both looked at me, and I shifted on my feet awkwardly. I didn't think this was something they wanted me to go to.

"Well, you guys have fun. I'll see you later," I said before stepping forward to give Hamilton a hug and a kiss on the cheek. I was still nervous for him, but I knew he was in good hands.

"I don't think so, princess. You better get on some comfortable clothes because it's girls against boys at paintball, and you can't run in those boots you're wearing," Jess teased while nodding at my feet.

"Really?" I asked. Admittedly, I had zero desire to shoot paint at people, but if it was what they needed, then okay.

Jess leaned over and playfully shoved my shoulder. "Get dressed. We're leaving in five."

22

*T*he restaurant looked cozy and romantic. It was dark inside, flickers of candlelight the only thing illuminating every table. The walls were lined with exposed brick, a warm red color. Arched windows lined a west-facing wall, showing off the last bit of light from sunset. It smelled delicious, robust Italian spices hitting my senses as waiters dressed in all black carried platters of authentic cuisine from table to table.

"This place is beautiful," I whispered in awe.

"It's the same as I remembered," Hamilton replied quietly while we waited for a table. I reached out and grabbed his hand, squeezing lightly. Today had been exhausting. Jess wasn't kidding when she said we had to fill every second with activities to distract Hamilton. Paintball was fun, though I already had bruises forming on my back from where I got shot. I sat out on rock climbing, and the hike wasn't a leisurely stroll. It was five miles on an intense incline with Hamilton practically jogging the entire way. Every muscle in my body was sore, and I knew that I'd be paying for our adventure for at least the next week.

I was surprised that Hamilton wanted to come here. It was his mother's favorite restaurant, and I felt conflicted about his motives. From what I gathered, Hamilton didn't want to think about her today. It's why Jess had a fucking itinerary full of things planned out.

"Did your mother used to bring you here?" I asked softly. Dealing with Hamilton today was like navigating land mines. I wasn't sure what was the right thing to ask and what would send him over the edge. I tried to stay attuned to his reactions, but his behavior made it difficult.

"I know you're worried about me," Hamilton said. "And I know this is confusing, and I should have probably given you a heads-up about today." I chewed on my tongue, forcing myself not to ask him another round of questions. "I didn't want to stress you out more than you already were. I thought I could handle it."

"It doesn't stress me out," I argued. "What stresses me out is not knowing what to expect with you. I don't want to say something that'll upset you. You spent an entire day avoiding the issue, then bring me to a place that reminds you of her..."

The hostess called someone's name, and a nearby party of four got up to be seated.

"Mom's best friend owns this place," Hamilton explained. "He and his husband moved away a while ago, but we would come here for everything. Birthdays. Thanksgiving. Christmas. Anniversaries. On the rare occasion I saw her happy, she was sitting in these booths. The night she died, we were supposed to go here to celebrate me scoring a goal in soccer."

"But you never came here that night because she..." I whispered.

"No. And I haven't been here ever since, either. I never really had someone that made me want to be happy again before. Jess tried. She thought I could get closure if I just finally went to dinner, you know? And I'm not stupid. I recognize that my coping mechanisms aren't healthy. I just wanted to do this with you. We don't have to talk about her. We don't have to remember her right now. We just have to be happy for a night. I think she'd really like that—she'd really like you."

"Beauregard, party of two?" The hostess said, drawing both of our attention. I stood up, though it felt like there was still so much more to say. Hamilton wrapped his arm around me before whispering in my ear.

"I just want to be happy tonight, okay? For her."

"Okay," I whispered back before he guided me through the restaurant toward our table.

Once we sat down, a waitress took our drink order. He got a glass of wine I'd never heard of before. I got water. "You did good out there at paintball. Though you kind of cheated by hiding for most of the game."

"You're just jealous that I was small enough to fit between those two boulders," I replied with a chuckle. I welcomed the change in pace of our conversation. "I'm worn out, though. Can you massage my shoulders tonight?"

"I'll do a full rub down on you, Petal," Hamilton replied before lifting his wineglass and taking a sip. His eyes were trained on me as he drank.

"Good. Because I'm sore all over. Jess is like a drill sergeant."

Hamilton tipped back his head and laughed, the sound melodic and tempting. "She takes today very seriously. I don't know what I would do without her, honestly. And I'm shocked that she included you in it. She's kind of...protective of that role. I've had girlfriends in the past, but she's never invited them."

Girlfriend? There was a lot to unpack with that statement. My eyes widened, but I tried to play it cool. "I like Jess," I replied, my voice nothing but a squeak.

"Is the girlfriend label freaking you out?" Hamilton asked with a smirk. Damn him for knowing what I was thinking.

"Last I checked, you didn't like labels," I countered. It felt like we were playing a game of chess, with the first person to admit their feelings losing.

"I like that we're doing plural things," Hamilton replied. "I'd like to do couple things more." I clutched my chest and stared at him. Hamilton was devastatingly sexy. He wore a suit for the occasion, his black hair combed to the side and the shadow of hair dusting his jaw giving him a dangerous edge. I could have crawled across the tabletop and kissed him. "Are you okay with labeling this? Are you prepared to go against your mother?"

I looked down at the table and took a steadying breath. "Yeah," I replied nervously. "I think I am."

"Look at me, Vera," Hamilton replied. I followed his directions with a frown. "There's no thinking. You either are or you aren't. Now you know my intentions. You know me. You know my pain. I'll give you time to decide, but I'm offering something real. Something that terrifies me because I have a habit of ruining all the good things in my life, but I want you, okay? I fucking want you. I just want to know that you'll be mine no matter what. And I don't think you will be until you pick up your phone and call your mother."

I didn't know what to say. I hated that I was still so controlled by a woman who had hurt me so much. I knew this limbo we were in had to end soon, but I wasn't ready to face it all just yet.

"Fuck," Hamilton cursed. He looked angry as he glared over my shoulder and across the room.

"What?" I asked while following his gaze. There, by the front door, stood... "Jack?"

"What the fuck is *he* doing here?" Hamilton growled.

Jack was standing alone by the front door, wearing a suit. He had his hands in his pockets and a nostalgic but anguished look on his face. The hostess smiled warmly at him and sat him at a corner booth by a window immediately. Hamilton watched as he sat down at a table across the restaurant from us. The waiter took away the other place setting, indicating that Jack was eating by himself.

A wave of sadness washed over me. Jack was absolutely a man tied to his responsibilities and status. I still wasn't thrilled that he'd researched my family so thoroughly, even though I realized now that it was a necessity. My mother had lied to the Beauregards. Maybe Jack wasn't intrusively crass after all, he'd just been conditioned to always be on the defense with his family because there were people constantly looking to take advantage of them. I'd only been in the family for a little while, and I had already been hounded and used.

But at the end of the day, I felt a sense of loyalty to Hamilton that spanned farther than just our relationship. He was deeply hurting. The loss of his mother affected him in ways I was still learning how to process. There was a reason he resented Jack so much. I was piecing it together and learning the road map that led to his bitterness toward his family. I just wanted to know what it was. I felt like understanding the dynamic with Jack would help me understand Hamilton.

"He has no right to be here," Hamilton gritted. He was clutching his wine glass with a death-like grip, his knuckles white as he stared across the restaurant. "This was Mom's place. This was the one place where she was fucking happy. He doesn't deserve it. He doesn't get to fucking ruin this for me too."

Hamilton stood up, and I quickly followed after him. Storming across the restaurant, Hamilton walked right up to Jack and slammed his fist on the tabletop. A few people gasped. I jumped and quickly thought of ways I could diffuse the situation. Hamilton had been on edge all day, and this felt like meeting his boiling point. "Hamilton!" Jack said while clutching his fist. "Did you get my invite? I wasn't expecting you to show up."

Jack had invited Hamilton?

Jack looked around the room nervously, as if expecting a scene. "I can have the waiter bring up a chair for you? Vera, I'm so glad to see you here too.

Your mother has been calling me about the two of you."

"I don't want to fucking sit with you," Hamilton spat. "I blocked your number ages ago so I wouldn't have to deal with your bullshit." I touched Hamilton's shoulder, but he shrugged it off.

"Let's not do this here, okay?" Jack said, his cheeks red with embarrassment.

"What? You don't want me to cause a scene, Jack? You don't want everyone to know how shitty of a husband you were—how shitty of a father?"

Jack cleared his throat and stood up. "You have every right to feel the way you feel right now. But this place is sacred. Let's not ruin it—"

"It's already ruined!" Hamilton yelled. "It was ruined when you cheated on Mom and forced her to raise me. It was ruined when she would sneak off to the bathroom before dessert to pop pills. It was ruined when she died, Jack."

"Excuse me, sir. I'm going to have to ask you to leave," the hostess said while approaching us. The entire restaurant was watching the exchange. The pain rippling throughout Hamilton's flexed muscles could be felt throughout the room.

"Hamilton. Let's go. Let's talk about this, please," Jack pleaded while reaching for his son.

"No. Fuck you. Fuck this place. Fuck everything. I hope you spend the rest of your miserable life with your miserable son. I hope you come here every year and think about the woman you ruined. I hope you think about me, too. How you blamed me... How you killed her!"

Wait...what? Jack killed his wife?

I grabbed Hamilton, this time my grip unyielding. The beautiful, strong man I was falling for broke at my touch. I pulled him in for a hug. It was like watching ice caps melt. He slowly softened. His hand rubbed my back. I lifted up on my toes and kissed his jaw. "Let's go home, Hamilton," I whispered. "Please."

When I pulled back from the hug, Jack was crying. He clutched a handkerchief to his face and stared at the ground, like it would swallow him up.

"Let's go," Hamilton whispered before threading his fingers through mine and pulling me through the restaurant. I looked over my shoulder at Jack just before disappearing through the front door, and to my surprise, his eyes were trained on me. I couldn't quite place the emotion bleeding through his gaze. Curiosity? Pain? Determination?

Something told me I'd learn soon.

23

The car ride home was stiff and silent. I stared out the window, watching the passing cars and lit up buildings while feeling uncertain how to help Hamilton. He was at a breaking point. How could someone that seemed so strong, so sure of himself, crumble so easily? Everything changed so quickly. His mother's death had a twisted hold on him. His family's legacy ruined him. I had so many questions about the relationship with his father and the accusations he screamed in the crowded restaurant.

You killed her!

I knew that Hamilton's mother was depressed because of her cheating husband. I wasn't sure if the overdose was an accident or not, but I knew that sometimes when people hurt, they liked to escape the heaviness of their thoughts. I understood why, in Hamilton's grief-stricken mind, he would blame his father—and he blamed himself. Seeing how toxic it was made me painfully aware of the mess I'd made of my relationship with my mother. I didn't want to get to this level, where every interaction was forced and full of hate. We had to get to a healthier place.

We pulled up to Hamilton's townhouse, but neither of us got out of the car. "So, that was..."

"Intense?" Hamilton offered. "All day has been very intense." He pinched the bridge of his nose and mumbled something under his breath. "I'm sorry our night was ruined."

"It wasn't ruined. Someday I would like to eat there. Maybe we can go on a calmer day?" I offered. "We can go on a regular Tuesday afternoon. Healing doesn't have to happen with momentous moments and anniversaries and decisions. It's the little steps, you know?"

"I'm never going back there. Jack ruined it for me," Hamilton whispered.

I debated on how to respond and decided to take a risk. "Maybe you and Jack should—"

"Don't you dare tell me that I should kiss and make up with Jack," Hamilton interrupted. "You don't know anything about our relationship. He doesn't deserve my forgiveness. He doesn't deserve anything. You don't know everything he's done."

"Because you won't tell me!" My tone was exasperated. "I'm not pressuring you to, but maybe things would be easier if you just talked to him? Get some closure? It's not healthy to live your life this way, Hamilton. I lo—care deeply for you. I hate that you go through this every year. I just think if you talked to him, it could help." I couldn't believe that I almost admitted that I loved him. Wasn't it too soon for that? Didn't we have too much to learn about one another still?

"Oh, like you talk with your mom?" Hamilton replied. "You've been ignoring her calls all week. You won't tell her about us. You won't call her on her shit for lying about the pregnancy and blackmailing you into cooperation. You're too scared to piss her off. What are you so afraid of, Vera?"

My eyes watered. "Look, you've had a rough day. I get it—"

"Don't patronize me."

"My relationship with my mother is my business. Even if I haven't talked about it with her yet, I'm still here. I'm still with you. I still chose you."

"You chose a dirty, secret fling that you'll drop the second your mother comes crying to you. I get it. I get it probably more than anyone else will. You feel like you have to be the best you can be. You shamelessly break your back for her because you feel obligated to make up for the fact that you exist. We've discussed it before. I know where I stand, and I can't hold a candle to your own insecurities and guilt. I don't even know why I try. This is such bullshit."

My throat seized up with emotion. It felt like I couldn't breathe. "That's not fair."

"What's not fair is you telling me to fix my relationship with my father when you have your own issues. I mean, seriously. It's fucked up, Vera. When are you going to realize how toxic it is? You can't live in denial anymore. It's pathetic. You're being pathetic."

"I'm ending this conversation before either of us say something we can't take back." I opened the door and got out of the car in a huff. Maybe I needed to go back to my apartment for the night and give him some space. Maybe dating Hamilton was a bad idea. This was a side of him that I knew had been lurking in the shadows of his soul, but now that I could see his demons in full bloom, it scared me.

"Vera?" A soft, whimpering voice called out. "Vera, is that you?"

I let out a shaky breath and looked toward Hamilton's front door where a willowy woman stood hunched over and clutching her stomach. Mom. Under the porch light, I could tell that her makeup was running down her face from the tears, and her glossy hair was pulled up into a messy bun. She clutched an oversized designer handbag filled with clothes that were practically falling out of the open bag.

I walked closer to her, nerves making me wince. "Mom? What are you doing here?"

She straightened her spine and swiped at the tears streaming down her face. "Hey, baby," she whimpered. The closer I got, the more her appearance shocked me. There was a blue-black bruise forming on her jaw. A cut on her lip that looked like a bite mark. There was a patch of hair ripped from her scalp, and she held her stomach tightly as if she were bruised there, too.

"What happened to you?" I rushed out before closing the rest of the distance between us. She needed a hospital.

"I had a little tumble, baby. Nothing to worry about." Her voice was scratchy. She looked too thin. Too broken. I knew she was lying. I could hear it in her tone and see it in the way she avoided my gaze.

It suddenly became very clear. "Did Joseph do this?" I asked.

"He's just a little mad at me... I was hoping I could stay with you for a couple of days while he calms down. I drove here."

My eyes watered. "Mom," I croaked. "He beat you." I went in for a hug, and she winced. The sad little sound that escaped her lips shredded my heart into pieces. "Why did he do this? I don't understand."

"He's been real mad lately, baby. My faked pregnancy is hitting him hard. He's stressed with work, and it's like he just woke up angry at the world. And also..." Her spine straightened with indignation. "He's very upset with you and

Hamilton. You never returned my calls. You've been staying here? What are you thinking? This was your fault, Vera."

I pulled away from the hug and stared at her.

"What?"

She licked her lips, making the cut there bloom red and spill a few droplets of blood. "You know what. I told you that we have to stick together, Vera. We had to be careful. Your little rendezvous with Hamilton has been very stressful for Joseph. I just knew it would blow up in my face. Now look at me." She lifted her arms up and dropped them helplessly with a groan. "You did this."

"I didn't do this," I whispered. "Joseph did it." Mom wasn't thinking right. She was badly hurt and forcing blame on me. I may have had a small part in the destruction of her happily ever after, but she had the starring role. A man is entitled to his anger, but he's not entitled to making others suffer as a result of it. It felt like somewhat of a breakthrough. For the first time in my life, I didn't assume responsibility for my mother's unhappiness and hurt.

"You did this. Hamilton did this," she snapped, her tone weak. I didn't know much about abuse victims, but I knew she wasn't thinking clearly. I couldn't hold her to a standard of sanity when she was this vulnerable.

I was about to demand that we call the cops when Hamilton started walking up the drive. "Oh look, a family reunion." He was staring at me, ignoring my mother's frail body beside me.

"Hamilton—" I began to explain, but he cut me off.

"Her or me, Vera?" he asked. The question caught me off guard. Seriously? He wanted me to choose? Now?

"I'm not choosing," I snapped. "It's incredibly selfish of you to ask."

Hamilton scoffed and shook his head, angrily mumbling to himself as he did. "You're just like the rest of them. Why bother prolonging the inevitable? You like going to an expensive school and staying in your expensive apartment. I thought you were different. I thought we could have had something, but the second she shows up, you forget about me. Just like Jack. Just like everyone else. Turning a blind eye—"

I'd had enough. From everyone.

"Joseph beat up my mother, Hamilton." My stark statement made a fresh wave of sobs break through my mother's lips. "I'm not choosing anyone or anything. I'm taking care of the only family I have right now. Stop projecting your issues with Jack on me. I'm not going to stand here and let you bully me. I'm going to take her to the hospital and back to my apartment because she needs me right now." Mom let out a choked sob. Hamilton's shoulders dipped.

"What?" he asked, the fog clearing on his anger as he took a step closer.

"Go to bed, Hamilton. Sort your shit out. I need to take care of her, okay?"

I gently grabbed my mother's arm and started guiding her toward her Escalade. "Shit, Vera. I'm so sorry. I didn't see. Joseph did this?"

"It's your fault," Mom cried out, her trembling legs nearly buckling beneath her. "It's all your fault."

Through the bright moonlight and streetlamps, I saw Hamilton grit his teeth. "Let me come with you, Vera. You don't have to do this alone."

I let out a shaky breath. I knew that my mother didn't want an audience to an already traumatizing experience. And Hamilton wasn't in the right headspace to be what I needed him to be. "Just stay here please and get some rest? I don't think you're capable of helping me right now. I just want to get her to the hospital."

"Vera. Please let me—"

"No," I snapped.

Hamilton helped me put Mom in the passenger seat. She was crying to herself, repeating the same thing over and over. "I hate you. I hate you both," she sobbed before putting her head in her hands. I swallowed that hate and buried it in my chest, suffocating the notion with determination. After shutting the passenger door, I stood outside with Hamilton for a moment, awkwardly wrapping my arms around myself and searching for the words to say.

"Are you sure I can't come with you?"

"Positive," I whispered.

Hamilton looked like he wanted to reach out and touch me but instead balled his hands into fists at his side. "Please call me if you need anything. I'll fix this, okay?" Hamilton said.

"I'm not going to call," I admitted.

"What? No. This is just a setback, Petal. I'm an ass. An insensitive asshole. I fucked up. I can fix this, Petal. I can take care of Joseph once and for all. I can make them all pay and protect you—even protect your mother." I didn't need his protection.

He reached out to grab my shoulder, but I shrugged out of his reach.

"I've got it all covered, Hamilton. I don't need you

to fix this. I need you to fix yourself." I let out a sigh, tears filling my eyes.

He looked down at his feet as I shoved past him to get in the driver's side. The moment I started the car, my heart sank. This felt like the end of it all, somehow. And I wasn't ready to say goodbye.

24

J'd seen my mother battered and bruised before. She once dated a married man and came home with a shiner on her face. The wife wasn't too happy when she found the two of them together in her bed. She also rode a bike to work when she couldn't afford a car and then crashed it into a ditch. Proud and determined, she came limping home with a broken foot and a bent bike frame. It never did heal right.

She handled pain. Delivered me without an epidural because she didn't want to spend the money. She endured bitter winters without a coat to save money. She had cigarette butt indents in her stomach. A ripped earlobe from when she had a stud yanked out.

But I'd never seen her like this. Cracked wide open. Raw. Bloodied. I wasn't sure if it was the physical injuries making her tremble and cry out. No, it was the mental anguish that had her twisted in knots.

Mom refused to go to the hospital, so instead, I took her to the apartment that didn't feel like mine anymore. I helped her into the bathtub and gasped at the number of bruises that littered her chest and torso. Most of them were easily hidden. Joseph knew exactly what he was doing. He had experience hiding his cruelty. I made out the imprint of fingerprints on her hips. Deep scratches along her sides. Dried blood between her thighs. "Mom, you have to go see a doctor. You need help," I whispered for what felt like the millionth time. My heart was breaking for her. All this time, I didn't see the signs. Her desperation to make sure we were making Joseph happy stemmed from her own sense of self-preservation.

"I don't want to," she snapped before easing into the warm water mixed with Epsom salts. Feeling helpless, I grabbed a washcloth and started gently running it over her skin. Without clothes, my mother looked too thin. I could count the bones in her spine, each disk protruding against her thin black-and-blue skin. She bent her knees and rested her chin against them, the bones cutting into her face as she let out a sigh. "I just have to stay here a couple days while he calms down. It'll get better, you know. I just need to let him relax. He doesn't want to see me like this. It hurts him to see me like this. I know he feels guilty. He loves me so much. I made him angry. It was my fault—"

"Mom," I replied gently, as if worried I'd spook her. "It wasn't your fault. You can't go back to Joseph like this."

"You don't get to tell me what to do, Vera," she gritted as I ran the cloth over a particularly nasty cut on her back. Some of her injuries looked older, like this had been going on for a while.

"Has this happened before?"

"Joseph is a passionate man," Mom mumbled. "He feels things stronger than everyone else. It's what attracted me to him. I like it rough."

I gagged. "This isn't rough, Mom. This is brutal."

A single tear fell down her cheek, and I wiped it away. "You can't go back there."

"And where would I go, Vera? I have nothing. We have nothing," she sobbed. "I can handle this, okay?"

I exhaled before lathering up shampoo in my palm and scrubbing her scalp. She jumped when my nails ran over a tender spot of baldness. He ripped out her fucking hair.

"How do I always end up like this?" Mom asked.

"Like what?"

"Helpless, letting my daughter clean up my mess."

I scoffed. "You had me when you were fifteen. You worked three jobs to raise me. You've always taken care of me."

"We both know that's a lie, Vera. You learned how to make dinner when you were eight years old," Mom replied. "You were folding laundry at six. Watching yourself, getting yourself ready for school when you were barely five." Soft tears sank down her defeated expression, but she looked proud of me in that moment. "You grew up fast. Faster than you should have."

"So did you," I replied warmly. "You took care of a baby you didn't want when you were just a baby yourself."

"You think I didn't want you?" Mom said, crying harder now. "Is that really how you feel?"

"I know who my father is. I know you didn't—"

"I wanted you, Vera. The moment I saw those two little lines on a cheap dollar store pregnancy test, I knew my life was going to change. Every good thing in my life starts and ends with you. You helped me find a strength within myself I never knew existed. Everything I do is because I want you to have a better life than I did. Because I love you so very dearly, baby. I might be a mess. I might not go about things the right way. I say the wrong thing. I let my ambition get in the way. And yes, I resent that my life was stolen from me, but I don't resent *you*. I have failed as a mother if you think for even a second that I don't love you."

I stopped washing her hair and leaned back, my own tears flowing freely now. "I've felt like this obligation. Something holding you back."

Mom reached out and cupped my cheek. "You push me forward. I wake up every single day knowing I have you in my life."

I hugged her wet body, not caring that she was getting my pajamas drenched. "You don't have to stay with Joseph, Mom," I whispered. "We were plenty happy before. We can be happy again."

"It's not that easy, baby. He's my husband."

"He's your abuser," I replied.

That word sent a shiver through her thin body. "I don't want to talk about this. He wouldn't be angry if you'd stop this nonsense with Hamilton."

It was like she slammed a wall between us, ruining the sentimental moment. Grabbing a nearby cup, she rinsed her hair of shampoo by dumping the water on her head like a baptism. I watched her for a moment before speaking. "I don't know what I'm doing with Hamilton," I admitted. It felt good to finally talk about him with my mother. Even if she didn't approve, I needed to get it off my chest. "Sometimes, it feels like he could be the one, Mom."

Mom's mouth dropped open, but she schooled her expression quickly. "You're too young to have *the one*."

"We have this connection I can't explain. I tried to stay away. It's not just physical. But sometimes, I feel like I don't know him. The Beauregards have a lot of secrets..."

"You don't know the half of it," Mom mumbled.

"What do you mean?"

Mom grabbed the conditioner and started coating the ends of her hair with it, working it up to her scalp with slow, methodical movements. "It's better if you don't know. I had no idea just how far their reach is..."

"More of a reason to get out while we can, Mom."

"It's too late for me, Vera," she croaked.

"It's never too late, Mom."

———

MOM AND I SPENT THE REST OF THE NIGHT IN silence. Every time I asked her what was going on with Joseph and the Beauregards, she closed off, sealing her mouth shut and refusing to talk to me about all of it. I wanted to pry the information from her lips, but I also didn't want to pressure her into telling me things she wasn't yet ready to share. She was hurting, she was a victim. I wanted to rush her to the police station and have Joseph behind bars, but I had to do things on her terms. In a time where her life felt out of control, it was important to make sure the decision to get help was in her hands.

When I woke up the next morning, I rolled over in bed, expecting to see my battered mother sleeping there, finally getting a peaceful night's rest. But instead of her snoozing frame, her side of the mattress was empty. I shot out of bed and started wandering the apartment, my feet shuffling across the wood floors. "Mom?" I called out. Nothing.

In the kitchen, there was no sign of her. It wasn't until I saw the scrawled note on the back of a receipt that I realized what she'd done.

Baby,

Joseph called. I got up early and drove home. Loved the girl's night. See you soon.

Xoxo,

Mom

I quickly grabbed my phone and dialed her number, but it went straight to voicemail. It was about a five hour drive from here to DC. What time had she left? Certainly she wasn't there already.

I didn't have a car, or I would have gotten on the road right then and chased her down. I needed more time to convince her that she deserved better than Joseph. This wasn't safe. What if Joseph killed her? Fuck! I knew how this would play out. Mom needed my support more than ever. I refused to let Joseph break her.

I didn't want to call Hamilton so soon, but I really did need his help. It wasn't like I could knock on Jared's door, and I didn't know Jess well enough to ask her to drive me to DC. I called him and was directed straight to his voicemail. "Where are you, Hamilton?" So much for, *call me if you need anything.*

Deciding that I couldn't just sit here waiting, I got dressed in a pair of dark jeans and a gray, knit sweater and slipped on some boots before ordering an Uber to Hamilton's townhouse. Much to my annoyance, the driver treated the ride like a leisurely stroll. My leg bounced as I rode. I clutched my cell phone in my fist and stared out the window at the passing buildings. The moment I pulled up to his neighborhood, I unbuckled and threw myself out of the car once we parked. Hamilton's motorcycle wasn't out front, but his Range Rover was. I knocked on the door, and the only thing to greet me on the other side was Little Mama's barks. I could hear her pawing at the door and whining to get to me. I didn't have a key, or I would have opened it up to check inside.

"Where are you, Hamilton?" I said with a curse before calling him once again. Maybe it was a bad idea to come here. Maybe I just needed to hop on the first train to DC and call the police. Fuck. I should have just taken her to the hospital last night. I was so scared that I'd push her away if I forced the issue, but she ended up leaving anyway.

But what would I do once I got there? Could I go

up against Joseph alone? If the Beauregard reach was as bad as everyone claimed, could I even go to the police? Where was Hamilton? I left him in rough shape last night. He was already struggling with the anniversary of his mother's death and seeing Jack. Then, I left him alone. What if he did something reckless?

I dialed his number again, and it went to voicemail. "Hamilton. Please call me back. Please. I'm sorry about last night, okay?" I paced in front of his house for a moment longer, and once I was certain that he wasn't home, I called Jess, who answered on the fourth ring.

"Hello? It's the asscrack of dawn, and I work tonight. This better be good." She sounded groggy.

"Do you know where Hamilton is?" I asked, my voice rushed and desperate. Jess must have picked up on the worry in my tone, because when she spoke again, she sounded more alert.

"I thought he was with you?"

"We got into a fight last night," I admitted. "My mom showed up. She needed medical attention and—"

"Wait. Slow down. What?"

Hot tears fell down my face, and I chewed on my lip. "I need to find Hamilton. I think he's the only person who can help me. Joseph hurt her, and she went back to him. Why did she go back, Jess? I could have helped her. We could have gotten through this. I don't know what to do."

"Where are you?" Jess asked.

"At his house. He isn't here. Where would he have gone?"

Jess went quiet for a long moment. "I'll come get you. I think I know where he is."

Breathing a sigh of relief, I replied, "Thank you, Jess. Thank you so much."

"Don't thank me yet," she snapped before hanging up the phone.

I had a plan. I had somewhere to go. I had help.

I just needed Hamilton.

25

*J*ess pulled her Honda Accord up to the gate in front of Jack's home where two guards stood scowling at her scuffed and dented ride. The cloth seats smelled like cigarette smoke, and she was wearing sweats, as if she'd rolled out of bed. I waited for her to pull up the drive, but she didn't. "I can't go any further. I was kind of banned from Jack's home three Christmases ago when I gave Joseph a black eye," she explained sheepishly. "But I'm willing to bet Hamilton is here."

"Why would he come here? Jack is home and he hates him. If anything, Hamilton should be avoiding this place."

She let out a sigh. "It's weird how the places that bring us the most pain can also provide us with comfort when we need it most, yeah? You called your mom when Saint was tracking you down. Hamilton comes here when his world is crashing around him. Go to the backyard. Follow the trail into the woods that leads to the community park. You'll find him at the base of a sycamore tree between Jack's property and the house next door."

"Isn't that your spot?" I asked.

"It is. But I don't think he needs me right now. I've never seen Hamilton give a shit about someone else besides me. He's always been too scared to. You should go. I think it will help him."

I nodded once. Although I felt pulled in so many different directions, I still wanted to make sure that Hamilton was okay. I ached to hop on a train and stop my mother from running back to Joseph. Part of me also craved crawling in a hole and processing everything that had happened these last two days. It was a lot. I hated it.

I pushed open her car door, and the movement made the rusted metal groan loudly. "Oh and, Vera?" Jess called just as I stepped out of the car. I straightened my shirt and looked at her.

She smiled softly. "If Hamilton has his head shoved too far up his ass to help you, I'll drive you to wherever your mother is, okay? I'll park right here and wait for you. I already called off of work."

I was speechless. "Really?" I asked.

She waved her hand. "Don't get all emotional. I like you. Infinity likes you. Sometimes I wonder if you have anyone looking after you. I guess I'm just trying to say that you aren't alone."

"Thank you," I replied before swallowing the emotion crawling up my throat, and shut the door. As promised, Jess moved to park on the street, and I watched as she pulled out her cell and started mindlessly scrolling, waiting for me.

The guards let me in after I showed them my ID. I was thankful that Jack still had me on the approved guest list. I wasn't sure how much longer he would allow that. Especially after last night. Between the faked pregnancy, my involvement with Hamilton, and Joseph's abusive ways, it was only a matter of time before shit hit the fan.

Following Jess's instructions, I walked around to

the back of the house and found the trail she spoke of. Trees lined either side of me as the eeriness of the quiet woods made my steps cautious, my heart a pounding, rebellious monster in my chest. Each shadow looming over me felt like it held secrets. Each step made my skin chill. Every muscle, bone, and tendon in my body was still and on full alert. Something was wrong. I felt like I was on the edge of something major, but I didn't know what.

"You're a joke. I'm willing to pay premium—" Hamilton's voice carried through the air, though it sounded far away and dulled by the wind and surrounding trees.

"You backed out of our last deal. It was supposed to be easy. One picture with you and Vera. Now you're asking for more when you haven't paid up."

The blood in my veins turned to ice. What? Who was he speaking with?

Leaves crunched under my boots as I walked closer. "Saint, I told you. I want Vera out of this. I have a good story that will ruin my brother."

Saint? No. No.

"Nothing will ruin your brother! You gave me the faked pregnancy scandal, and Jack had it shut down in minutes. I'm blacklisted from most publications, and the ones I *am* allowed to work with aren't reliable, trustworthy, or meaningful enough to make a difference. There's no merit in trash."

"He's beating his wife," Hamilton growled.

"Not to sound heartless, but people won't give a shit unless you have proof. A video. Pictures of it happening. No one ever believes the victim when the monster is a man in a position of power. It takes concrete evidence, and even then, you still have to smack people upside the head with it. It won't do anything. I'm in fucking hiding now because approaching Vera put me on the radar."

"Yeah, well your theatrics are to blame for that," Hamilton replied, his tone sarcastic. I pressed on, hiding behind the large trunk of a tree while peering at them. Hamilton was wearing the same outfit as last night, and Saint was sitting at the base of a large tree, picking at his nails.

"Look. I'm glad you got the story on the faked pregnancy. Only you could weasel information out of a bridesmaid while fucking her. You must have a magic dick, because she spilled *everything*. Honestly, that story probably saved what little of a career I have left. I can't believe Lilah Beauregard went to such lengths to fake a pregnancy. Maybe she deserves a shitty husband. I'm a firm believer in karma."

Hamilton kicked Saint in the shin and growled. "No one deserves Joseph's cruelty. Even Vera's shitty mother."

Saint groaned and rubbed the spot on his leg where Hamilton kicked him, while peering up at Hamilton with a scowl on his thin face. "I'm just saying. You wanted a scandal. You fucked your niece —numerous times—for the cause. I could have had that taboo treat on the cover of at least a few publications, but you vetoed it. It wouldn't have ruined the Beauregard name completely, but it would have at least made your family look bad. We tried. Unless you're willing to pull out the big guns or take down Joseph yourself through illegal means —which is still an option—there isn't much I can do anymore. My reputation as a journalist is in the toilet. I don't blame you, Hamilton. You're my brother, man. I'm here for you. Jack did our mom dirty. I still think you could weasel out a scandal from Vera. I mean her mother had her when she was fifteen. If the court records weren't sealed, I bet that would be something worth sharing. Jack wouldn't have done that without a reason, you know?"

Hamilton frowned. I could see the way his beautiful mouth turned sour. "Vera is off-limits."

Saint rolled his eyes. "You get a taste of pussy and

grow weak. I thought we were going to bring down Jack for our mother?"

"*Your* mom. My mother is dead. I'm not doing this for the woman that gave me up. I'm doing this for—"

"Nikki. Yeah. I know. We all know. I tried, okay?"

Silence greeted me as I processed it all. Saint was Hamilton's half-brother? It was all a lie.

It was all a motherfucking lie.

I stepped out of the shadows and toward the two of them in disbelief. "Was I just a joke to you?" I asked, my voice wavering with anger and disgust. At my words, Hamilton snapped his gaze to me, his determined face falling at the sight of my tear-stained cheeks.

"Petal." My nickname sounded like a plea. A prayer. A cry for help.

"Don't call me that," I snapped. "Don't you dare."

Saint stood up and let out a sigh. "Hey there, Vera. I'm so sorry for my role in this. It's nothing personal, you see. Just trying to do right by my mother."

"You're brothers," I commented.

"Only by blood," Hamilton explained.

"Only by any way that actually counts," Saint replied. "I'll let Hamilton explain everything. I can't stay in one place for too long. Ever since the faked pregnancy exposé, Jack's put the pressure on the police to have my head. I'm not yet sure if I mean that figuratively."

Saint got up, wiped his hands on his jeans, and whistled while walking away. "You sent him?" I asked. "The man who has been stalking me— harassing me—the man who wrote an article painting my mother and me out to be gold diggers is your brother. Someone you hired." I was in shock. I clutched my chest while staring at an uneasy Hamilton. I couldn't tell if he wanted to hug me or run from me. "The night at the club. With Jess and Infinity. You set that up, didn't you?" Though my tone sounded like a question, it was rhetorical. I already knew the answer.

"Vera. I'm so sorry—"

"Were you just going to kiss me? Share our fuck fest scandal and let the world gossip about us?"

"I decided that night not to go through with it. I swear I didn't want to hurt you," Hamilton rushed out.

"Right. How can I believe you, Hamilton? And you're the person that leaked my mother's fake pregnancy? You knew? All this time you fucking new."

"Colleen told me the night of the wedding," he explained. "She was drunk and feeling chatty after we had sex. I wasn't expecting to find anything out. I went there to stir up some drama, get drunk, and remind Joseph that I knew the truth. I never planned on learning what your mother was doing. It just kind of snowballed from there. I started talking to you because I thought maybe you had some insider information I could exploit. I saw an opportunity."

I nodded and wrapped my arms around myself. "So I was an *opportunity*? Even better. Were you thinking about revenge when we fucked, Hamilton? Were you thinking about destroying the Beauregard name when I was riding your face? Was I an easy target?"

"No. No. Maybe at first but—"

"Fuck you. Tell me why. Tell me what was so important that you took my heart and stomped on it."

"Joseph was on drugs," Hamilton cried out. "Probably still is. He's gotten better at hiding it now. You can put addiction in a designer suit, but it's still addiction. I hate him. He used to beat the shit out of me. Every fucking day. Jack was juggling two monsters. Mom's depression and Joseph's demons. I was caught in the crossfire of his image, and I hated it."

I refused to soften my heart at his story. I refused to feel empathy for the man who used me.

"I'm sorry he beat you up, but what does that have to do with my mother and me?"

"I saw him at the wedding. I saw the smug look on his face. I saw the way he held her close. Jack looked so fucking proud. He looked like a real family man. I knew the truth. He doesn't deserve a happily ever after. He doesn't deserve his dream job. He doesn't deserve any of it."

"So you want him to be miserable?" I asked. "You missed your mark, Hamilton. The only people suffering are my mother and me."

"Jack started focusing more on Joseph. His anger issues. His sociopathic tendencies. He considered Mom a lost cause." Hamilton looked like he was on the verge of tears. His hands were balled into fists at his sides. "The drugs Mom overdosed on? She got them from Joseph. She stole them from under his mattress. Jack had to cover it up to save his precious son from being at the center of it all. She even left a fucking note. She said that she couldn't stand to look at the psychopath she birthed, the bastard she was raising, and the cheating husband who resented her."

I knew that something was inherently wrong with Joseph, but to hear that Mrs. Beauregard's last words were calling him a psychopath just increased my concern for my mother. I tried to remain calm. "You have every right to feel the way you do, Hamilton. I have a lot of sympathy for you, okay? But this doesn't make up for the fact that you used me. And for what? What did you accomplish here, Hamilton? You wanted to make them look bad? The only people you hurt were my mother and me."

"We can still do something. Your mother could come forward about the abuse. I could—"

"My mother is driving back to DC as we speak. She's in no place to go against the Beauregards. She still thinks she loves the asshole. You want to make a difference, Hamilton? Talk to your father. Sort your fucking shit out. It's too late. Your mother overdosed. There is nothing you could have done differently." Hamilton walked over to me and reached for my arm, but I took a step back. "I should have never trusted you. You didn't just hurt me. Joseph beat up my mother. She had cuts and bruises all over her body, Hamilton. Because of us. Because of your fucked up family. You knew what your brother was capable of, and you still let me pursue this. You put us at risk. You used us for some ridiculous vendetta."

"I'm just tired of everyone thinking my family is perfect!" Hamilton roared. "He doesn't get to just live his life. Joseph once snapped my arm in the door. He'd knock me down, then kick me in the stomach. And Jack had his head shoved so far up his ass that he didn't once take my side. And then Mom died. And shit got worse."

I swallowed my emotions. "I'm sorry, Hamilton. I'm so sorry. But this is just too much." Straightening my spine, I gave him a cold look before saying goodbye. For good. Forever. "Don't talk to me again. I'm going to get my mother out of this mess, and I'm going to forget you ever existed. I hope you get whatever closure you're looking for, Hamilton. But I'm not going to let you ruin me to get to it."

"Petal, no. Please! I love you."

His declaration did nothing. I had no sentimental reaction to his affections, only rage. "You're not capable of love. You wouldn't know what it was if it slapped you in the face. Petals aren't meant to be plucked, Hamilton. When you love something, you let it bloom."

26

I couldn't go back to Jess's car. Not only was I devastated by the revelation about Hamilton, but I quickly realized that Jess was probably in on it too. There was no way she didn't know about Hamilton's plan. They were best friends, and she was probably in on it from the beginning. I felt like such a fool. I couldn't go back to Greenwich. I couldn't go back to my apartment. I wanted out of this mess of a family.

I walked through the woods, leaving Hamilton to stand there alone, his hands outstretched for mine but only clasping air. He didn't chase after me, though. How could I have been so foolish? How could I have ignored all the signs? My mother warned me. Even though Joseph was a monster, he warned me, too. I was starting to realize that everyone was a villain. Everyone had an ulterior motive. There were no innocents. I should have seen Hamilton for what he was.

And even though I was angry, my heart still hurt for the boy who shared the trauma of Joseph's abuse.

When I saw the Beauregard's home, I pulled out my cell, fully prepared to call an Uber to my apartment so I could pack a bag and take the train to DC. I didn't exactly know what I'd do once I got there, but I had to convince my mother to leave Joseph. No amount of financial security was worth being with a monster.

"The guards told me you were here," Jack said. I hadn't even noticed him sitting on his back porch. He was clutching a glass full of amber liquid in his palm and staring out across his property at the tree line. I'd never seen him dressed so casually, with a black shirt and sweatpants; he looked normal, almost. "Is Hamilton at the sycamore tree? He always loved it there."

I debated on ignoring him. Jack had a role to play in all of this. He supported a monster. But my need for answers outweighed my sense of self-preservation. "Did you know?" I asked while marching up the steps. "Did you know that Joseph is a psychopath? Did you know that my mother showed up on Hamilton's doorstep yesterday bruised and bloodied? You're a hypocrite, Jack," I added before sitting down in the chair beside him. I didn't want to look at him—I couldn't. So instead, I stared out over the swaying blades of grass while finding my bearings. Ten more minutes couldn't hurt. Ten minutes of sitting and searching for answers before I'd figure out what the fuck my mother and I were going to do.

"I'm the worst kind of hypocrite," he admitted. I didn't have to pull the admission out of him. He readily agreed, like it was a plague on his mind he needed to sweat out with a fever. "I did you and your mother a disservice. I sat there, pretending that it was my son who needed protecting from your mother, when in fact it was the other way around."

"He beat the shit out of her, Jack. How can you

just sit there, knowing what he's capable of, and still support him?"

"I suppose the same reason you still love a woman who lied about her pregnancy so she could marry into my family for money."

I sputtered. "It's not the same."

"No. I suppose it's not. Yet here we are. Stuck." Jack lifted his drink and took a sip. "I learned to prioritize from my father. The day I started working for him, he told me that every thriving business has a million problems under its belt. The key to success is finding the biggest one and focusing on it. And if it isn't fixable, you move onto the next."

"Is that how you approach your family, Jack? You treat your children like problems you can't fix?"

Jack smiled. "You're a smart woman, Vera. I can see why Hamilton is so fixated on you." I bit my tongue. "I'm a bit wiser now, though. Nikki and I realized something was wrong with Joseph when he was three. He used to break every single toy we ever gave him. He was attracted to dangerous things. Fire. Needles. Electrical sockets. Nikki blamed herself. I suppose Joseph's *problems* started her spiral. We went to therapists, but he outsmarted them. He learned how to appear normal. He mimicked empathy, wore kindness like a mask. I ignored the deeper problem because it was easier.

"Nikki then became my bigger problem. I'd catch her staring at Joseph with her fists clenched. She feared him. I couldn't understand why she wouldn't just let it go. My wife and I grew apart. And by the time I told Nikki about my affair and Hamilton, I'd lost her completely. No amount of therapy, antidepressants, or help could save her. So I treated her like I treated my business. I focused on the other problem."

I swallowed and turned to look at Jack. Hearing his version of events added a sense of clarity to the story that I'd been craving. "If you can't fix it, move on," I echoed his earlier sentiment.

"Hamilton was like a Band-Aid. He won't believe me, but she loved him. In fact, she probably loved him more than she loved Joseph. She resented me, but oh, she loved Hamilton. He was a second chance. He breathed new life into her. She took him in as her own. Our only rule was that he could never know of his birth mother. It was an easy enough agreement. I was happy to forget about the one-night stand. We settled. Closed case. Non-disclosure agreement. I paid a lot of money to make sure Nikki had full parental rights. She still had moments of weakness, but I had faith that we'd be a family again. Hamilton is under this ridiculous belief that everything was perfect between the three of us before he came along. He doesn't realize that he *saved* our family."

"Joseph must have been jealous," I whispered.

"Incredibly so. Joseph has so much anger. He's the one who leaked the truth to the press about Hamilton's birth mother," Jack replied. "Nikki was never the same after that. She spiraled. Sometimes..." Jack stopped to adjust his collar. "Sometimes I wonder if he put the drugs somewhere Nikki would find them. I knew they belonged to him. She'd dabbled in temporary relief before, but the drugs in her system were Joseph's beast of choice."

It terrified me to think that my mother was married to someone capable of so much evil. "Why does Hamilton blame you?"

"Because I clean up Joseph's messes. Every. Single. Time. At first I did it for the sake of my legacy. How can I build an empire when I can't even manage my own family? Then it just became a habit. Second nature. Instinct. I'd tell you all the things I kept hidden, but I'm afraid you'd hate me more than you already do. I don't know how to be a father. I know how to fix problems. I know how to bribe, lie, and steal. I sent Hamilton away, and now I'm an old man who's made a habit of saving the son who doesn't deserve saving and hurting the son I should have protected. All the while, I'm balancing a fortune and legacy that only makes Joseph more powerful. I have half a mind to cut him off just to save the rest of the world from him."

"Why are you telling me this?" I asked.

Jack took another drink before tossing the glass into his yard. It shattered on impact, but the crashing sound was absorbed by dirt and grass. "I want a relationship with my son, Vera. You get through to Hamilton in a way I've never been able to. I saw the way he calmed down when you spoke to him last night at the restaurant. I don't care about the papers. I don't care about the reelection. I'm withdrawing from the race. I want to fix my family before it's too late. Last night was a wake-up call. I can't keep sweeping Joseph's mistakes under the rug." Jack paused to clear his throat. "Hamilton blames me for Nikki's death. He thinks I should have done more. I should have handled Joseph better. I shouldn't have cheated. I loved my wife, Vera. And if she could see the mess I've made of this family, she'd be ashamed."

"I'm assuming there is a reason you're telling me all of this."

"I can bring your mother here. I can give your mother space and time away from Joseph and keep her safe. He won't hurt her if she's here. Joseph doesn't have genuine feelings. He goes through the motions. He thought she was pregnant, so he thought he was supposed to be a family man. But he can't keep up with the charade for long. If she's here, he's free to do whatever he wants. He'll agree to it, especially if I suggest it. I'll give her a job here. Something where she can earn honest money. Give her the opportunity to get a clear head."

"Are you doing this for her or for Joseph?" I asked.

"For both. Once he has someone, he picks at them like they're scabs. Hamilton probably knows that sad truth better than anyone else. It's always the people closest to him."

Once more, my heart bled at the thought of Joseph abusing Hamilton. "I'm assuming you want something in return?" I asked. Jack was a politician through and through.

My grandfather let out a sigh. "I want you to help me mend my relationship with Hamilton. I'll give you everything you could possibly want. School. Your mother's safety. Your apartment paid for. When you graduate, I'll make sure you have whatever job you want. I'll keep Joseph away. I'll do everything in my power to give you a good life. All I ask is that you help me fix things with my son, Vera. I know you're capable of it."

"I can't, Jack," I choked out. I hadn't even realized that tears were streaming down my face. "He betrayed me. He was using me to hurt you."

"He has to care about you, Vera."

"He doesn't," I sobbed.

"The second Joseph told me that Hamilton had his eye on you, I knew it was all a ploy. This isn't the first time my son has lashed out. I didn't think anything of it. But then I noticed a shift last night. I know my son. Hamilton loves fiercely, and Vera, he loves you. I can see it clear as day."

I crossed my arms over my chest, letting the chill of the air wash over me. "I don't love him."

"You can't bullshit a bullshitter, Vera. You love him too."

"It doesn't matter!" I yelled. "I can't be with someone who hurt me like that."

Jack pressed his lips into a fine line. I waited with bated breath for him to speak. "You're going to have to get over that. If you want to protect your mother and finish your degree, you'll help me. I might be a changed man, but I'll still do whatever it takes to fix my family. I don't care how your feelings have changed. You want your mother out of that house with Joseph? You *will* stay. You *will* fix things with Hamilton."

I stood up and paced the deck. How could Jack ask this of me? What was he thinking?

Debating my options, I realized I didn't have much of a choice. I needed to get my mother out of that situation. I needed to finish school so I could be self-sufficient. Could I help Jack while protecting my heart? Could I honestly try to fix years of pain? "I'm not even sure I'm capable of mending your relationship with Hamilton, Jack."

"All I ask is that you try. All I ask is that you stay."

"You can't force me to love him, Jack."

"I'm not asking you to. I'm just asking you to give our family a second chance."

I looked up at Jack, seeing him with fresh eyes and a hardened heart. I knew my answer would change the trajectory of my life. Once again I had a decision to make. My mother's safety and happiness, or mine. It was a tragic sacrifice. A consequence. I spent so long running from my feelings for Hamilton, and now his family *wanted* me to run headfirst back into his welcoming arms.

Rustling in the distance drew my attention back

to the tree line. Hamilton emerged with his shoulders slumped. I could sense his pain even from here. Broken. Hardened. Defeated. Even now, I wanted nothing more than to run to him. I wanted to be better again. I wanted to seek the comfort of his arms and dive into the compatibility we shared.

But if I were going to do this—if I were going to help Jack and save my mother—then I'd have to do it with a clear head. I refused to give Hamilton my heart again.

"So?" Jack asked. "What's it going to be?"

I let out an exhale. "I want Mom here by tomorrow," I replied. "And I don't want you to punish either of us if I fail."

"Deal."

I stared at Hamilton once more. His hungry eyes were locked on me. Pain felt like a tangible entity between us. "I'll try."

A NOTE FROM THE AUTHOR

Thank you so much for reading. Thorns and Forgiveness, the conclusion to Hamilton and Vera's story, will release February 4th, 2021.

Preorder your copy:
www.authorcoraleejune.com

ACKNOWLEDGMENTS

This book would not have been possible without the support and love of Christina Santos, as well as Christine Estevez with Wildfire Marketing.

I would like to especially thank Katie Friend, Meggan Reed, HarleyQuinn Zaler, Savannah Richey, Lauren Campbell and Claire Jones for beta reading.

I am grateful to all of those with whom we have had the pleasure to work with during this book. I'd like to especially recognize my editor, Helayna Trask. She always takes the time to dive into the worlds we create and make sure they are perfect for you all. I would also like to thank all the dedicated members of The Zone and Cora's Crew. And finally, thank you again to HarleyQuinn Zaler for this drool-worthy cover.

I started writing this book almost a year ago, and picked it back up on a whim. I had zero plans of releasing it this year, and wasn't sure I could get inside Vera's head. But the second I started writing, I just couldn't stop.

I can relate to Vera in many ways. There comes a time in all our lives when we stop seeing our parents as super heroes and start seeing them as humans— and humans are beautifully flawed in so many ways. It can be jarring when you catch your first glimpse of their shortcomings. I once read a quote that said, "We always talk about how parents get to watch their kids grow up, but kids get to watch their parents grow up, too. They just don't realize it."

Disclaimer: I promise that this book is entirely a work of fiction. Lilah was not modeled after any of the people that raised me. I have four amazing parents. It's just...the older I get, the more I realize that my perceptions of normal were shaped by incredible people that worked hard to give me a safe childhood. A lot of times we look at our parents strengths and how they shaped us, but I think it's important to recognize that their weaknesses help us grow, too.

Vera's journey made me examine my own role as a mother. While writing the tail end of this book, I had a very devastating miscarriage that rocked me. I sat on my bed and sobbed for what felt like hours, and hadn't noticed my oldest daughter sneaking into my bedroom with a candy bar to make me smile, and a roll of toilet paper to wipe my tears. We cuddled. She asked why I was crying and I told her that sometimes Mommies get sad, just like everyone else.

She saw a bit of my humanity that day. I hope every crack in my armor shapes her into a compassionate person, just like every little vulnerability that my parents were brave enough to show me, helped me grow into the woman I am today.

ABOUT THE AUTHOR

CoraLee June is an international bestselling romance writer who enjoys engaging projects and developing real, raw, and relatable characters. She is an English major from Texas State University and has had an intense interest in literature since her youth. She currently resides with her husband and two daughters in Dallas, Texas, where she enjoys long walks through the ice cream aisle at her local grocery store.

Stalk Me:

Facebook:
https://www.facebook.com/AuthorCoraleeJune/
Instagram:
instagram.com/authorcoraleejune
BookBub:
https://www.bookbub.com/profile/coralee-june
Newsletter:
www.authorcoraleejune.com